MAX ALLAN COLLINS

and

MATTHEW CLEMENS

YOU CAN'T STOP ME

PINNACLE BOOKS
KENSINGTON PUBLISHING CORP.
www.kensingtonbooks.com

PINNACLE BOOKS are published by

Kensington Publishing Corp.
119 West 40th Street
New York, NY 10018

All Kensington titles, imprints, and distributed lines are available at special quantity discounts for bulk purchases for sales promotions, premiums, fund-raising, educational, or institutional use. Special book excerpts or customized printings can also be created to fit specific needs. For details, write or phone the office of the Kensington special sales manager: Kensington Publishing Corp., 119 West 40th Street, New York, NY 10018, attn: Special Sales Department; phone 1-800-221-2647.

ISBN-13: 978-0-7860-2134-5
ISBN-10: 0-7860-2134-9

First printing: March 2010

10 9 8 7 6 5 4 3 2 1

Printed in the United States of America

For Lee Goldberg—
who really knows TV

Seeing a murder on television can help work off one's antagonisms. And if you haven't any antagonisms, the commercials will give you some.
—ALFRED HITCHCOCK

If you die horribly on television, you will not have died in vain. You will have entertained us.
—KURT VONNEGUT

ONE
The Crime

Chapter One

John Christian Harrow had never much cared for the Iowa State Fair.

He was uncomfortable around throngs of people, and the cacophony of chatter, ballyhoo, and music always put a crease between his eyebrows. The skyline of vast barns, art-deco pavilions, Ferris wheels, and even a mammoth slide held no magic for him; overhead open-air cars of airsick passengers swaying like fruit about to ripen and fall made him question the general sanity of the human race.

The smells, whether the stench of farm animals or the lure of frying batter, did not appeal—they made him neither want to milk a cow nor risk his arteries on a funnel cake. And now and then an unmistakable upchuck bouquet would waft across his nostrils. At least the day wasn't sweltering, as August often was here. It was eighty and humid and no picnic, but this wasn't heaven, this was Iowa.

At six-two, barely winning the battle to stay under

two hundred pounds, Harrow might have been just another farmer gussied up to go to town, forty-something, short brown hair, penetrating brown eyes, strong chin, high cheekbones, a weathered, slightly pockmarked complexion, tie loosened and collar unbuttoned.

But J.C.—as anyone who knew him for more than five minutes called him—was not farmer but a detective. He was in fact a seasoned field agent and criminalist for the Iowa Department of Criminal Investigation. And right now he detected a damp stripe down the spine of his dress shirt, and wished to hell that the Kevlar vest underneath came with pockets for ice bags. His sun-soaking, unbuttoned navy suitcoat concealed his holster and nine-mil, clipped to his belt, riding his right hip.

This was no day off to take in the state's most celebrated festivities. And it wasn't the normal work-day where he found himself either at a crime scene or in a lab or even in the field interviewing witnesses and suspects.

Today Harrow had drawn a special assignment as part of the extended protection team working on the President of the United States's visit to the nation's most famous state fair.

Usually cops augmented the President's Secret Service detail, but the events of September 11 had changed that. Ever since that tragic day, security weighed heavily on the minds of most Americans, and the government had become more creative in ways to protect those in their charge. They kept cops on the streets when they could and when necessary, used qualified others, like DCI Field Agent Harrow, to fill in.

The rule was, you had to have a badge to work protection detail.

Today, his DCI badge—probably aided by the fact that he had a background in local politics—seemed to make him the perfect candidate for this particular task. Which sounded far more exciting in practice than it really was. He'd done very little in the morning other than walk around the fair and assess threats.

He had deemed the cow sculpted from butter as non-menacing unless the President decided to ingest it, in which case it would be death by cholesterol overdose. In the afternoon, before the President was introduced, Harrow stood on the stage, eyes processing possible troublemakers in the crowd, then maintained his vigil from stage left throughout the Commander in Chief's address.

A thin man with too heavy a jacket for an August day, another who seemed jittery, a woman with a purse big enough to hold a gun or a bomb or God knew what . . .

Harrow saw them all and reported them up the food chain to Secret Service. A certain amount of stress came along with searching for a potential assassin, but on the whole this was a vacation day with pay for Harrow. Despite his general disregard for politicians, and his lack of love for the fair itself, the DCI agent felt honored to be entrusted with a small part of his President's welfare.

After a well-received speech, the President was led down the stairs by the Secret Service contingent at stage right. Secret Service eyes quickly scanned left, ahead, right, and back again. Several more agents eyeballed the crowd on the other side of the wire fence between the audience and the backstage area. Trailing this group, still on stage, Harrow looked out over the still-cheering crowd.

Despite the chest-high wire fence, the throng pressed forward, each citizen wanting to shake hands with the leader of the free world, some wearing sunglasses, some not, some wearing hats, farmers, businessmen, housewives, women in power suits, young, old, middle-aged, an ocean of faces and bodies surging for a chance to press the famous flesh, or to get at least a closer-up glimpse of the President. Most were smiling, some looked confused, and some even afraid as the crush of people pushed toward the fence.

Then Harrow picked out a face—really, an expression—of anger. But all that watching had sent Harrow's eyes sliding past before what he'd seen registered, and the DCI agent's eyes darted back, scouring the crowd for the unhappy man.

Seconds crawled like minutes until he again located the face in the crowd. The man was dressed like a farmer—bib overalls, T-shirt, sunglasses, and a cap with CONTINENTAL PEANUTS stitched across the front.

Several things about the farmer made simultaneous *blips* on Harrow's cop radar: The hat was for a peanut-seed company, one of the biggest in the country, but peanuts were a crop not grown in Iowa; the man was Caucasian and about forty; the sunglasses were not typical—the generation of farmers younger than Harrow's father had learned the value of UV protection, but many farmers Harrow knew never wore sunglasses.

The loudest, biggest *blip* came from the soft, white skin of the man's bare arms—not even a hint of tan, and a farmer who had not been outside by August was not a farmer at all. A glance at hands soft enough to belong to a perfume-counter clerk told Harrow this "farmer" had not done a real day's work in his life. . . .

Harrow's processing of all this took a second or two, and then the fake farmer's hand slipped into a pocket and came out with something that glinted in the sunlight. Harrow didn't even have time to use the little communicator that ran down his arm inside his suit.

He yelled, "*Gun!*" as the angry face in the crowd lurched forward, right arm coming up. Harrow knew at once that the man's hand held a small-caliber automatic pistol.

Harrow leapt from the stage, arms in front, feet splayed wide behind him, the faces of the people below etched in expressions of surprise, fear, and confusion as he flew over them, his only thought to get to the weapon.

Everything seemed to stop for a second or two, Harrow feeling he was hanging in air, watching as the would-be assassin slowly squeezed the trigger. The agent seemed able to see each fraction of an inch the trigger moved in its inevitable journey.

Just as Harrow grabbed onto the man's arm, flinging it upward, the gun fired, the shot flying harmlessly over the barns of 4-H animals, creating a muffled but immediate symphony of whinnies and grunts. . . .

As Harrow and the man crashed to the ground, the world went from slow motion to fast-forward as Harrow found himself suddenly aware of several things happening at once: People broke their fall, and the crowd separated like a welcoming gate only to dump them on the gravel-packed ground; panicked bystanders tried to escape the wrestling bodies and the sight of the gun that Harrow and the shooter still fought over even as several Secret Service agents crashed down.

A knee dug into Harrow's back and fingers clawed not only at the shooter's hands, but at Harrow's, trying to pry the pistol free. Even under the pile of writhing bodies, Harrow managed to twist the arm back, the shooter screaming in pain and releasing the pistol into Harrow's grip.

A Secret Service agent said, "I'll take that," and Harrow handed it over, as another agent asked, "You all right, buddy?"

"Yup," was all Harrow could manage.

Final tally: one wild shot, and no injuries to the President.

Who was whisked away so swiftly that Harrow almost missed the moment where the most powerful man in the free world locked eyes with him and mouthed: *Thank you!*

Several Secret Service agents had received a few scrapes, and a handful of fairgoers did suffer injuries, the most serious a young woman who broke an arm in the panicked trampling that followed the gunshot. Harrow himself was unscathed but for a bruise on his back from that overzealous Secret Service agent leaping on him.

The would-be assassin, like the young woman, had a broken arm, thanks to Harrow, not that the perp received any sympathy from the crowd watching him get hauled away.

That was when Harrow found himself the center of attention, questioned first by the Secret Service, then by the national media, and, finally, by the *Des Moines Register* and local news crews before he was able to extricate himself for the drive home.

Though the outside temperature was only about seventy, the Ford F-150's air conditioner ran full-tilt. In the pickup, Harrow relished the blast of cold as he sailed north on I-35, the night swallowing the lights of Des Moines in the rearview.

Although he'd always thought of himself as a cop first, until five years ago Harrow had made his living in politics, twice winning election to the office of sheriff of Story County. But he still considered himself basically apolitical.

Deciding not to run for a third term, Harrow had hooked up with the DCI in 1997 and had been much happier ever since. The job change had saved his marriage too—otherwise, his wife of twenty years might have wound up divorcing him and taking their son, David, with her.

Ellen had never asked Harrow to quit, not in so many words, but had wholeheartedly supported his decision when he finally smartened up. His petite brunette wife had been the prettiest girl at Ames

High and then Iowa State University, and one of the smartest too, smart enough anyway to see long before Harrow the strain the sheriff's job had inflicted on him.

Only after he'd taken the DCI job did his wife finally confess how close she'd come to leaving him. Being married to a cop was hard enough—being married to one who spent half his time running for reelection had become unbearable.

Now they were happy as newlyweds. The family hadn't moved to Des Moines when he took the DCI gig—fifteen-year-old David was thriving in the tiny Nevada (*Nuh-vay-duh*) school district, just thirty miles north of the capital, and Harrow wasn't about to pull his popular, athletic son out just as high school was kicking in.

They'd moved from the county seat to a secluded farmhouse that cut fifteen minutes from his commute, and, anyway, plans were afoot for the crime lab to move to Ankeny, in a couple of years, which would shorten the ride even more.

Harrow knew he should be hurrying home— Ellen would be breathless to find out whether or not he'd shaken hands with the President (he had) and if the man was as handsome in person as she thought he was on TV (actually, more). Certainly, she would grill him about that even harder than the Secret Service and the media had.

He'd been trying to call ever since the so-called "State Fair Incident" had gone down, but the answer machine was full and Ellen didn't carry a cellular. He was a little surprised she hadn't called him on his cell—maybe she hadn't been near a radio or TV.

The home addresses of DCI agents were a closely guarded secret, especially from the media, and Harrow hoped the national news hadn't pulled strings or done computer hacking that would mean he'd arrive home to a surprise party of CNN, MSNBC, and Fox news trucks.

That possibility aside, pulling off the interstate, heading east on Highway 30, he found himself not surprisingly anxious to get home. And, as usual, though he enjoyed the unwind time of the commute, the closer he got to home, the more eager he became.

He exited 30 onto Six-hundred-twentieth Avenue, turning back south on the two-lane blacktop with just a couple farms on either side, the last few miles of his drive. He killed the air, rolled down the window, and let warmth rush over him.

He yearned for a smoke, but if he lit up, even just a precious few drags, Ellen might smell it on him. Then she'd be pissed even if he had saved the President, and he didn't need that tonight. He glanced wistfully at the glove compartment, where half a pack and a cheap lighter kept a low profile under a map of Iowa.

Smash in the door of a crackhouse? Say the word. Confront a PCP-pumping gunman holding a pistol to the head of an innocent hostage? No problem. Stop a presidential assassin? Even that had seemed easy today . . . but let Ellen catch him with cigarette smoke on his breath?

No way, no chance, no how.

Another left, and he was heading east on Two-hundred-fiftieth Street. The lights of their house, settled mostly by itself out here in the country south of Nevada, would be visible when he topped the next hill. As the idea of a cigarette drifted away like so much smoke, he crested the rise, looked to the left for the familiar glow, and saw only the mercury vapor light stationed atop the garage.

No house lights—that was odd. He wondered if Ellen had mentioned going out tonight. He didn't remember her saying anything like that, but sometimes words went in one ear and out the other, when you'd been married as long as they had. David could be most anywhere, with his buddies or his girl. . . .

Well, at least the national news boys hadn't been waiting. Harrow slowed at the turn up the long driveway to the house. Turning just past the mailbox, he felt something inside him catch.

The door of the mailbox was closed.

Ellen always left it open, after removing the mail, her signal to him that he didn't have to stop for it. Had he forgotten a dinner out she'd planned, or one of David's many ball games? She was active with a couple of women's groups and the PTA—maybe she'd gone to Des Moines to shop or run errands, and went straight to whatever it was.

With a shrug, he put the truck in park and climbed out to get the mail.

If the mail was still here, though, that meant she had been gone since mid-afternoon at least. He opened the box, pulled out its contents, and headed back to the truck.

He climbed up and in, tossed the pile of bills and magazines and so on onto the passenger seat, and eased the truck into gear, then crept up the long blacktop driveway. The two-story house was dark, which made him uneasy.

If Ellen was home, the lights would be on; but even if she was going to be gone, she would have left one light on for him. It was just something they did for each other.

Something was wrong.

Chapter Two

Harrow gunned the truck up the short hill, pressing the garage-door opener and painfully counting the seconds as the door slid up. He still couldn't see anything. He cursed himself for not replacing the opener's burned-out bulb.

The hill was steep, and the garage sat at a slight angle to the house. He would not be able to tell if her car was inside until the truck's lights hit the garage. He crested the hill, and, as he feared, her car sat parked in its space.

What the hell was going on?

Where *was* David? If something was wrong with Ellen, if she'd gotten sick or been injured, why hadn't David called his dad's cell? Nearing the garage, Harrow kicked the brake and threw the truck into park, the sudden stop almost hurling him into the wheel.

He hopped out, pulled his pistol, and circled

around the back of the truck. Anxiety gripped him and his cop senses were tingling; but he hadn't defaulted to cop objectivity—*this was his home.*

Resisting the impulse to run, but still using the vehicle as cover, he crept around the truck, checked the windows in the house, saw no movement in the dark, then crossed the short distance to the back door.

You're being a dumb, over-reacting shit, he told himself.

Still, he had the pistol ready as he opened the screen door. . . .

Then, his hip holding it open, he reached for the knob of the inside door with his left hand.

The knob didn't turn.

The door was locked, yet another bad sign. They never locked the doors when they were home. Acid poured into Harrow's stomach, his chest tightened, and his eyes burned. This afternoon had been about instantaneous action—leaping to stop an assassin a nearly instinctive move.

This was different.

Entering his own house had become about caution and danger, his mind flooded with possible outcomes, none good.

In his gut, he already knew that tragedy was waiting. That didn't stop him from praying that he was wrong as he unlocked the door. Entering the landing, he looked straight ahead at a family photo on the wall, Ellen, David, and himself smiling at the lens. His mother had snapped the photo at a family picnic a year before she died.

He glanced left, down into the darkened basement, then turned right and went up two steps into the kitchen.

Normally a bright room, with its yellow walls and white trim, now an inky threat, with no lights on, every shadow a trap. In the half-light that filtered in through the open curtains of the corner window over a small breakfast nook, knives in their wooden block on the counter to his right took on malevolence. Harrow glimpsed the moon through the window, a full fat moon, a butcher's moon.

Fitting then that he also noticed that the butcher knife was gone from its slot in the block.

He moved past the stove on his left, the sink on the right, the big side-by-side refrigerator/freezer straight ahead. His rubber-soled shoes padded silently across the floor. Every nerve in his body strained, on alert for the slightest movement, the smallest sound. At the doorway, he could go right down a short hall to a bathroom and a downstairs bedroom that now served as a home office. Straight ahead lay the dining room.

He wasn't going to turn on the light, just in case. On TV, the criminalist would have used a mini-flashlight to find his way around. Never mind that said criminalist made himself a target by using the flash, giving away his position to any potential attacker. Television never showed the *real* use of the flashlight, which was to find the goddamned light switch. . . .

Not that he needed light getting around his own

home. Still, this was not city dark, which wasn't darkness at all, really—this was country dark.

The house remained eerily silent except for the ticking of an old-time mantel clock atop the wood sideboard. As his eyes struggled to find clues in the darkness, he slowly slid forward past the formal oak dining set. The only illumination came from the tiny amount of moonlight and rays from the garage light that sneaked in through cracks in the curtains in the dining room windows.

Gun up now, moving toward the living room, Harrow heard the thundering rush of his own blood and felt sweat streaking down his forehead; and, too, he heard his heart's sledgehammer pounding. Just short of the living room, his foot touched something, and he looked down to see one of the chairs on its side under the table, a spindly wooden leg sticking out.

He wanted to scream for Ellen and David, but something was wrong here, and if there was an intruder, Harrow couldn't know if the bastard was still around.

That meant doing things by the book.

Finally, cop objectivity settled in. Moving slowly, his eyes well adjusted to the dim light, he eased into the living room.

Moonlight spilled through the half-open curtains of the picture window and played like a grim spotlight on the face of Ellen on her back on the floor beside the coffee table, a dark pool on the rug around her body, her lifeless eyes staring at Harrow, begging to know where he had been when this terrible thing happened to her. She wore a cardinal-red ISU T-shirt and blue jeans, her dark hair framing her face. Two holes darkened the shirt like a huge snake bite near her left breast.

Kneeling beside her, only vaguely aware of the tears running down his cheeks, he checked for a pulse, knowing already he would find none. Her skin felt cool and slightly rubbery—like meat left out to thaw on the counter.

No pulse.

Also, no wedding ring. It wasn't like her diamond was anywhere near big enough to inspire a robbery.

He swallowed and rose. Moving, Harrow looked through the entryway and saw David crumpled on the floor in front of the stairs to the second floor, a dark puddle around him too, the butcher knife on the floor nearby.

David was on his back, eyes closed peacefully, two black holes piercing the first *A* and the *D* in the Nevada T-shirt that he wore over knee-length denim shorts.

Looking at the knife on the floor, as clean as it had been in the block, Harrow knew instantly that David had been in the kitchen when he heard the first shot and had grabbed the knife in a vain attempt to protect his mother.

Harrow checked for a pulse, found none, paused long enough to run a finger through his son's fine brown hair, then rose and checked the rest of the house.

Assured that he was alone, he punched 9-1-1 into his cell phone.

Then he found a chair and positioned it between

his dead wife and son. This was a crime scene, and even that small act was out of bounds, but he did not care. He was not about to leave them alone.

Harrow felt empty inside, hollow, but the emptiness, the hollowness, was Grand Canyon vast; echoes of screams and gunshots he'd never heard filled the abyss within him.

Cops were crawling all over the house now, every light turned on, the windows bright in the darkness. The first uniforms to arrive, in a blur of flashing red and blue were Johnson and Stanowski, the deputies who had worked under Harrow when he had been sheriff. Johnson confiscated his gun and walked him outside to take his initial statement in the yard.

Under the garage light, Lon Johnson, a rail-thin twenty-year vet with light green eyes and sandy hair, shook his head as he looked toward the house, his skin pale and a sickly yellow under the mercury vapor light.

"J.C., I'm sorry. Christ, I'm sorry. Do you have any idea what the hell happened in there?"

Harrow shook his head.

Night-shift sergeant Stanowski, another longtime vet, was heavyset, his crewcut tinged with silver. "No questions, Lon. Not till the detectives get here."

"Jesus, Stan," Johnson said to the sergeant, "this is family."

Stanowski gave Johnson a sharp look that said, *Family or not, he's still a suspect.* In the sergeant's place, Harrow would have done the same.

Johnson seemed about to say something to his sergeant, and Harrow held up a hand. "Lon, take it easy. Stan's just doing his job. Wants his ducks in a row."

"I know, J.C., but . . ."

"No buts," Harrow interrupted. "You want to do me a favor? Do this by the book."

The sergeant tried to hide his embarrassed smile at the show of support from the man who, if you went by the book, was their prime suspect.

Looking at Stanowski, Harrow said, "Any chance I could get into my truck?"

"Not before it's processed. Why?"

"Cigarettes in the glove compartment."

Stanowski pulled a pack from his shirt pocket and shook a smoke out for Harrow. The sergeant knew Harrow supposedly had quit, but had the decency not to point it out, and lit up the former sheriff.

Harrow took a long drag, letting the smoke fill the emptiness, as he wished nothing more than for cancer to strike him instantly, right at this moment, right here in the goddamn yard, and kill him. A second later, however, the thought dissolved, like a hailstone battered by rain, replaced by another one: *Someone had to find the person who had killed his family.*

And in that moment, the decision that would inform years to come was made: if it took every second of the rest of his life, he would find the killer of his wife and son.

"J.C.," Johnson asked, "you all right?"

Harrow just stared at him.

After a moment, the deputy blanched and said, "Sorry, stupid damn question."

The detectives drove up then, putting the awkward moment out of its misery, and Harrow was left alone to finish his cigarette as the two deputies talked to the investigators.

The secondary was some young pup that Harrow never saw before—short black hair, a suit that probably cost almost a month's pay, and the well-scrubbed shine of someone who didn't like getting his hands dirty. What the hell was he doing in this job?

The lead detective Harrow knew. A short, wide-bodied man in jeans, an open-collar shirt, and a cheap sportcoat, Larry Carstens looked like the one-time college football player he'd been—close-cropped blond hair, wide forehead, wide-set brown eyes, formless nose, and lips as thin as a cut.

Carstens had been a uniformed deputy under Harrow, and had made detective three years after Harrow's departure. In the last couple of years, they'd even worked a couple of cases together, Harrow representing DCI.

When they had been filled in by the uniforms, the detectives walked over to where Harrow stood next to his truck, his eyes darting between them and the house, which seemed to call to him in a low whisper.

"Larry," Harrow said with a faint nod.

Carstens returned the gesture. "J.C., we're all very sorry about your loss."

Harrow gave another nod, but said nothing.

"We'll do it by the book," Carstens said with a world-weary sigh.

"Please."

"I had patrol cars set up a half-mile in either direction. Any reporter, national or local, that wants to turn this into a circus will have to hike his ass in."

Harrow sighed. "Appreciate that."

"Tell me what happened. I know about this afternoon—it's been all over the media. Start with leaving the state fairgrounds."

Harrow told Carstens what little there was, right up to the 911 call.

"Let's back up," Carstens said. "Take from the morning till the presidential assignment kicked in."

Harrow did.

Finally Harrow said, "Look, Larry, you've got my gun. Run it, and you'll see it hasn't been fired."

Carstens nodded absently. "By the book, J.C. We'll want to do a GSR test too."

"Fine, then where the hell is Ogden?" Harrow referred to the only real criminalist employed by the Story County Sheriff's Office, the man who should be doing the gunshot-residue test.

His eyes narrowing in the darkness, Carstens took half a step toward Harrow. He kept his voice low, tone clipped but not disrespectful. "Try to remember, J.C., you're not running this investigation. For now, in fact, you're a suspect."

Harrow stepped back, stubbed the cigarette out under his foot. "Okay, I'm a suspect. You're right. But can I ask one question?"

"You can ask."

"Was there any sign of robbery in there?"

"Nothing so far, unless precious items turn up missing. You have a safe, or a locked box with jewelry or money or anything in it?"

"No."

Carstens frowned. "Then why the question?"

"Ellen's wedding ring is gone."

". . . Could she have taken it off to do the dishes? Maybe it'll turn up on her nightstand or—"

"No. She never took it off. She had a thing about that."

"Was it valuable?"

"Not particularly. Less than half a karat. She'd never let me upgrade. She was . . . sentimental."

Carstens swallowed. "J.C., I'll look into it."

"Please."

When the crime scene van did turn up, Harrow was surprised to see not Story County's criminalist Ogden, but a crime scene team from the state Department of Criminal Investigation, his own employer.

He watched with detached professionalism as the DCI crime scene team, people he had known for decades and worked with for years, started in. Several went into the house, while others worked the exterior and the driveway. They all scrupulously avoided making eye contact with him. To them, at least for now, he was the invisible man.

The flashlights in the yard and on the driveway bobbed around, wielded by techs who seemed little more than silhouettes in the dim moonlight. Inside the house, every light continued to burn—

idly Harrow recalled that the only times every window in a home burned with light were when a party was in progress or a tragedy had just occurred.

The night insects were silent, almost as if they respected the seriousness of the situation. The temperature had dropped, but the cold that Harrow felt emanated from within not without. A crop-riffling breeze carried the smell of someone barbecuing nearby. A family having a meal. The familiar scent took on a strange bitterness.

Eventually, the crime scene investigators started toting out his life, and the lives of Ellen and David as well, in plastic and paper bags, boxes, and envelopes. He had never been on this end of a crime scene and, for all his familiarity with the process, felt violated watching these people, his friends, going through his family's things and carting off anything that might prove him either innocent or guilty of the murders of his wife and only child.

He wanted to scream for them to stop. Christ, they *knew* him, didn't they, they *knew* he couldn't have done this, but he also understood they were just doing their jobs, and that job was neither to convict nor to exonerate, but to discern the facts.

Harrow held up pretty well, standing there in the yard, watching them pore and pry over and through every private thing in the house, at least until the coroner's crew brought out the first gurney.

A sheet was drawn up over the face, but Harrow instantly knew the body beneath the sheet was his son. Wetness striping his face, he took two steps toward the stretcher before Carstens eased a consoling arm around Harrow's shoulder and turned him gently away.

"Smoke, J.C.?"

Harrow accepted the cigarette automatically and held it between trembling lips as the detective lit him up.

"You found him. You saw him. You don't need to see him again, not that way."

As if anything could erase that horrific image burned forever into his brain.

Under their white sheets, David and Ellen would join the others now. They would both be in there with all the other ghosts he'd met over the years at crime scenes. Ghosts that sometimes came when he slept . . .

. . . *the little girl that wanted to know why he never caught her killer; the old woman who had died of natural causes but hadn't been found for three days, the only ones aware of her passing her four unfortunately very hungry cats; the twenty-one-year-old wife who had been stabbed to death by a husband who accused her of cheating, even though he'd been the one having the affair.*

Hundreds of ghosts.

And now David and Ellen, too.

As he heard the second gurney on the sidewalk, he turned his back to the house, sucked on the cigarette, and did his best to ignore the sound of the wheels rolling along over the concrete. With all his heart, he wished Ellen would sit up and tell him to put out his damn smoke.

Carstens said, "You'll have to come in with us, J.C.—there's going to be more questions."

Harrow nodded. "The sooner you finish with me, Larry, the sooner we can go after the real killer."

The detective said nothing.

There *was* nothing to say, Harrow knew. Even in his own ears, "Go after the real killer" summoned images of O.J. Simpson on a golf course.

Hell with that. The only thing that mattered to Harrow now was getting through with this bullshit so he could bury his family and, if DCI and the sheriff's department didn't find the son of a bitch, start his own search.

When Harrow and Carstens finally entered the sheriff's office, only a couple of hours lacked before sunup. By Harrow's calculation, he'd been up for just short of twenty-four hours and, oddly, felt not so much as a hint of exhaustion.

The deputies and other staff were scattered throughout the lobby, the corridors, the break room; they and the bullpen got an eyeful as Carstens and Harrow marched through on their way to the interview room at the rear. Unlike Harrow's compatriots, who had avoided his eyes at home, these folks, some known, some not, stared openly.

And for those several long moments, J.C. Harrow felt not like a cop or a father or a husband or a victim, much less the hero who'd saved the President.

But another suspect.

Chapter Three

David and Ellen were buried in a cemetery in Ames, not far from Ellen's parents. A huge crowd, too many of them media, turned out for the funeral. The nation mourned with him—the tragedy that befell the man who had saved the President. But even on that sacred day, consumed with grief, Harrow heard the whispers.

He hired it done.

The coroner was an old pal who covered up for him.

It's all *a cover-up, so no one would know the kid killed his mom and then himself.*

Though they all kept their voices low, every allegation screamed at him.

As Harrow had predicted to Carstens, his firearm test came back that his pistol had not been fired. He also tested negative for gunshot residue. The Secret Service had video of Harrow on post for the hour on either side of the approximate time of death determined by the coroner at the autopsy. Everything about Harrow and his story checked out, and still the rumors continued.

The DCI worked the case hard, but there were just too few clues. The best one, a tire track lifted from the driveway, led nowhere—a P235/75R15, the most popular passenger car tire sold in the United States. Harrow knew too many knockoffs were out there for anybody to even be sure of a brand.

The story ran big. Not just in the *Des Moines Register* and statewide media, but *USA Today* and CNN and every other cable news outlet. When Harrow was exonerated, leaving the DCI to search for, as *NBC Nightly News* put it, "a killer in the heartland," the story began to attract international attention.

The mail had started then, some accusing him, the far larger percentage telling him the nation shared his grief—the man who saved a president only to have his family murdered the same day had become something of a national celebrity.

His friends, the people he'd worked with for most of his adult life with either the sheriff's office or DCI, busted their asses for him. They wanted to find the murderer who had killed the family of one of their own. Months passed, then a year, with no new leads.

Harrow's law enforcement brethren wanted to help, but they had other crimes on their hands, and of course the national media had a finite attention span.

Finally, J.C. Harrow returned to the decision he'd made in his front yard on that terrible night: David's father, Ellen's husband, would track down the killer himself.

He had no idea how, but he would find a way.

Sell his car or sell his soul, he would find a way.

TWO
The Team

Chapter Four

Though he'd never admit it, not under threat of torture or *death* even, Jeff Ferguson loved his older sister.

She'd just helped him with his sixth-grade math homework—he felt a grudging respect for Jessica and her ability to do the kind of complex story problems that a calculator couldn't dent.

Like everything with Jessica, her aid came at a price. Jeff would be taking his sister's shift doing the dishes every other night. That meant dishes duty for a solid week.

Jeff's dad, the town marshal, would call this cheating. But it wasn't like Jessica had just filled in the answers for Jeff—she'd shown him, as they went along, how to solve the complicated problems. In fact, he had done the last two on his own, Jess watching over his shoulder.

Blond and blue-eyed, the pair could have been clones of their mother, a successful real estate agent here in Placida, Florida. Jessica was in the eighth grade, but seemed older than that to Jeff.

Sometimes, though, she seemed really immature to him. She texted constantly during various stupid shows that she and her clique of girlfriends found "awesome," always about girls their age or a little older and a lot richer. Jeff had agreed to make sure Jess didn't get busted by Mom for texting when she was supposed to be doing homework—that was the second half of his payment for the math boost.

Even in the family room, where he sat curled on the floor in stocking feet with his math book, Jeff could detect the wafting aroma of spaghetti and meatballs, a family favorite. The tomato sauce would mean extra scrubbing when he did the dishes tonight, but why complain? He was guaranteed an A on his math homework, and he loved spaghetti.

Then he heard the sound of trouble—Mom's heels clicking in the hallway.

"Jess," he hissed, voice low.

His sister, eyes glued to the family room's big TV, didn't hear him, or those clicking heels either.

"Jess," he tried again, struggling to keeping it low enough to avoid their mother's radar-like hearing, but loud enough to snap his sister out of her texting trance.

Still no response.

Panicking now, knowing that if he slipped up in his guard duty, Jess would make his life eternally miserable, the boy did the only thing he could think of: he hurled his pen at his sister's noggin.

After the pen careened off her skull, she spun on him, her eyes wide with homicidal rage.

Making a terrified face, he pointed violently toward the hallway, and Jess's expression melted immediately. She fumbled for, and got, his pen, tossed it back, hid the offending phone under a pillow, and turned down the TV to a more reasonable volume. She also managed to pick up a history book and appear to be enthralled.

The whole series of actions seemed to Jeff like a great baseball play—Evan Longoria, his favorite player, diving to his left to stop a hot grounder, then rising, stepping on third, and throwing to first to complete a double-play.

Mom strode in—slender, blond, blue-eyed, wearing the slacks and blouse she'd worn to work—and moved immediately to Jeff's side. She tousled his hair and gave him a huge smile that he couldn't help but return.

Jess smiled at her mother too, but to her brother it seemed forced.

"What are you reading, dear?" Mom asked her.

Holding up the book dutifully, Jessica answered, "American History."

Mom didn't miss a beat, glancing at the screen and saying, "Like the invention of lip gloss?"

Jessica, her mouth moving, couldn't find words.

Trying extra hard not to laugh as his sister got busted, Jeff buried himself in his math book and did his best to look both busy and completely disinterested in Jessica's fate.

"Let's turn off the TV," Mom said, "and get ready for dinner."

Jessica didn't argue, simply used the remote.

Mom asked Jeff, "How was your day?"

He shrugged.

"Did they teach you brain surgery or anything?"

"Mom," he said, drawing out the last letter.

Jessica fell into line behind their mother, who led the way out of the family room, Jeff trailing. Mom was making her usual left turn to the kitchen, Jess about to head over to the stairs to the bathroom, Jeff ready to head down the hall to wash his hands when the front door opened.

Jeff at first thought it was his father, but this figure was skinnier, and maybe not as old, and held a pistol, which Jeff's dad would never do in the house.

The man's entrance was so sudden, Jeff was more surprised than afraid, stunned to see the stranger step inside and close the door behind him, as casual as if this *were* Jeff's father.

Mom, however, seemed to instantly see that something was very wrong and moved between the intruder and her kids.

Looking past his mother, Jeff watched in silent horror as the stranger brought the pistol up and pointed it at her.

"No," Mom said, holding up a hand like the crossing guard at school, and the man fired the gun.

Orange and yellow flame and sparks erupted from the barrel like the sparklers last Fourth of July. . . .

Mom took an involuntarily step back, her other hand coming up as if to protect herself, but it was too late. A tiny pink misty cloud hovered as she teetered.

Jessica screamed—it was shrill and almost fake-sounding.

"*Mom!*" Jeff shouted, his voice barely a whisper in his own head as his ears rang from the roar of the pistol in the enclosed space.

Frozen, Jeff watched as the stranger with the gun swivelled toward Jessica. Down on the floor, Mom had stopped moving, her eyes open, staring but not seeing.

Another loud pop turned Jessica's scream into a gurgle, as she made a slow pirouette, her shirt blossoming crimson as she held out her hand to her brother, then sagged to her knees, then fell onto her side.

As the stranger turned in his direction, Jeff ducked into the bathroom and slammed the door. He managed to push in the knob lock and twist it, but knew the killer wouldn't need long to get through. Only one thing to do—the bathroom had a window overlooking the fenced-in backyard. Jeff's only chance.

He heard two more pops and dove into the tub. Peeking, he saw holes in the door, around the knob. . . .

. . . but for now the barrier held.

The boy climbed up onto the toilet, stretched to unlock the window. Though seldom used, the mechanism worked fine. Lifting the window, though, proved harder—stiff in its tracks, the thing did *not* want to *move.* . . .

Jeff glanced toward the door just as two more bullets punched through. They barely missed him, thunking into the wall beside him, cracking wall tiles like eggs. Blinking at sweat, heart pounding, Jeff gave a mighty tug, and the window moved just enough.

He grabbed the frame and swung through feet first, kicking out the screen, even as he heard the bathroom door splinter open.

He flew through the opening, his back scraping the bottom of the frame, and dropped into dusk that was almost darkness, landing with a jolt on the grass, a good six feet below, his stockinged feet stinging. He rolled and came up running, his legs hurting, his back burning, as he half sprinted, half limped around the corner of his home. Not home free, however—the backyard was enclosed by a six-foot wooden privacy fence.

He hoped the bathroom window was too small for the killer to get out—if so, that would give the boy more time. More time to do *what*, he didn't know. He had no idea why this was happening or what was really going on. His mom and sister were dead; despite all the gunfire and blood, that tragedy seemed abstract to the child, though he did sense he was next on the stranger's list. *Why* he was next, he had no idea.

That was the extent of his mental processing of what had happened to bring him to this moment. And now that moment, and the moments tumbling thereafter, were all that concerned him.

If he tried to get to the neighbors, could he make it? From the fenced-in backyard, he could get into the garage, and out onto the driveway. Dad's shed, back here, led nowhere, a dead end. But the fence between the house and its freestanding garage had a gate—through there, Jeff could get to the street and the neighbors.

As he neared that gate, however, Jeff heard the

back door swing open, nearby, and light poured out. If the boy went through, he would walk into the stranger's path. In any case, the killer would turn toward the fenced-in yard and come through, looking.

Jeff figured if he ducked into the shed, he could at least hide in there long enough for the killer to go in to check the garage. Then the boy could make a run for the gate and the neighbors.

That seemed his best chance.

He slid open the shed door as quietly as he could, then squeezed into the hot, musty-smelling metal structure and just as carefully closed the door. Dad's lawn mower shared space with a roto-tiller, a weed-whacker, and some garden tools inside the dark, cramped space.

He prayed that his father was on his way home from work. His father was a marshal. His father had a gun. Again sweat ran into his eyes, and he rubbed them furiously, trying to get them to stop burning, but they only burned worse.

Straining to hear any sound beyond the door of the shed, Jeff wondered if maybe the killer had gone. Other than the pounding of his own heart, he heard nothing. Maybe the killer had given up and gone away. . . .

Jeff allowed his eyes to slowly scan the walls of the shed, and they came to rest on his mother's gardening shears—the ones Mom used to clip off flowers. She kept them very sharp, he knew. He reached across, trying to not make the slightest noise, and plucked them off the wall.

If the killer was still out there, maybe Jeff could

stab him or poke out an eye or something. His father said a man had to defend himself.

And Jeff intended to try.

He listened for what seemed like a very long time and heard nothing—not the garage, not the gate; even the shed door didn't open.

Moments became minutes, and he was sure the killer must be gone. . . .

Carefully, Jeff cracked the shed door and looked out. Darkness had taken over the yard, normally such a friendly playground for him and his sister over the years, now barely visible in blue shadows.

But he could not make out anything except his house beyond. None of the shadows seemed to be a person.

He allowed himself a brief relieved exhale, then continued to slide the door open ever so slowly, still being careful to be quiet about it. . . .

His eyes quickly scanned the yard as the opening grew, but he saw nothing, no one. He finally allowed hot tears of grief and fear to run down his cheeks. For a moment, he wondered if he'd dreamt the whole thing, maybe this was a nightmare, maybe he was napping in his room, and Mom and Jess were downstairs right now.

Taking one tentative step, he felt moist grass bleed up through his socks—Mom kept the grass watered and green. The wetness felt cool and almost soothing. The threat was gone. The nightmare might be real, but it was over.

Still, he listened with the ears of a rabbit, the shears in one gripped hand, ready to protect him. No sound, not even crickets or night birds or wind.

Even his footsteps were silent. He took another, then another. He was into the yard now, and there was no stranger. He turned toward the gate, took one quick step to start running the short distance, but his second step hung in the air, foot wriggling there, as something, *someone*, grabbed him by his head of hair . . . felt like it was being pulled out by its roots!

He howled, but a hand clamped over his mouth and his protest was swallowed. He kicked and fought, but nothing did any good, his captor far stronger. Bringing up the shears, trying to jab them at the arm holding him, Jeff found no target, the stranger throwing the child to the grass. The stranger simply muscled the shears away with one hand and cuffed him with the other, knocking Jeff into a whimpering pile.

The fight was out of the boy. Defenseless, he squeezed his eyes shut as the stranger lifted him and carried him back into the house. Jeff wanted to scream, but nothing would come out—nothing was left. Once inside, the stranger tossed the child like a doll into the hallway and Jeff plopped next to the bloody corpse of his sister.

Not just a bad dream after all.

Looking up, finally, he could see the barrel of the pistol, a big black eye staring at him, inviting him, forcing him, to stare back.

Another Fourth of July flash, and the nightmare was over.

*   *   *

Taking a step back, the man who thought of himself as the Messenger wiped sweat from his forehead with a sleeve. Wasn't supposed to be this hard. His message should be easier to deliver.

The Messenger felt admiration for the boy. He had fought back. He'd had spirit. A pity such a strong child had to be sacrificed; but nothing was free, not in this life, at least. And he had a job to do. A message to get across.

He gazed down at the woman. Pretty, and the spitting image of her two kids. His eyes fell to her left hand. To the wedding ring on the fourth finger.

This wouldn't be the first ring he had taken. In the beginning he hadn't taken any, but he'd thought he could get his point across better if he began taking them, and something in him liked having souvenirs of his efforts.

Still, for all its obviousness, no one seemed to be deciphering his message.

Maybe it was time to start making the message more clear. More emphatic. Without really thinking about it, he withdrew from his pocket the garden shears the boy had tried to use on him.

Maybe this brave boy had been sent to deliver a message to the Messenger.

Perhaps it was time for him to spell the message out. Hadn't his own marriage been severed?

Just taking the ring was not a strong enough sign. He understood that now. He bent down, as if proposing, and took the woman's hand in his. It was still warm. Placing the fourth finger between the blades of the shears, he squeezed.

It took more effort than he had expected, but in the end, the finger crunched and snapped like a thick twig, the ring and finger coming off as one, the blood spill minimal since the heart no longer pumped.

He found a plastic sandwich bag in the kitchen, slipped his prize inside and put the shears back in his pants pocket. He had a new trophy, in the ring finger . . . and a new tool. Despite the trouble he'd gone through, and the sacrifice of a brave child, this message had been successfully delivered.

If only someone out there could understand. Only then could he stop.

Chapter Five

The day began as uneventfully as any of Carmen's, or yours, for that matter. But this seemingly routine day at the office would mark the real start of Carmen Garcia's life, which, coincidentally, was what the eventual cost of her big break might be.

A tall, reedy brunette in faded jeans and an Ozomatli T-shirt, hair tucked up in a loose bun, Carmen tightrope-walked to her cubicle, towering triple mocha latte clutched in a death grip in one hand, stack of folders tucked precariously under her opposite shoulder.

Her doe's brown eyes gave her an earnest, innocent look that belied an ambition to get to the top of the television news game, her high cheekbones and heart-shaped face aiding in that effort.

So many piles of papers covered her desk that Carmen could only wonder if she were personally responsible for the death of an Amazon rain forest. She dropped the wad of folders onto the dead trees, flopped into her chair, slid her purse off her shoulder onto the floor, and sipped the hot latte with the passion of a true addict.

Carmen had climbed aboard a plane the day after graduating summa cum laude from the television production school of Columbia College in Chicago, and moved here to LA, where she'd gotten a job as a production assistant with *Crime Seen!*, a first-year reality-crime show for the faltering UBC network.

The United Broadcasting Company had run sixth in a six-network race for so long, they were threatening to get lapped, the network such an industry joke that Carmen knew getting a job there might hurt her résumé more than help it.

But *Crime Seen!* had sounded interesting . . . in addition to being the first and, yes, only show to look past her lack of experience and make her a job offer.

So UBC it had been. At least United was an over-the-air network, and not cable. Even a sinking ship in the broadcast ocean carried more prestige for your average rat than cable—not much of a rationalization, she knew, a sinking ship being a sinking ship whether the *Titanic* or a tugboat. . . .

Now, nine months later, she found herself enjoying working on the show. This was in part, of course, because *Crime Seen!* was UBC's surprise ratings winner.

In one season, the series—which brought coverage of interesting local crimes to a national audience—had led to the capture of over a dozen felons in half a dozen states. No small feat in only twenty-one airings since last August.

Two wife beaters, three armed robbers, four burglars, two scam artists, two serial drunk drivers, and three murderers had been apprehended thanks to *Crime Seen!* The show was moving from hit series to national phenomenon, and now—with two weeks to go before the season finale (airing live as a ratings grabber)—everyone was busting their butt, following the example of their boss.

J.C. Harrow was not your typical celebrity host. Coming up on six years ago, the former Iowa sheriff turned criminalist had become a tragic American hero when—on the very day he saved the life of the President—his wife and teenage son were brutally murdered. The case made national headlines when the criminalist, briefly a suspect, launched his own investigation into the deaths of his family.

Even though the killer's trail went cold, Harrow's search for his family's murderer continued to fascinate the public, generating an acclaim that led to UBC approaching him to host *Crime Seen!* At fifty, Harrow possessed the charisma and rugged good looks of a natural TV star with his piercing blue eyes and a wavy shock of dark brown hair just now going gray at the temples.

Being on prime-time television kept his family's case alive, but through the first twenty-one episodes of *Crime Seen!*, Harrow had not once mentioned the tragedy on air. Instead, he and the show's staff had tracked down other felons, often with Harrow there to capture their arrests on camera. To UBC, it was reality show heaven.

As for Harrow, well, Carmen couldn't exactly say what he was getting out of it.

She cleared a small space for her morning's monster latte, turned on the computer, and shifted the piles of paper as the machine booted up. As usual, show-runner Nicole Strickland had funneled all the fan mail to production assistant Carmen, whose inbox was jammed.

The e-mails ran the gamut from "love the show," to "hate the show," from "screw Harrow," to "I want to screw Harrow." Suggestions how to make the show better ranged from showcasing more sexually oriented crimes to actually gunning down suspects on air. Some wanted signed pictures from Harrow or a segment host, of whom there were four: Angela Batten, Steven Wall, Carlos Moreno, and Shayla Ross.

Naturally, each host had his or her own strengths and weaknesses, though Carmen felt the only advantage they had over her was experience. True, former network White House correspondent Moreno brought an undeniable gravitas to each story, but the others were local news veterans plucked from obscurity more for their looks and camera ease than any journalistic chops.

For the next four hours, Carmen dealt with the e-mails until yet another paper pile had grown, this one outgoing mail, mostly cheap black-and-white photo reprints of on-air personalities with stamped autographs. Requests for Harrow's pictures made up a considerable pile of their own.

Those requests went to Harrow's desk, where he

actually signed each photo and often enclosed a note himself. Whether two requests or two hundred, each day their star personally dealt with his own fan mail. She liked that about him.

With a Diet Coke and a salad a co-worker brought her from the commissary, the production assistant worked through lunch. She was back on the Internet doing research into various crimes around the country when something about a small town in Florida caught her eye.

The wife and two kids of the town marshal of Placida had been murdered.

Everybody on the staff looked sideways when the family of a cop got killed—their relationship with Harrow made that natural. But, as they'd all learned over the past six months, these types of crimes, while uncommon, were not unheard of.

Still, for the next hour, she dug into everything she could find about Placida, Florida, and the crime. She printed dozens of documents, gathered them into another pile—working on her second rain forest—then started at the top and began studying, instead of just swiftly scanning.

Placida was a Gulf Coast town of less than a thousand souls. Maybe fifty miles south of Sarasota and just north of Ft. Myers, the hamlet lay on a jut of land out into Charlotte Harbor. Local law was a town marshal and three part-timers. For any *real* trouble, the Charlotte County sheriff handled it.

The median age of the citizenry was just a hiccup short of sixty. The average income was twenty-five thousand dollars above the national average because 71.2 percent of the population had white-collar jobs. Placida was a classic bedroom community—or anyway it was until the night town marshal Ray Ferguson came home to find his family murdered near their kitchen.

The murders took place back in September, not long after *Crime Seen!* first aired. When Carmen went to start an electronic file on the case, she noticed one already existed. She opened it and read it quickly: in early October, segment host Shayla Ross had done a cursory study of the case, then abandoned it as a dead end.

The dirtiest little secret about *Crime Seen!* was the mandate to choose crimes that had enough threads for their team to follow. Cold cases were avoided, as were crimes where no suspects were on the horizon. TV viewers wanted closure, and soon.

As Carmen pored over material from the case, she could not shake the feeling that some important detail had been overlooked. Something small and insignificant to Shayla and the investigators, but enough to set off a tiny if mournful alarm in the back of Carmen's mind, a foghorn on a faraway shore.

She stopped, rubbed her eyes, shook her head, then rose, stretched, and walked to the break room for a soda—maybe a little distance would shake something loose. She fished change out of her pocket, got a Diet Coke from the vending machine, and tapped lacquered nails against the lid as she mentally riffled through thousands of bits of information she'd read about the Ferguson murders.

At the end of his shift, Ray Ferguson had come home in a well-tended Placida neighborhood.

Though he didn't make nearly as much money as the other members of the community, his real-estate agent wife, Stella, did. The Fergusons had two kids, a boy, Jeff, eleven, and a girl, Jessica, fourteen.

Like Harrow's wife and son, mother and children had been shot in the chest. Unlike Harrow's family, each was only shot once. Also unlike her boss's case, these victims were shot in one room, apparently executed in turn—Harrow's wife and son with a .357, the Fergusons with a nine millimeter (though in the latter case the efficient assassin had gathered up his shell casings).

A gruesome touch set the Ferguson killings apart, however—the fourth finger of Stella Ferguson's left hand had been cut off, post-mortem. Forensics indicated a gardening tool had been used.

As at the Harrow home, no fingerprints were found, the only piece of evidence (if that) turning up on the Fergusons' driveway: a leaf from a corn plant. As far as the investigators were concerned, that leaf might have come from anywhere. But Illinois farm kid Carmen discerned a clue.

Some quick work on the Internet garnered Carmen more—seemed Florida produced more corn than she'd have thought, nearly one hundred thousand acres in all. But compared to the *twelve million* acres harvested in Harrow's home state, that wasn't much. . . .

And a particular photo at the *Placida News* website sealed her suspicions—it showed a transparent plastic evidence bag with that single corn plant leaf inside.

Rural kid Carmen recognized the difference between a sweet corn plant and a field corn plant. Charlotte County, Florida, home to Placida, was on the northern edge of the highest-producing area for sweet corn in Florida. Virtually no field corn was grown in the northern half of the state. The state's small field corn crop, produced in the southern end, centered on the ocean side, not the gulf.

Why, in a county that grew exclusively sweet corn, was Carmen looking at the leaf of field-corn plant?

She couldn't answer that question yet, but she knew one thing: city kid Shayla, formerly of Boston, would never ask it.

Carmen needed help, and she knew precisely who to ask. But she would do more than just ask—this was her shot—this was her chance. . . .

The PA found Harrow, back in his office after lunch, dutifully signing publicity photos. She knocked on the jamb of the open door, then smiled when Harrow looked up.

"Got a minute, boss?"

Carmen knew that many TV stars made outrageous demands for their offices, turning them into virtual apartments. Harrow's was quite the opposite. A glance would make any visitor think Harrow was nothing more than your average corporate attorney. Furnishings were nice enough but not extravagant, bookshelves filled with research material, his desk a mahogany island mid-room, piled with papers that marked this a workplace and not a showplace. Two leather chairs sat opposite him.

Harrow tossed his Sharpie aside and smiled. "I can spare a minute just to avoid the writer's cramp." He nodded to a chair.

Carmen sat on its edge. "Around the fourth or fifth episode, we were in a production meeting where you mentioned a DCI case you worked involving the specificity of plant DNA."

Harrow gave her a sideways look. "That's not a question."

"No. It's a preamble."

Wearing half a frown and half a smile, he said, "Fourth or fifth episode. How do you remember stuff like that?"

She shrugged. "You never know when 'stuff' will come in handy—like today."

"Today, huh? What are you up to, today?"

She told Harrow what she'd found so far. No places, no dates, just the circumstances. She connected no dots, however, between the Ferguson and Harrow murders.

"So," he said, softly, eyes tight, "this was *Shayla's* story. . . ."

"Yes, sir. And she thought it was a dead end."

"'Sir,' yet. I *am* in trouble." He shifted in his leather chair. "And you went in on your own, and maybe found something?"

"I think so, but I need that plant expert you told us about last year to verify my theory."

Harrow studied her for a long moment. Carmen might have been a slide under the criminalist's microscope.

"Then," he said, "once you've found out you're right, you'll hand all the information over to Shayla—correct?"

Carmen sat silently for a moment. This was her opening, and she knew it.

"If this pans out," she said, "I'm hoping you'll make me the reporter who covers the story."

After a long silence, Harrow said, "You know I can't promise you anything."

"If you tell me you'll try, that's all I ask."

She could tell he was intrigued; but was he also irritated?

Giving away nothing, he said, "And why do you think this nearly eight-month-old case is so important that it merits you a promotion from PA all the way to on-air personality?"

"It's a juicy murder case we can feature on the live show."

"We've had those before."

"Not ones that might be related to *your* case, as well."

And there it was: out in the open.

She said, "You heard the circumstances. You can see the similarities. And the link back to Iowa, or anyway the heartland, if that plant is what I think it is."

Harrow's eyes held hers. Was he trembling? If so, was it with anger? Had she gone too far?

He said, "You think that would influence my decision?"

She stared right back at him. "Frankly, yes."

He began to protest, but Carmen cut him off. "J.C., I know you're not like most people in this business. . . ."

"And yet," Harrow said, exasperated, "you're trying to blackmail me."

"I don't consider it that." She risked a tiny smile. "Maybe . . . manipulate you, a little?"

He just looked at her.

She gestured, and her nervousness showed. "J.C., you've told me a dozen times you believe in my potential. I'm just asking for the chance to prove you right."

Was that a smile? Small, barely discernible, but . . . a smile?

She sat forward. "Give me the name of the man at that seed company, and I'll follow the lead wherever it goes. I'll give you the info, *all* the info, and you can decide who deserves the story—Shayla or me. Is *that* blackmail?"

He considered that, then asked, "Why didn't you just ask me for the name of my plant guy? Make up a reason, or just not go into what you'd found?"

"I owed you more than that."

Harrow grunted a laugh. "Call Settler Seed in Dekalb, Illinois—your old stamping grounds. The man you want is Dr. Brent Caldwell. Tell him I sent you. See what you can get, and be back here within twenty-four hours."

She burned with pleasure, pride, enthusiasm, and outright glee, but remained coolly professional as she said, "Yes, sir."

Rising slowly, forcing herself to move deliberately, she eased toward the door.

The sound of Harrow's voice stopped her. "Carmen?"

Turning, she said, "Yes?"

"The killer cut off Mrs. Ferguson's finger. My wife didn't suffer that . . . indignity."

"No."

"But her killer *did* take her wedding ring."

"Mrs. Ferguson's killer did too—he just took the finger along with it."

A deep crease formed between Harrow's eyes. "Why, do you suppose?"

"If it's the same killer . . . and I think it is . . . he's devolving."

"And if he's devolving . . ."

"He'll accelerate. There'll be more killings. Soon."

He was nodding, slowly. Then he said, "Get back to it."

And she did.

Chapter Six

Shortly before the special live-broadcast season finale of *Crime Seen!* went on air, Dennis Byrnes—early forties, close-clipped black hair, languid gray-green eyes, five o'clock shadow, thousand-dollar Armani suit (charcoal)—surveyed his kingdom.

During a broadcast, the control room was surprisingly silent but for the piped-in studio sounds, even though a dozen technicians hovered over control boards and personal monitors, the audio world sequestered in a booth off at right. The near silence was punctuated by commands from director Stu Phillips, who perched stoically in the center of the back of three tiered rows—the eye of the storm. In his late fifties, Phillips had been at both NBC and CBS, where his fortunes had fallen in favor of younger men, and thanks to the competition's shortsightedness, UBC had snagged a real pro.

Byrnes liked to brag that "UBC is a young network, but we don't put up with ageism," though he neglected to mention that he could get away with paying older pros like Phillips half, or less, of what the big boys had.

Behind the director, show-runner Nicole Strickland leaned against the back window wall, her arms folded, her mouth a tight, thin, straight line. The slenderly shapely, striking woman's tousled red hair vied for attention with her green eyes. This evening she wore a sharply cut, cream-colored Dolce & Gabbana suit with matching Jimmy Choos. Byrnes relished having a beautiful woman as his hatchet man.

Also against the back wall, in the center where an aisle cut down the three tiers of techs, stood Byrnes himself, with a perfect view of the large plasma screen (labeled: PROGRAM) above the bank of similar oversized monitors, whose screens were sectioned into eight windows reporting individual camera shots, remote feeds, and cued-up prerecorded material. The PROGRAM flat-screen reflected the finished product going out over the airwaves.

Crime Seen! had saved two very juicy cases for the finale, and Byrnes would be shocked if this were not the highest-rated episode of the season. He watched with half-lidded eyes as Carlos Moreno demonstrated that two young girls had not been kidnapped, as their mother had reported, but were murdered by her and buried on a piece of farmland owned by the mother's parents. Footage of her arrest—not seven hours before—was the capper.

In the second segment, Angela Batten outed the

CEO of an insurance company that for years had been defrauding its policyholders by substituting new language in renewal documents—just the sort of story of corporate greed getting busted that tapped into Main Street America's rage against Wall Street. Few in the viewing audience were aware that *Crime Seen!* itself came to them courtesy of the big oil corporation that was UBC's Big Daddy.

Byrnes knew these two juicy and very different stories would each be front-page fodder on tomorrow's *USA Today*, with *Crime Seen!* getting plenty of play. He was neither psychic nor overconfident— just this morning, the network prez had been interviewed for both stories.

Finally all that remained was J.C. Harrow's season farewell, which, as scripted, was a laundry list of the miscreants the show had helped bust, all wrapped up in Harrow's rugged, Midwestern "I'm a victim too, but I'm getting back at 'em" persona.

With pleasure if not affection, Byrnes regarded his unlikely, ruggedly photogenic star on the monitor, where Harrow could be seen casting a film noir shadow against a brick backdrop with a single barred window—cheesy but effective.

The former lawman sported a navy blue blazer that looked unpretentious, although it was no off-the-rack number, worn over a lighter blue button-down dress shirt, open at the collar; his jeans were faded, worn—Everyman attire that Wardrobe had slaved over.

Piercing blue eyes stared out at America as Harrow said, "My colleagues in the booth are going to have to forgive me for breaking from script . . ."

Byrnes, paying half-attention before, suddenly stood as straight as an exclamation mark, and was heeding his star's every word, every pause, every gesture.

". . . but some late-breaking news has changed the circumstances of tonight's live broadcast."

Byrnes snapped at the director, "What the hell?"

Phillips, in a headset, his eyes blinking a Morse code SOS, glanced back helplessly at his boss.

Byrnes leaned so far forward at the top of the aisle, he had all his weight on the toes of his four-hundred-dollar Bruno Magli loafers. He might have been a diver preparing for a double gainer.

"You all know that, for almost six years, I've been searching for the person or persons who killed my family."

In the booth, the director couldn't help himself, and told his cameraman to push in closer on their host.

"Recently, a member of the *Crime Seen!* staff found what she thought might be a clue tying another crime to the deaths of my wife and son. This is the first new evidence that's been turned up in the case in many, many months."

Byrnes yelled, "Did you know about this? Did any of you *know* about this?"

The director shook his head, but his attention was on the drama unfolding before them all. Those involved in technical aspects of the broadcast ignored their big boss; others, just standing observing—like show runner, Nicole Strickland, now edging away from the network exec—merely shook their heads and melted into anything handy.

"Next season," Harrow was saying, "we will be following this clue, and working hard to uncover other evidence, in a concerted, focused effort to track down the killer or killers of my family. . . ."

Byrnes said, "*Great* idea, Nicole, bringing in a live audience for this episode."

"And we'll be doing it right on this show. You will be with us every step of the way—helping us track down the murderer of my wife and my son."

Gasps from the studio audience interrupted the star.

Picking up, Harrow said, "UBC has pledged to buy us the equipment we need, and to pay for the finest crime-scene team I can put together to investigate this case—a veritable superstar task force of criminologists and crime fighters."

Byrnes threw his hands up. "UBC pledged what?"

"We'll start assembling the team, and investigating, as soon as the show ends tonight . . . and we will work as long as we have to. Join us in September when we start *Crime Seen!*, season two, by bringing you up to date on our progress on this case over the weeks ahead."

His eyes narrowing, Harrow added, "Finally, a special message to one person—the killer of my family. I'm coming for you . . . and I'm coming soon."

Then the credits were rolling, which often signaled the control room getting rowdy, but right now it was like church—in more ways than one, because several people were praying.

The screen faded to black as the show went off the air.

Byrnes said to Nicole, "Get him. Now."

She nodded, cell at the ready, turning away, speaking quietly; then, cupping the phone, she said, "He'll be in his office. He says . . . he's expecting you."

"No shit."

Soon the exec was moving down the corridor, which would normally be filled with staffers quickly finishing up and getting the hell out. With the season over, the network had arranged a wrap party at the newest swank LA bistro, El Viñedo, to which they should all be on their way.

But Byrnes found the hall lined with cast and crew.

As his gaze swept over them, their eyes either found something very interesting in the carpeting to focus on or turned toward lead reporter Carlos Moreno.

Byrnes's frown withered his staff the way sunlight did vampires. "What's this about?"

But Moreno, six feet tall with short spiky black hair, was impervious to the exec's gaze. His eyes locked unblinkingly on Byrnes's. "We're here to support our boss," he said.

Byrnes never flinched. "That's very gratifying, Carlos . . . since *I* am your boss."

"We support J.C."

A few nervous nods backed up that claim.

"All right, duly noted," the network president

said, keeping his tone even, nonconfrontational. It was a union town, after all. "I'll see you all at El Viñedo."

People peeled off the wall and headed down the hall and around the corner—hostages released after a siege—though Moreno stood firm.

Byrnes met the man's gaze. "You don't think I should fire J.C.'s ass?"

"Nope."

"What *do* you think I should do?"

"Give him what he wants. He's an accidental genius. He didn't mean to, but he just handed you and me and all of us the biggest potential ratings winner in history. If he'd come to you first, you—"

"But he didn't come to me."

"Dennis! So what? He isn't your standard TV whore. You were well aware when you hired him that J.C. took this show hoping to find his family's killer."

"And here I thought it was the truckload of money we backed up and dumped at his feet."

The reporter rolled his eyes. "Right, Dennis. Money. *That's* what makes J.C. Harrow tick."

Byrnes frowned, but had no response ready before the reporter gave him a little salute and ambled off down the hall.

The exec strode down the corridor to the dark-wood door with the name J.C. HARROW in banker-like gold lettering. For a split second, Byrnes considered knocking, then decided *screw it,* and went in.

Behind his desk, J.C. Harrow appeared as relaxed and confident as a man who had just scored his biggest success, and not committed career suicide on national television.

Byrnes didn't bother to sit down, just strode up to the desk and gave his star a cold, confrontational glare.

"I just want to know one thing," Byrnes said.

Harrow did not take the bait. He just waited silently, leaning back in his chair, his expression not quite smiling, but certainly self-contained.

"Why did you piss it all away on a whim, J.C.? You could have come to me, we might have put something together, instead you skyjack the airwaves. Weren't we *good* to you?"

For a long time, Harrow said nothing, then, "That's more than one thing, Dennis. If you want an answer to any of those questions, pull up a chair and sit down."

Byrnes had a moment—a moment where he had to choose between losing it entirely, going off like a geyser, or behaving like a grown-up.

So he pulled up a chair, crossed his legs, folded his hands, and (*goddamnit!*) smiled at his star. "Please, J.C. Enlighten me."

"UBC has been great," Harrow said. "The money is generous, and I like the work. But, Dennis—I didn't piss *anything* away."

"Nothing but your career and your starring gig on the number-one-rated show on this network."

"Explain," Harrow said, not at all confrontational.

Byrnes shook his head. "Can you really think there's any reason I'm here other than to fire your ass?"

"You wouldn't need to be here, if firing me was all you had in mind. Or anyway, you wouldn't *still* be here."

Byrnes had no response to that.

Harrow shrugged, rocking slightly in his chair. "Anyway, why would you fire me? . . . I may be a relative novice in this business, but I know enough to be sure of one thing—I just guaranteed to double your ratings in the fall."

Byrnes sat forward, seething but in control. "You go on the air and commit my network to unknown, enormous expenses, you rewrite—off script and on air—the format of our top show, and you wonder why would I fire you? Do you think when word gets out any network would ever trust you in front of a camera again?"

"Maybe not a *live* camera," Harrow said, with a puckishness unusual for the ex-cop. "Anyway, Dennis, I don't think you'll let the word get out. You know that I wouldn't take as much blame for this as you would—for allowing it to happen. *I'm* not where the buck stops."

"That sounds uncomfortably like extortion."

"Dennis, much as I like you, I'm not much for taking lessons in morality and business ethics from television executives."

". . . Maybe there are circumstances where I'd consider putting you back on the air . . . but I'm not paying for some 'superstar' private forensics team or any other wild-eyed ideas. . . ."

Harrow sat back again, shrugged. "You can take me off the air, Dennis, but I'll have another network signing me up for a new show by end of work-day tomorrow . . . on my terms, right down to the 'superstar' forensics team."

Byrnes started a sigh somewhere around his toes, and finally it emerged. "Why didn't you come to me with this idea?"

"And have you say no? And hold me to my contract? I do apologize for the tactics, but they were necessary. Your priority is the show—mine is finding my family's killer. I believe I came up with a way that serves both our interests."

Byrnes shook his head. "I can't believe you would commercialize the murders of your own family. . . ."

Harrow's laugh was a bitter thing. "Give me a goddamn break, Dennis. You've been commercializing my family's death since day one of this show. And I've been letting you do it, because it's a relatively harmless means to an end that is everything to me."

For the first time he could remember, Byrnes found himself in a room with someone he could not stare down, facing someone who wasn't afraid of him. Like any jungle predator, Byrnes could smell fear and pounce. Only this time, the fear he sensed in this room was his own.

"You played me for a fool tonight," Byrnes said.

Harrow shrugged. "I know, Dennis. And if that means you have to let me go, to save face, and let the chips fall wherever the hell, well then . . . no hard feelings. You're doing what you have to do. Like I am."

The star rose, and came around to extend his

hand toward his seated boss. "Whatever you decide, I owe you for the platform you've provided me. Thank you."

Stunned, Byrnes took the proffered hand, shook it, and said, "I'm not going to fire you, J.C.," the words almost a surprise to himself as they came out. Without letting go of his star's hand, he said, "But ever screw with me again, J.C., and I will end you in this business. Do you understand?"

"I understand."

"I do have to say this, though."

Harrow was returning to his chair as Byrnes said, "Do you have any idea what you're proposing, how much a production like this would cost?"

"Actually, yes," Harrow said. "That's frankly part of why I sprang it on you the way I did. Dennis, it was an ambush—I make no pretense otherwise."

Byrnes was unprepared for what happened next. Harrow handed him a fat spiral-bound document—a budget proposal.

The exec began flipping through the pages—the numbers were large, but actually less than he might have anticipated. Still, tomorrow the UBC board would be giving the exec the kind of bad time he'd just given Harrow.

After another endless sigh, Byrnes said, "All right, J.C.—we'll do it your way. You'll get your toys. I'll even go to bat for you with the board. I'll tell them you told me your plan ahead of time, and take the heat that should be yours."

Harrow frowned, confused. "Why would you do that, Dennis?"

"Because I back my people. We're a team. We're a family . . . and I'm Daddy."

He waved the budget at the host.

"But if this half-assed scheme fails, and ratings fall? It's your ass, and your whole crew's."

Harrow's mouth made the thinnest line of a smile. "Sounds like 'Daddy' is strict."

"Daddy spanks, yes. And Daddy also has chores for you. We'll do things your way, J.C., just as you've requested."

"Thank you."

"Don't thank me yet. You do things your way, hire who you want within these budget parameters . . . but you will also be available for any and all publicity we deem necessary."

Harrow's face tightened. "You know I find that distasteful. My contract—"

"Screw your contract. This is another unpleasant means to an end that you're going to have to put up with."

"Any and all publicity," Harrow said hollowly.

"Any and all—if this is going to work for both of us, I've got to be able to pump the ratings as much as possible."

Harrow sat silently for several long seconds. Then he shrugged. "You're right, Dennis."

"All right, then." Byrnes slapped his thighs. "If we're going to do this, let's make *Crime Seen!* a bigger hit than it is already."

The exec rose and moved toward the door, and Harrow said, "There's one more thing, Dennis."

Turning back, the network president said, "Don't you think you've been greedy enough?"

"Not a matter of greed," Harrow said. "But I want a new segment host."

"Why?"

"I need to reward the talented PA who found the clue that set this in motion."

Byrnes smirked. "Funny, you want to reward him—I'd just as soon throttle him."

"It's a *her*," Harrow said. "Carmen Garcia."

The exec frowned. "Isn't she Nicole's mail girl?"

"Yes."

Byrnes closed his eyes. "Brother—Nicole's going to *love* that."

"Why, Dennis, are you suddenly afraid of Nicole?"

". . . I have to ask, J.C.—is this personal?"

Harrow looked at him blankly. "What?"

"Jesus, man. Don't make me pull teeth—are you sleeping with her?"

His eyes narrow, Harrow said, "Christ, Dennis—she's young enough to be my daughter."

Shrugging, Byrnes said, "Which in Hollywood is a plus."

Harrow shook his head glumly. "You've been out here too long. You think everybody is an amoral scumbag."

"Hollywood gets to us all, J.C. Just tonight, for example, *you* screwed *me* over. . . ."

Harrow had no response to that.

Byrnes threw up his hands. "All right. I'm tired. You win. I'm going home and see my wife and two daughters, who are just fine, thanks so much for asking. I'll let Nicole know that you have a new segment host."

"Thanks, Dennis."

"You're welcome, J.C." He beamed at his star. "Screw me again, and you'll find out just how amoral a scumbag I can be."

Chapter Seven

The room was stuffy, the weather warm for May, the humidity heavy, the smell of rain hanging in the still air as the Messenger (as the killer thought of himself) found the spot on the videotape and cued up the ending of *Crime Seen!* yet again. He had not prayed in years, but he did now. Maybe, finally, someone was getting the goddamned message!

"Recently, a member of the *Crime Seen!* staff found what she thought might be a clue tying another crime to the deaths of my wife and son."

Watching in his living room, the Messenger smiled.

"Next season," Harrow was saying, "we will be following this clue, and working hard to uncover other evidence, in a concerted, focused effort to track down the killer or killers of my family. . . ."

About damn time, the Messenger thought.

"And we'll be doing it right on this show. You

will be with us every step of the way—helping us track down the murderer of my wife and my son."

He took in Harrow's words like clues that each needed close examination, and he wondered if it was possible that after all this time, the dumb shit-kicker he'd transformed from a retired county sher-iff into a national celebrity was finally, *finally* getting a clue himself.

If so, maybe there was even more work to be done than he had planned on.

That was all right. He had been waiting years for someone to raise the stakes, and, thus far, no one had. He had sent message after message over the last ten years, and, until now, no one had discerned their meaning.

It wasn't as if Harrow had been the first. Far from it. By August of 2002, the Messenger had already delivered two other communications without any-one understanding what he was up to; and since Harrow's family, there had been more.

Many more.

He wound the tape back slightly.

Harrow said, "You will be with us every step of the way—helping us track down the murderer of my wife and my son."

If you're smart enough, he thought, going back to his plans for his next message. *If you can read the writing on the wall. . . .*

Chapter Eight

First thing Saturday morning, J.C. Harrow was on UBC's small corporate jet, heading to Waco, Texas.

He hadn't slept well. On some level, he supposed, he had won, but Byrnes had been right to liken what his host had done last night to hijacking the show and blackmailing the network. Had he gone to the exec with his "catch a serial killer" road-trip concept, Harrow might have been embraced as a visionary . . . or rejected out of hand.

And he had not been experienced enough in the business of show to calculate the odds. Just going for it, on live television, seemed the best way to acquire the wherewithal to track down the bastard who had stolen Ellen and David's lives.

So he had stooped to commandeering his own program, and putting the man who'd hired him in a hell of a spot with the network. Now, on the Cessna, he sat with the other three passenger seats unoccupied, the two pilots his only company. He didn't mind the solitude—it helped him get the bad taste out of his mouth, over how he'd gotten here; and he could study the files of the team he hoped to assemble—hard copy in manila folders, not his laptop. He was no Luddite, but he preferred the Old School approach; he still chose a morning paper over a news website.

When he got to Waco, he learned from his PD contact that Laurene Chase—the best forensics investigator in central Texas and maybe the entire state—was working a crime scene; he would not be able to talk to her until the next day. That was disappointing, but he was okay with it—he was still prepping, and one thing that TV and law enforcement had in common was that solid preparation was key to success.

After a solo dinner, Harrow spent the evening in his room going over the files. The names he was considering were all people he knew personally, professionally, or by reputation. They were not in every case the number-one person in their fields, but all were eminently qualified and, more importantly, were people Harrow felt he could work well with, and trust.

He started with a baker's dozen files; when he was finished, he had a smaller stack, and began to make a list on a yellow pad.

Laurene Chase was at the top. In descending order came Michael Pall, a DNA scientist with the Oklahoma State Crime Lab; chemist Chris Anderson from Meridian, Mississippi; Billy Choi, a tool mark and firearms examiner from New York; and computer forensics whiz Jenny Blake, Casper, Wyoming.

The taller stack of files had other strong possibilities, and he would not be distraught if he had to return there. In any case, he would have a better chance of making this work with a dependable number two who would keep her head when all about them, especially her emotionally invested boss, might be losing theirs.

The biggest liability would be if he was unable to assemble the right team—and the chemistry between team members was something that could not be predicted. A second major liability was himself— no police department anywhere would dream of assigning a crime scene analyst to investigate the murder of his own family.

He'd already heard from Carmen that this morning's media outlets were rife with editorials and interviews with experts condemning his participation—on MSNBC, a retired LA detective turned bestselling author said, "I've heard of having a fool for a client, but this is ridiculous."

Beyond any ethical or practical concerns, having such an emotionally involved crime scene analyst on the team was one thing; having that analyst *head up* the team was another. It could easily be a recipe for disaster . . . which was why his choice for a second in command was key.

The first name on his list.

Laurene Chase.

* * *

By mid-morning Sunday, Harrow found himself leaning against a rented Lexus at the far end of the parking lot of Our Savior Baptist Church on the northeast side of Waco. He blew out a ribbon of smoke from his second cigarette. The sun was bright but pleasant, the temperature in the mid-seventies, Harrow enjoying a breeze. Spring in Texas included the scent of flowers Detective Harrow couldn't identify, though the evidence was pleasing enough.

These days, Harrow was smoking again, but out of a sort of half-assed respect to his late wife, he tried to keep the habit at bay. He wore a navy blue polo, jeans, and black Rockys, the cop shoes he seemed to have worn every day of his adult life.

As the congregation emptied out of the brick church down wide cement stairs, Harrow stubbed the cigarette out under his toe, then stood a little straighter, searching for his friend. This was a mostly African-American congregation, dressed in Sunday best and proud of it, parading past the pastor after a brief exchange, then mingling with other worshipers below a while before slowly dispersing to their cars.

Harrow liked black churches—right now, there were smiles and laughs and loud talk and hugs and backs getting slapped. Predominantly white churches he'd attended since childhood had always seemed stiff and vaguely guilt ridden. And at this kind of church, the women, older ones anyway, wore hats! What the hell ever happened to white women in hats?

Last out was a tall, slim, milk-chocolate woman

in a fitted gray business suit and open-collared pink dress shirt under a gray vest. Her long black hair was battened down in tight cornrows, and she wore tiny silver hoop earrings that caught sunlight and glinted. That same sunlight made the woman squint, but her oval, black-framed glasses took up the battle, tinting darker against the brightness. When she glanced toward Harrow, she added a wide smile to her ensemble.

She started toward him, and he met her halfway, next to a silver Toyota Camry that would prove to be hers.

As she neared, her smile turned sly, and she said, "Not too often do we get a real, live TV star out here in the boonies."

"Waco's hardly the boonies, Laurene."

"Maybe not. But I sure didn't expect to see a Hollywood type like you turning up at a church."

"Outside a church. Wouldn't want to risk lightning." He grinned and extended a hand. "Good to see you. Really good."

She knocked the hand aside and gave him a big, warm hug. She smelled better than the flowers in the breeze.

"Been too long," Laurene said. "When was the last time, anyway?"

He thought for a moment. "Probably that IAI conference in Dallas."

They were both members of the International Association for Identification, an organization made up of some seven thousand forensic investigators, examiners, techs, and analysts worldwide.

"Doesn't *that* seem like a lifetime ago," she said.

"Laurene, I'm sorry about Patty."

"I know you are. I got your flowers and the card. Meant a lot, J.C."

Laurene's life partner, Patty Moore, had passed away not quite a year ago from cervical cancer.

"I'm just sorry I couldn't make it down here," Harrow said.

"It's all right," she said. "I know you're a busy guy."

Harrow glanced around. "Can I take you for Sunday lunch or brunch or something?"

"Sure. And I know just the place."

They walked two blocks to a Popeye's Fried Chicken. She knew Harrow was a sucker for the onion rings. They shared a big basket of them and some hot wings and laughed about the prospect that food like this would kill them before some bad guy did. Seated at their little table by a window, the view obscured by restaurant adverts, they wiped off their fingers with paper napkins, and the talk turned serious, as if a switch had been thrown.

"I should have got down here," he said, hardly able to meet her eyes.

"You didn't know Patty that well."

"That's not the point."

"What you wrote? On the card? It really did mean a lot, J.C. Hell . . ." She sighed, and her eyebrows flicked upward. "You understand loss better than most. But you know how it is—you shake it off, and get on with it."

"You do?"

"Yeah. Sure."

"I, uh, checked up on you, kid. I know."

"You know."

He nodded. "I know. I know you went back to work less than two months ago."

"Come on, J.C. I needed time."

"Time to grieve."

"Right."

"I need you to level with me, Laurene."

"Why?"

"We'll get to that . . . *if* you level."

Laurene seemed to stare out the window, though she was really looking at a poster advertising buffalo shrimp. "I got to where I could barely get out of bed, J.C. Clinical depression, the medics call it. Damn near lost my job."

"Funny. I almost lost mine the other day."

The dark eyes sparkled. "You? How does a *TV Guide* cover boy almost lose his job?"

"Haven't you been watching the show?"

Her half smile added up to a whole smirk. "Right, I'm gonna watch some jive-ass reality show, after I been out on the street all day and all night, busting bad guys in the flesh."

"Oh . . . well . . . I can under—"

"J.C.!" Her laugher was sharp, little knife jabs of glee. "You can't tell when I'm *playin'* you? There is not a week goes by when I don't time-delay your ass. Me skipping commercials doesn't offend you, does it?"

Now he laughed, embarrassed. "No. Not at all. Did you, uh . . . catch the show the other night?"

"Yeah, I saw it. This is how they do the ratings now? Send the star door to door?"

He leaned in. "Now I *know* you're playing me, because, if you did see that show, you must already know why I'm here." He locked eyes with her, and nothing jokey remained in her expression. "Laurene, I need a second-in-command. A second I can trust not to bullshit me, and let me know when I'm out of line."

She sipped Diet Coke through a straw; her eyes were not on his now. She was thinking.

"You know what I'm asking, Laurene."

She sighed. Shrugged. "J.C., I have a job. A job I haven't been back to for long, and probably shouldn't risk."

"I don't want you to risk anything, Laurene. But with your background and abilities, you could work anywhere. You're damned good at what you do. But you are also underappreciated and underpaid."

"It's 'cause I'm a local girl. But I like helping out where I grew up."

"I'm not asking you to leave Waco forever. But I *am* offering you a raise."

She stretched her arm across the table and put a finger to his lips. "I'm not worried about the money, Handsome. Long as there's health. I learned the hard way what happens when you don't have that kinda coverage."

"UBC treats its people well, far as perks go. They have a deserved rep for underpaying the help, but *I* will set your salary."

"Suppose I don't care about coming back to Waco."

"What do you mean?"

"I mean, does this gig have legs? Will it last past this one case?"

Harrow shrugged. "I don't know. I suppose if we're successful, anything is possible. But with the TV exposure you'll have, a lot of new possibilities are going to open up."

"Right. Maybe I'll star in *Foxy Brown Part Two*."

He laughed. "Hey, I would pay to see that."

She laughed too, then got very silent, wheels turning.

Finally, she said, "If I can wrangle a leave of absence, you'll guarantee good PR for the Waco PD? Give them some kind of love on the air?"

"Hell," Harrow said, "I can probably get them a screen thank you in the credits every week."

This was the kind of request Dennis Byrnes would love—the kind that didn't cost a damn thing.

She thought a while longer. Then: "All right, Sweet Talker. I'll hit up my boss. If they don't put up too big a fuss, I'll do it. What are we talking, nine months?"

"That's the maximum, unless we decide to take this concept onto a second case. But I'm not thinking in those terms, Laurene. This isn't about television, not really."

Quietly she said, "I know what it's about."

"Thanks, Laurene," Harrow said. "You're a lifesaver."

Laurene smiled and shook her head. "You want saved, you saw where the church was. . . . Notice you didn't come in. Let me guess—last time you set foot in church was at the funeral. Right?"

"God and I," Harrow said, "are not on speaking terms."

"I been there. But God didn't do this."

"He didn't prevent it."

"No. No. But it was some sick monster that did this, J.C. And we need to find him, so he doesn't do it to anybody else."

"Amen," Harrow said.

From his hotel room in Oklahoma City, Harrow called Michael Pall. The scientist seemed pleased to hear from the lawman turned TV star, and agreed to meet him in the hotel bar for a drink later that evening.

Harrow was already seated in a leatherette booth when Pall came in around seven. Only five-six, the middle-aged Pall was no Superman, but did resemble an aging Clark Kent with his black-frame glasses and thick comma of dark, dangling hair.

Then Harrow shook hands with the guy, and began to wonder if Pall—however short he might be—might be Superman, at that. He had a vice-like grip, and Harrow used a ploy taught to him by another cop buddy back in rookie days. *When confronted with a death-grip hand-shaker,* the cop had told Harrow, *just extend your forefinger.* This made it impossible for the other man to crush your hand. Harrow didn't know all the physics of it, but damned if it didn't work.

"Damn, it's good to see you, J.C.—how long's it been?"

"Something like ten years."

"So why do you look just the same?"

"It's a good thing Oklahoma pays you to go after the truth, Michael—'cause you don't lie for shit."

"Isn't that, J.C.—I just don't have much imagination. Just the facts, ma'am, like they used to say on *Dragnet.*"

"Watch it, buddy—you're betraying both our ages."

They smiled and got settled into the booth.

Though Pall said little, his résumé spoke volumes. For one thing, he'd been part of the team that brought peace to families by identifying victims in the 1995 bombing of the Murrah Federal Building in Oklahoma City. And, although it never played into the trial, he also had developed evidence that implicated Timothy McVeigh. He was slightly older than Harrow.

They ordered drinks and made small talk for a few minutes. Finally Pall asked, "Are you gonna tell me why?"

"Why what?" Harrow asked.

Pall looked at Harrow over the top of his glasses.

Harrow said, "You know about the show."

"I live in Oklahoma, J.C., not a cave."

"You follow it?"

"I saw Friday's episode. You think it's a good idea, J.C., investigating something so close to you?"

"It's a good idea if I surround myself with the right people."

"Have you eaten? I could eat."

Pall called a waiter over and ordered salad, steamed vegetables, and a small rare filet.

Harrow said, "Make it two."

When the waiter was gone, Harrow said, "Michael . . ." No one called Pall "Mike" that Harrow knew of. ". . . have you thought about retirement?"

Pall studied Harrow. "And here I thought you came to offer me a job."

"You've got your time in, and qualify for a full pension. You're single, at least as far as I know, which means you'd be free to travel. I'm here to offer you a chance to do a little moonlighting."

"How many months you guaranteeing?"

"Nine. But it will mean more money than two full years at your current job. And there's a possibility—just a possibility—that we might keep the team together, if we're successful."

"The team? Or the 'act'? This sounds like show business to me, not law enforcement."

"You know me better than that, Michael. This will be professional all the way."

"Who else do you have?"

"My second is lined up—Laurene Chase."

"Oh. Well. That's a very good start. Here's our food!"

They ate.

They had a drink after. They had another drink, and after Pall finished his, he asked, "When do you need an answer?"

"The sooner, the better," Harrow said. "You're

my first choice in this position—but I have other names I can go to."

"I'm the first you've approached?"

"In this slot, yes. Only other team member signed on is Laurene. We go to work June first."

"I'll let you know," Pall said.

When Harrow left the meeting, he had no idea which way the scientist was leaning. Pall was a lot of things, but easy to read was not one of them.

The next stop took Harrow to Shaw and Associates, a commercial crime lab in Meridian, Mississippi. Sixty-five, with white hair and an easygoing smile that spoke of confidence and success, Gerald Shaw had left public life for the private sector over twenty years ago. Now, his crime lab was the most respected of its kind in the nation, if not the world.

After small talk over a cup of coffee, Harrow got to the point and asked for the loan of chemist Chris Anderson.

"Loan?" Shaw asked, arching a black eyebrow that seemed stark next to the white swooping over his forehead.

"We'll pay him," Harrow said, holding up a palm. "You can take him off salary and even bennies, while he's with us."

"Well, doesn't that sound like a sweet little deal," Shaw said genially. "And just who's gonna cover his workload?"

Harrow had known Shaw was a sharp business-man, and was prepared for the haggling. "We'll pay for a sub. If you have any expenses lining up a sub, we'll pay that, too."

Shaw grinned sleepily. "Well, that does sound a little sweeter. But it's up to the boy himself. If Chris wants to go, fine—you got yourself a deal."

Born and raised in Tuscaloosa, Alabama, Chris Anderson had played basketball in high school well enough to make All-State, but not to get a scholarship. His grades, though, had been another matter—exceptional in math and science, Anderson had earned a full ride at the University of Alabama right there in his hometown. He took his first trip north to attend graduate school at the University of California-Berkeley, probably the nation's best chemistry grad school.

Tall, with blond bangs, Anderson had the playful brown eyes and wide smile of a boy-band singer. Not yet thirty, he was something of a prodigy in the forensics field—Shaw paid the young man double what he could have made in public law enforcement.

After Harrow outlined the plan, Anderson—who had never watched *Crime Seen!*—turned to Shaw. "Mr. Gerald, how do you feel about this?"

A hand settled on Anderson's shoulder. "Might be a good idea, Chris. I've known J.C. for years. He's a good man, and it'd get you out of the lab for a while. Some field work would be good experience for you."

The young man considered that. "And my job would be here when I got back?"

"You bet, son," Shaw said. "Whenever you want it."

Turning his fresh face to Harrow, Anderson said, "Well, then, sir—when do I start?"

Two days later, in New York City, Harrow found himself in a rundown Brooklyn tenement building, standing in a dark hallway in front of apartment 406.

He knocked and waited.

Nothing.

He was just getting ready to leave when the door swung slowly open and he found himself staring at a bleary-eyed young man wearing only a bed sheet wrapped around him like a sarong. The son of an Asian father and Caucasian mother, Billy Choi was an ex-New York cop and former Golden Gloves boxer. Harrow had run into the criminalist at various IAI functions, where they'd shared war stories over drinks, even teaming up for conference role-playing sessions.

"J.C.," Choi said, rubbing the sand from his eyes, his normally swept-back jet-black hair a bird's nest. From the lack of surprise, the guy might have seen Harrow five minutes ago.

"I come in?" Harrow asked.

Choi stepped out of the way, gestured with one hostly hand, and Harrow entered. To call the place a rathole would have been an insult to rats, the young man's housecleaning skills limited to hiding the real mess beneath empty pizza boxes and dirty dishes.

"Is it helpful in your work, Billy?"

"Is what?"

"Living at a crime scene?"

"Pretty funny, J.C. When I wake up, I might laugh."

"Mind a question?"

"Hit me."

"Can you play nice with others?"

Shrugging, Choi said, "Not according to the NYPD. Gross insubordination, they call it."

Harrow gave him a long hard look. "They also call it striking a superior officer."

"Nothing superior about him," Choi said.

"Oh?"

"Well, maybe. As in King Asshole."

"Ah."

"J.C., I just hit him. *You'd've* killed his ass."

But Harrow merely looked at the young ex-officer. "No, I wouldn't."

Choi could not take Harrow's gaze, and his eyes dropped to the floor. "Yeah, man, I know—I screwed up royal."

"Question stands. Can you play nicely with others?"

"Does it matter?"

"Might. You watch my show?"

"I've seen it. Hey, nice gig, bro."

"You see Friday's show?"

"What's today?"

"I'll take that as a 'no,'" Harrow said, and brought him up to speed.

"I'm in," Choi said.

Harrow shook his head. "Answer the question first."

"I can play well with others," Choi said, a kid forced to recite in front of the class.

"No bullshit, Billy—I've got the second chance you've been looking for. But if you screw me over, you won't be able to land mall cop."

"No bullshit, *sensei*," Choi said, earnestly. "I promise ya, J.C. You give me the chance, I'll be a right guy. No more screwin' up."

"And you would walk away from all this?" Harrow asked, gesturing around the dire apartment.

Billy grinned. "For you I would, J.C."

Harrow was halfway down the crummy corridor of Billy's building when his cell chirped. The caller ID said it was Pall.

"Michael," Harrow said. "Good to hear from you."

"Thought you should know," Pall said, "I put my papers in this morning—end of the month's my last day."

"You heading for a beach, or coming aboard?"

"Send me an airline ticket. If it's to Hawaii, I'll head for the beach."

"And if it's to LA?"

"Then I'll come work for you."

In Casper, Wyoming, at the state crime lab, Harrow met up with the last candidate on his Dream Team list—Jenny Blake.

A petite blonde with blue eyes, Blake was painfully shy, and Harrow was well aware that her limited social skills could hamper her in the over-the-top world of television.

That limitation aside, the twenty-five-year-old had tremendous computer skills. As a teenager, she had used those skills to lure child predators to her foster parents' house in Casper, Wyoming, before calling the local police. Her legend spread to the Wyoming state crime lab, where a friend had passed the story on to Harrow. After college, Blake joined that same Wyoming crime lab.

Of all the potential members of the team, the shy Blake would likely be the hardest to convince to join up.

Their mutual friend introduced the pair over coffee in the crime lab's breakroom, then excused herself.

Harrow laid out his pitch with quiet intensity and what he felt was sincere eloquence . . . and Jenny Blake turned him down cold.

Her shyness made her tremendously uneasy about the whole television aspect of the job, but having been raised in foster care, she had as much empathy for a parent who had lost a child as she did for the children who were preyed upon by adults.

"Jenny, this isn't about television," he told her. "That's only a means to an end. Thanks to the network, we can afford the best people in their fields—like you."

"I'm happy here," she said.

"I just need to borrow you for a while. Jenny, this person, these persons . . ."

"Unsub," she said.

"Yes, this unknown subject killed my wife and my son. David had a great future in front of him, and it was taken from him, stolen from him, and . . . we believe this unsub has killed many others, young people like my son, children too. And this is my chance to stop him."

"Here," she said. She was handing him a napkin.

"What?"

"You're crying."

He didn't realize. He dried his eyes.

"I'll do it," she said.

Chapter Nine

Harrow had seldom set foot in the conference room used by the top UBC execs and, for that matter, the board itself. You could have played touch football in here, if it weren't for the long narrow table of dark polished wood bisecting the space. The walls were beige and blank, lacking even framed posters bragging of hit shows, not that UBC had many. Tables in a back corner held shining stainless steel urns of coffee, orange juice, ice water; and offered baskets of breakfast pastries, fresh fruit, and yogurt cups on ice.

At the front of the room, behind Harrow, was a mammoth plasma screen that could display one huge image or dozens of smaller ones. Just behind Harrow at his left was a cameraman capturing his every move, and at his right, a female audio guy's boom was a sword of Damocles over his head. Two more cameramen were positioned on either side of the table—not directly across from each other, of course—and a male sound guy with a boom was catching the talk at the table.

Way at the back, near the craft service area, stood network president Dennis Byrnes in a light gray Brooks Brothers, black shirt, and charcoal tie, arms Superman-style at his waist; next to him, of course, was Nicole Strickland, arms folded across the admirable shelf of her breasts, like a bodyguard in Donna Karan.

Harrow turned his attention to the people seated at the table. Nearest were the five forensics experts that made up his dream team; farther down were Carmen Garcia and a contingent of top production personnel.

They were chatting among themselves, the ones already acquainted taking the lead. One thing law enforcement professionals and TV/film people had in common was an affinity for taking advantage of any free food and drink on deck, and this group was no exception.

"All right, everyone," Harrow said, loud, firm, but not unfriendly, and the group settled down. "I'll start with my thanks to all of you for walking away from other work, at short notice, to be part of this innovative, and likely history-making investigation."

He gestured toward the back of the room.

"I also want to introduce you to the two people who have made this possible—network president Dennis Byrnes and our executive producer, Nicole Strickland."

Polite applause rang in the room, like friendly

fire, the faces of the new people turning toward the execs.

Harrow gestured. "Would you like to join me, Dennis?"

The cameraman closest to the execs swung his attention their way, as did the boom operator.

Byrnes smiled and shook his head and raised a palm. "No, J.C. I'd just like to say that UBC—from Nicole and me to every member of the board—is behind the *Killer TV* team all the way."

Some curious frowns appeared, and the faces turned toward Harrow again.

"That's how our remote segment is labeled," Harrow told them, his embarrassment showing through. "*Killer TV* . . . we're a kind of show within the show. It may be a little undignified, but Dennis tells me it's tested well. . . ."

"Certainly has," the exec affirmed.

". . . and of course that's the be-all-and-end-all in television." Harrow gave up a wry smile. "And, anyway, it's a small concession, considering the financial support the network's providing."

Nicole spoke up, her alto a musical, lovely thing (at least when she wasn't berating or firing somebody): "You'll all receive directories of the numbers back here at home base, including mine. While I'd appreciate you staying, whenever possible, within the chain of command . . . I have five assistants, who would also appreciate you helping justify their salaries. . . ."

A few polite laughs.

". . . do not hesitate to call me directly, if there is

a matter of urgency. Six o'clock Friday night comes promptly at six o'clock every Friday night . . . meaning we do not stand on ceremony. We don't have that luxury."

"And now," Byrnes said, "we're going to do our job, which is to get out of your way and let you do yours."

The execs made their exit to one last nice round of applause, the enthusiasm of which may have been influenced by relief to see them go.

Harrow took the seat at the head of the long, narrow table. "Now that the two two-hundred-pound gorillas are gone, we should start by acknowledging the four-hundred-pound gorilla still in the room."

No one said anything, but their eyes were on him like magnets on metal.

"I'm heading up an investigation into a crime in which I carry an enormous emotional stake. It breaks a rule so basic, hardly anybody bothers formulating it *as* a rule."

Kind smiles.

"So here is your fallback, people. If the need arises, Plan B is to remove me from the case, and Laurene Chase will take over as lead investigator. Laurene?"

Nearest him at right, she stood, and nodded at him, and then at everyone around her.

Harrow went on: "I can be replaced at the network's whim . . . no, no! No argument there, that was a basic part of the agreement to fund our efforts. And I can be removed at Laurene's directive."

Laurene said, "The man speaks the truth."

Harrow said, "If you have concerns that you don't

feel comfortable expressing to me, I understand—you won't be going behind my back, because we'll just call it part of that chain of command Ms. Strickland mentioned. Go straight to Laurene."

Billy Choi said, "Laurene, fire J.C.'s ass, would you?"

Everybody laughed. Harrow gave Choi a tiny look that said, *Thank you,* for breaking the ice.

"The second thing," Harrow said, "is that we're going to be on camera pretty much every second we're working. You will not be followed into restaurants, your hotel rooms, or restrooms. And your free time, what little there'll be of it, will be your own. Everything else is fair game . . ." He looked right at the camera. ". . . unless either Laurene or I say otherwise."

Harrow rose and walked deeper into the room, his camera- and soundman following. "I want to start by introducing you to the crew who'll be keeping us company. There will be others, but these five on camera and sound are among the best in the business, as some of you already know . . . and they're the ones who'll be trailing us the most."

As he made introductions, those seated at the table craned when necessary to take in their electronic shadows.

"First, sneaking up behind me, is a thirty-year veteran in the business, including ten years at UBC—Maury Hathaway."

Maury peeked out from behind the shoulder-held camera, and smiled and nodded, and people said, "Hi," "Hey, Maury," and the like. The husky Hathaway wore khaki cargo pants and an open-front button-down shirt over a Grateful Dead T-shirt, his blond hair graying around the longish edges.

"Working sound for Maury is Nancy Hughes."

A slender young woman, blonde hair tied in a loose ponytail, dipped her boom to them and gave them a toothy smile. She wore jeans and a loose white T-shirt.

"Across the way is Tim Ingram."

A wiry black guy who looked barely out of his teens gave the group a boom bob and a wave. He wore a brown T-shirt with a white silkscreen of some hip-hop star not on Harrow's radar.

"Down and across from me, that's Leon Arroyo."

Cameraman Arroyo's smile was huge, his teeth very white. A light-skinned Hispanic with wavy black hair and a full beard, Arroyo wore baggy shorts and a multicolored rayon shirt that looked slept in.

"Down at the far end of the table—close to the food, you'll note—is Phil Dingle."

Dingle, a spade-bearded, affable, not quite heavy-set six-footer in a black shirt and chinos, came out from behind his eyepiece to grin and say hey. "You won't know I'm here," he said.

Harrow moved down the table. "Our lead investigative reporter and segment host is Carmen Garcia. She found the clue that jump-started the investigation."

The group turned to her, and she gave them a megawatt smile and a crisp nod. The Ozomatli T-shirt and jeans were gone, replaced by a designer suit that cost probably ten times her old weekly salary.

The tousle-haired, well-scrubbed Midwestern girl

had been replaced by a stylishly coiffed California female with flawless makeup and freshly lacquered nails.

The willowy brunette rose and said, "I'm not going to lie to you—this is the biggest job I've had in broadcasting, and I owe J.C. a debt of thanks for believing in me. I'll have some production assistants, who aren't here today, who you'll meet later. But to echo Nicole—we can't stand on ceremony. Come to me with anything. Anything."

She introduced the newcomers to two Avid editors, three post-production sound editors/mixers, and three writers, who would be accompanying them all the way.

"We are doing more than investigating," Carmen said. "We are creating a segment for a weekly reality show. Some of what we do will go out live, but many of our interviews will be edited along the way, and ready for air."

Laurene said, "Ms. Garcia—"

"Carmen."

"Carmen—our job has to be finding, and stopping, this killer, or killers. That's our primary concern."

"It's a concern we all share. But you're also the stars of our show. And the show pays the freight. You saw how positive the network president was about what we're doing. J.C., would you care to tell us all why Mr. Byrnes is our biggest fan now?"

Harrow, who had made his way back to the head of the conference room table (his camera and audio shadows too), was just taking his seat.

"Glad to, Carmen. And if your dignity was bruised

by *Killer TV*, I'm here to tell you we're largely under-written by toilet paper, among other enthusiastic sponsors."

A mix of laughter and groans greeted that.

Harrow was saying, "We are making a lot of money for UBC, or at least right now we are. If we don't deliver, the financial plug could get pulled."

Carmen picked up (and all eyes followed): "You'll take time out for interviews, sometimes in advance of air, sometimes live, and you'll be giving a certain amount of your time over to working with our writers, who'll make your expert findings and opinions user-friendly to laymen."

Billy Choi said, "We'll be scripted?"

"You will at times read off teleprompters, yes. And when you speak 'off the cuff,' it will be on approved subjects, and within parameters approved by UBC Legal."

"Don't tell me we're gonna travel with lawyers?"

Harrow said, "Not yet, Billy. I talked Byrnes out of that. But if we overstep, intentionally or not, that could come."

An uncomfortable silence draped the room.

"All right," Harrow said. "Some of you know each other, by reputation anyway. But I don't believe anyone here but me is familiar with *all* of you. So I'm going to ask you each to introduce yourself and give us a little backstory . . . as they call it in the TV game."

Without prompting, Harrow's second-in-command—sleek in a lavender silk blouse and black slacks—rose and cast a cool, professional smile on her colleagues, her cornrows of ebony hair shimmering. "Laurene Chase, chief crime scene investigator, Waco PD. Currently on leave of absence."

Next to Laurene, the short, short-haired, bespectacled, broad-shouldered Michael Pall rose. He appeared vaguely nerdy in a nice but clearly off-the-rack blue suit with blue and red striped tie. He gave his name, tagging on only, "DNA scientist, Oklahoma State Crime Lab."

Billy Choi pointed a finger and fired it, gunlike, at Pall saying, "Federal Building—'95. Helped put McVeigh away. Nice job, man."

Pall tried not to react, but a smile flickered.

Next to him sat Chris Anderson, the improbably handsome Beach Boy of a chemist and lab tech from Meridian, Mississippi. He half rose, and introduced himself in his soft southern accent, but when he mentioned the Shaw and Associates lab, the other forensics experts sat up a little.

Across from Anderson sat Jenny Blake, her blue eyes studying the tabletop as her fingers fiddled with a ballpoint pen.

"Jenny Blake, computer stuff," she said, not rising, without really looking at anyone at the table.

Harrow barely nodded at the next-in-line criminalist when Choi popped up and said, "Billy Choi, crime scene analyst, tool mark and firearms examiner formerly of the Big Apple, now of sunny Los Angeles and . . ." He turned straight to the nearest camera. ". . . breakout star of *Crime Seen!* on You Bee Cee. *Book 'em, Danno!*"

This goofy performance cracked up the whole team, even Jenny and Harrow. It was just the tension break they needed, and once again the team leader sent Choi a little appreciative smile and nod.

As the *Book 'em, Danno* laughter subsided, Harrow patted the air and said, "All right, all right . . . let's get down to it."

Anderson sat forward, his intensity undercut by his Southern drawl. "Where do we start, Mr. Harrow?"

"It's J.C, Chris."

"Yes, sir."

Everyone laughed.

"And you all know the basics already—so let's start with our new evidence. Carmen, you found it—care to walk us through?"

Carmen was ready with a remote. The massive screen behind Harrow came alive and showed the evidence bag that held the single leaf.

She said, "This corn leaf was found in the driveway of a home in Placida, Florida. Stella Ferguson and her two children were shot in their home in a manner very similar to J.C.'s family."

He felt eyes flick toward him, but remained neutral.

"Stella's husband, Ray, was town marshal of Placida."

This news narrowed the eyes of the other forensics experts, and their attention was rapt as she went on to explain the circumstances—including the severed wedding-ring finger—and how the case had gone cold, until she'd spotted the leaf.

Laurene asked, "How did you even know to look at that leaf? Even the state investigators missed it."

Carmen's grin was not terribly professional, if very winning. "Hey, I'm a farm kid. You use what you know. And I knew that leaf was wrong . . . but that was all I had for sure. I took it to J.C., and he was able to hook me up with the right expert—Dr. Brent Caldwell at Settler Seed."

Slack-jawed, Choi asked Harrow, "You knew lookin' at the leaf what *seed company* made it?"

Before Harrow could explain, the DNA scientist, Pall, did it for him: "No, but he knew that Settler Seed would have DNA samples from every plant put out by every commercial seed company in the world. Naturally, they have samples from every plant they manufacture; but also samples from every competitor's plant. They need to make sure that they don't infringe on someone else's patent and, likewise, to make sure the competition isn't infringing on theirs."

Choi said, "Chess club, right? Captain?"

Pall frowned. "Chess club, yes. Captain, yes, but not of chess club—wrestling team."

Choi held up his palms in mock surrender.

Anderson said to Carmen, "Very nice thinkin', Miz Garcia. But what d'yall find out?"

"As it happens, this particular leaf came from Settler itself—field corn KS1422, which is sold exclusively in Kansas and is, as I said, field corn *not* sweet corn, which is the type grown in that part of Florida."

Choi said, "I know there's sweet corn and popcorn, but what the hell is field corn?"

Everybody gave Choi a look.

"What?" he asked, injured. "Where I come from, corn's in a can or frozen or frickin' microwavable."

Harrow held up a palm. "Billy, you're doing exactly what I expect from you, and everybody on the forensics team."

"I am?"

Harrow's eyes traveled around the table. "I don't expect any of you to know everything. God knows, I don't. And if you don't know, for God's sake, say so. Screw your ego—we have a killer to catch."

Laurene said, "J.C. is right—we're all going to have holes in our game that the others of us'll need to fill."

Harrow asked, "How many people saw that corn leaf and saw nothing but a leaf, until Carmen came along and saw something different?"

Choi opened his hands and said to Carmen, "So? Enlighten the ignorant."

"Field corn," she said, "is grown for uses other than human consumption—animal feed, some plastics, biofuels such as ethanol, although it's used as fuel in bio-gas plants in Europe, where it generates power."

"Thanks," Choi said. He said to the others, "That wasn't so hard, was it?"

Carmen said, "Anyway, the point is, this is a type of field corn sold exclusively in Kansas."

"The question that comes to mind is," Anderson said, "how does a leaf from a corn plant grown in Kansas wind up in a cul-de-sac in Florida . . . a state where they only grow sweet corn?"

"That," Harrow said, "is what we're to find out."

Pall said, "If the killer left that leaf behind—whether accidentally or on purpose—it's a reasonable assumption that his area of operations extends beyond Florida."

"Yes," Laurene said. "It extends to the Midwest, where we have a similar crime, in another corn-growing state—Iowa."

Choi said, "How do we know the Florida victim didn't have an Uncle Silas from Kansas who walked that leaf in? Helluva leaf of faith, guys. Sure you want to make it?"

Carmen said, "I've already researched the families of the victims, and of the neighbors, and there's no Kansas tie. Trust me. None."

"Okay," Harrow said, shaken a little by Choi's valid undermining of their clue. "Anybody think this lead is too thin to be worth taking?"

No one did. *Thank God.*

"All right, then," Harrow said with a sigh. "Jenny?"

Jenny looked up quickly, a rabbit who'd heard the bark of a nearby dog.

"Use those computer skills to find me a link between my case and the Ferguson murders in Florida."

She nodded and reached down for the briefcase that held her laptop.

"Also, check for similar crimes, particularly in the Midwest. The Florida case slipped through our fingers for a while, so maybe there are more."

Jenny was already getting out her computer. She gave Harrow another quick nod and turned to her keyboard and monitor, focusing on her task.

"Laurene," Harrow said, "as our chief crime scene analyst, I want you on a plane to Placida today. Find out what else they missed."

Laurene nodded, asked, "When was this murder?"

"September," Carmen said.

"Not what you'd call a fresh trail."

"Billy," Harrow said, ignoring that, "you and Carmen will go with Laurene—I want you two to interview the cops and any potential witnesses. Treat them right—they worked hard on the case. They'll look at you as poachers, so play nice."

Choi crossed his heart. "My best behavior, boss."

"Now I can sleep better, hearing that. Oh, and see what you can get on the guns too."

Choi nodded.

Pall asked, "What about us?"

"Michael, you and Chris do lab analysis of the evidence from both the Iowa and Florida cases. Make sure nothing else has been missed."

Anderson's expression was lazy, but his eyes were not. "Where *is* the evidence?"

"In your lab."

"We got a *lab*?"

"Sure."

"You're not talkin' about a retriever are you?"

"No, Chris. A fully pimped-out crime lab."

"Here at this TV studio?"

Harrow shook his head. "Outside."

Chapter Ten

The forensics team, the camera crew, and Carmen and her little army all followed Harrow out, paraded down the hall and through double doors into the bright LA morning sunshine. The smog had rolled back to cast a brighter light for the occasion.

Parked before them were a semi-trailer rig and two tour buses, each vehicle bearing *Crime Seen!*, *Killer TV*, and UBC logos.

"Am I seeing things?" Pall asked, staring wide-eyed, hands on hips, tie flapping a little in the breeze, seeming very Clark Kent to Harrow. Mini Clark Kent. . . .

"Not a mirage, Michael," Harrow said to the DNA expert, and led the team to the semi-trailer first. "And there'll be a makeup/wardrobe motor home, and a satellite uplink truck joining the wagon train, when we head out."

Though they stood on the driver's side of the

trailer, their attention was on the drone of a motor, just out of sight.

"The motors you hear," Harrow said, "are the air conditioner and refrigeration unit for the crime lab that takes up the trailer's front three-quarters."

The whole team seemed dumbfounded, and were exchanging colorful reactions, the TV crew catching it all.

Toward the front of the trailer, three metal stairs hung down. Harrow climbed them, pulled open the door, and led the team inside the white-walled world, neat work stations set up on either side: a fingerprint hood, a drying closet, a gas chromatograph-mass spectrometer, an AFIS, NIBIN, CODIS station, and a water tank to catch bullets fired for testing also lined the walls. Three long tables ran down the middle, one a regular work table, another a backlit table with bulbs under the surface, a third holding a Kodak MP3 evidence camera in its stand.

The team looked around in wonder. Most came from state crime labs that weren't nearly this up to date.

Anderson asked, "Who the heck's footin' the bill for all this?"

"UBC and our sponsors," Harrow said. "And much of the equipment here was provided by the manufacturers in exchange for a mention in the end credits.

Choi said, "The way they squeeze the credits down these days? What good's that kind of unreadable plug do them?"

Carmen said, "We provide the companies with footage of you 'stars' using the equipment, and it becomes part of their promo package when they go out to state and local crime labs around the country, and the world."

Shaking his head, Pall said, "Weird way to stop a killer."

"That's entertainment," Laurene said. She swivelled to lock eyes with Harrow. "Which brings us to something else, J.C."

Harrow felt the camera move in on him as he said, "What?"

Ignoring Hathaway and his video eye, Laurene asked, "How long is this season supposed to last again?"

"Twenty-two weeks," Harrow reminded her.

"And what happens if we haven't found the guy?"

Harrow didn't duck her gaze. "We keep looking."

"Can we be cancelled?"

"Any TV show can be cancelled. But we've got at least twenty-two weeks, guaranteed, and even if we aren't finished then, we should be able to keep going. As long as, well, we've been . . ."

"Entertaining?"

"I was going to say 'make compelling viewing.' I believe we'll be allowed to keep up the search—too much of an embarrassment to the network not to. On the other hand, I don't figure we'll need more time than we've been given."

"Cool," Choi said. "But what happens if we nail our guy in, oh, two weeks?"

After all these years of looking for his family's killer, and now finally having one clue that might be a genuine lead, Harrow had never contemplated the possibility that the case might now come down quickly.

"That would be great," he said. "Sooner the better."

Laurene asked, "Oh? And how's the network going to feel about that?"

"Well, they'd be thrilled, I'd think."

"Really? They promote something as a season-long serial only to have it wind up in two weeks? Wouldn't that cut into their profits?"

Harrow finally saw where Laurene was headed, and the truth was, he didn't know the answer. "Maury, turn off the camera."

Hathaway's head peeked around the edge of the camera. "J.C., this is good stuff."

"You know the rules, Maury. When I say 'cut,' you cut. I won't abuse the privilege. Shut it down and kill the sound too."

Hathaway did as he was told. So did Hughes.

Choi asked, "You want them out while we talk?"

"No," Harrow said. "Anyway, it's Maury I want to talk to."

"Me?" Hathaway asked, setting the camera on a nearby table. "What did I do?"

"Nothing. I just want an expert opinion."

"I'm no expert," the heavyset cameraman insisted. "I never saw *CSI* in my life. I don't even watch television. I *make* it."

That got chuckles all around, but uneasiness was in the air.

"Maury, do you think the network would ask us to withhold evidence, to . . . parcel it out, time its release, for dramatic effect? Just to keep the show going?"

Hathaway's eyes widened, and his mouth dropped—not a typical reaction from a seasoned vet like him. "Hell, I never thought of that."

"Me neither," Harrow admitted. "And what's more, I haven't been here long enough to know the answer. Maury, you've been at UBC for ten years. You know everything and everyone—what do you think?"

The cameraman took a long silent moment, glanced at Hughes, who seemed similarly flummoxed. Finally, he said, "Nicole never would pull anything like that. Not that she's honest, but I don't think she's got the power or the cojones to go that far."

The team looked relieved, if somewhat skeptical.

Harrow asked, "What about Byrnes?"

"Him I'm not so sure," Hathaway said. "I mean, the guy is all about the bottom line. But his reputation—and my experience with him? He's honest, as far as it goes."

"What does that mean, Maury?"

"It means—it's Hollywood."

This did not ease Harrow's concerns.

Laurene asked, "So, if we have misgivings about the networks and its priorities—what's the impact on how we proceed?"

"We handle all the evidence ourselves," Harrow said, "or at private labs we trust, like Chris's employer, Shaw and Associates."

Choi was frowning, his expression close to pissed

off. "Would these UBC SOB's tamper with evidence?"

Harrow shook his head. "I don't believe they would, Billy. But it will be better if we can keep the situation from arising. I believe we can address any attempt to have us hold back evidence—"

"Like for sweeps week?" Choi said, only half kidding.

"Like for sweeps week," Harrow said. "We can head that off by getting the lawyers involved. Obstruction of justice trumps ratings, every time."

Laurene seemed satisfied with Harrow's take on the network situation. "Okay," she said. "Then I have another question, J.C."

"I'm not surprised," Harrow said patiently.

"If . . . *when* . . . we catch this killer—who has jurisdiction?"

"We'll see about that when we know more," Harrow said. "Let's catch the bastard first, then we'll worry about who gets to try him. Certainly we'll be cooperating with state and local, and sharing any glory."

Shaking his head, Pall said, "Nobody's ever attempted anything like this before, J.C. But you know as well as any of us . . . if you were this asshole's lawyer? You would say you couldn't get a fair trial anywhere in the United States."

All eyes were on Harrow.

Pall went on: "A top-rated TV show used its hunt for him as a ratings boost? Think there'll be twelve licensed drivers anywhere in the country that won't be prejudiced against this guy once we do catch him?"

Harrow put up his hands in surrender. "I'm the first to admit I haven't thought of everything involved here. Maybe I got blinded by finally seeing a pinpoint of light, after years of darkness."

And as far as the network and Dennis Byrnes were concerned, Harrow had known when he signed on that he was inking a deal with the devil. Now, he just hoped he wouldn't get tripped up by the fine print.

"First, let's find the guy," he told them. "Let's stop him and expose him, and trust that matters like jurisdiction and fair trials don't trip us up."

Laurene said, "These are dark waters, J.C. Choppy too."

"I know. But I couldn't ask for a better crew to help make the voyage."

Choi grunted a laugh. "Good thing I know how to swim."

Harrow said, "Just so you don't jump overboard on me, Billy. . . . Maury, turn the camera back on, and let's get down to work."

Chapter Eleven

The motel room was dark, the flimsy, filmy curtains pulled tight against the fading afternoon sun as the Messenger kicked back on the bed, thin pillows piled behind his head as he watched the national news on UBC.

Outside, what passed for rush hour in Socorro, New Mexico, was under way, which meant maybe ten cars on the street, not five. Still, with only nine thousand souls, Socorro was still way bigger than his own hometown.

Made him wonder—if the rights of people could be so blatantly trampled on in a little town like his, with no repercussions, how could people's rights ever be protected in a town twenty-five times the size? Or in a really big city, like New York or Chicago? Possibilities for corruption there were mind-boggling.

That thought only served to reinforce why his work was so important—why he needed to keep leaving messages around the country, until someone was smart and capable enough to understand their importance.

Sad that he'd had to go the way he had, but he needed help, and the normal routes for gaining assistance had paid him no heed. The messages he was delivering seemed the only reasonable way to recruit the help he so desperately required.

On the tube-television screen, Carlos Moreno was doing a satellite interview with J.C. Harrow, host of *Crime Seen!*

"Has anything like this ever been attempted, J.C.?"

Outdoors in what seemed to be Southern countryside, Harrow—in a corny Robert Stack-style trenchcoat—said, "No, Carlos, this is a first. We've assembled some of the best forensics talent in the nation, and tonight we'll share some of the exciting work we've been doing, while *Crime Seen!* has been away."

The Messenger farted with his lips over the rest of the interview, and laughed out loud at how uneasy stately anchor Jackson Blair seemed, when he was forced to close the broadcast with a blatant plug: "Be sure to stay with UBC tonight for the season premiere of *Crime Seen!* with J.C. Harrow and his crack criminalists, as they close in on the murderer of the host's family, nearly seven years ago."

If Harrow and his team of "crack criminalists" were "closing in on the killer," it was news to the Messenger, who had seen no sign of them.

No one had come to his hometown, no one had approached him on his travels to deliver his messages, and no one was anywhere near him now, unless they were being good and goddamn secretive about it. As if to prove the point, he got off the bed, walked to the window, and peeked between the thin curtains.

He sure as hell didn't see Harrow out there, or any "crack criminalists," or even criminalists on crack, much less any of those dopey-looking buses and trucks that had been featured all summer in those ridiculous commercials promoting the show like it was the second goddamn coming.

What he did see was fading sun, a sky turning purple, and headlights starting to snap on in passing cars as darkness descended on Socorro like a soothing blanket. Any sense of comfort in this community, however, was a false one; this was a night that would wake this town up forever.

Though thus far no one seemed to be getting his messages—well, they received them, but they didn't *get* them—he still held out hope. He would continue his quest until someone acknowledged his messages and did something to right the wrong.

He'd thought Harrow might be that man. But as the summer passed with nothing but ludicrous publicity for the show's *Killer TV* segment, it seemed more and more likely that Harrow couldn't make out the messages either. The former sheriff might be sincere in trying to find the Messenger, but was clearly being used by the television network in a cheap, sleazy, distasteful stunt for money and ratings.

Still, Harrow had come the closest of anyone, so far at least, and the Messenger realized that a personalized refresher might be just what was needed to jump-start the ex-sheriff, and nudge him in the right direction. He wondered if Harrow might have other family, to help make that point—brothers, sisters, father, mother . . . ?

There had to be some appropriate target on the map that would send a more pointed message to the UBC superstar. Research, investigation, would be needed, though that would have to wait. . . .

First, he had already devised a message for delivery here in New Mexico.

He returned to the bed and picked up the copy of *TV Guide*—with Harrow and his team's picture on it—that had been tented over the .357 Magnum. The six-shot Smith and Wesson pistol had been utilized twice before, sending previous messages.

Each message delivered had become an indelible memory, not memories he cherished at all, rather burdens to bear. One such memory bubbled up as he watched another in the seemingly endless parade of *Crime Seen!* spots that rolled across the small faded screen.

August, six years ago. A house, bigger than his own, sat on a hill in Iowa, off Highway 30, back in the sticks between Ames and Nevada, the owner a retired Story County sheriff, living there with his wife and son. The home had belonged to J.C. Harrow, the man he had made a star—devil his due, Harrow had saved the President's life in a crazy coincidence that had, weirdly, served both the Messenger and his future nemesis.

Harrow's fame had been an unseen outcome of that particular message. You couldn't always know the ways in which your actions might impact the world. Making presidential hero Harrow a major celebrity, by having his family murdered the same day, had been one such instance.

As he checked the load in his revolver, and his backup in his speed-loader, he frowned, mildly surprised that—despite how many messages he'd delivered—each one remained distinct in his mind.

He took no pleasure in reliving these events, but he owed it to those who conveyed his messages for him not to forget their sacrifice. Without them, he would be nothing; without them, no point could be made.

The key, he knew, was that each delivery was cataloged in his mind by the gun he'd used. That was why, at the beginning, he had not needed to take souvenirs to help him remember and keep straight the calls he made. He was not, after all, some FedEx man with a computer to keep track.

But with each specific gun, he could look at it and remember each message just as he had delivered it, despite a certain sameness that had quickly crept in. That house in Iowa wasn't so much different from the one he would visit tonight in New Mexico.

Both were two-story family homes, away from town, the Iowa one on a hill, this one down in a valley. The houses, except for their age (Iowa being older), were very similar, as were the families inside. Though retired Sheriff Harrow had only the one child, this family had two. And like Harrow, this man—George Reid—was a civil servant, the lead accountant for Socorro County.

And the Messenger knew all too well how much trouble accountants could cause.

Even now, the .357 pressing against his side as he drove to deliver the Socorro message, he could feel the similarities between the two messages weaving within him, a reflection on a past delivery and a briefing for the upcoming one.

In Iowa, he parked one road north of his target, and left the nondescript Chevy sitting by the side of the road as he took off cross-country, making his way through the neighbor's cornfield that stood between him and the back of Harrow's house.

In New Mexico, he killed the headlights and turned into the Reids' long driveway, coasted out of view from the road, killed the engine, climbed out of the car.

The Iowa breeze was warm, the sun bright, as the Messenger made his way through corn taller than him, careful to guard his face and hands from the slash of stalks, the air smelling like a summer Sunday from back when life was good.

Tonight the breeze in the Rio Grande Valley was cool, blowing gently from the Cibola National Forest to the west, hinting of a late-season forest fire. Darkness had settled in, but a bright moon and a million stars made it easy to navigate the gravel drive.

When he got to the edge of the cornfield, he'd peeked out at the back of the house—shut up tight, air conditioner humming. No other sounds, movement. He expected a barking dog, a passing car, something, anything; but nothing—nothing but the steady beat of his own heart.

The drive here was lined with Mexican pinyon

trees, providing plenty of cover as he made his way. The night was a calming cloak, the lights of the house visible through the trees.

He'd moved around the Harrow house to the east, using the cornfield for cover till he was behind the garage, where he could step out, without anyone seeing him.

Here, the garage was attached to the house, one door open on the empty space of George Reid's SUV, the other door closed, the wife's car obviously within as usual.

He'd felt the sweat beading his brow and trickling down his back, but it was just the August heat, not nerves. He was just a postman on his rounds, delivering bad news. Internally, he was so cool, it was as if he already stood within the air-conditioned walls of Harrow's house.

On this New Mexican night, he was so experienced at his mission that he didn't even feel warm, despite wearing black jeans, a long-sleeved black T-shirt, and black Reeboks. Even the stocking cap didn't seem to generate any heat on his forehead. He was far cooler than he'd been in Iowa, and dressed differently.

At Harrow's, he'd straightened his narrow black tie, and glanced again toward the house, where he saw no movement through curtained windows. He carried a pair of Watchtower pamphlets and wore the plain dark suit suitable to a Jehovah's Witness. This, he felt, was a perfect disguise. Even if he knocked on the wrong door, no one ever remembered the earnest anonymous face of a Witness thrusting the Watchtower at them; and very seldom was anyone rude enough to slam the door in a religious face. Usually he could easily get in the door, selling one message before switching to his real one.

This message he would deliver without guile. He had scouted this house, just as he had all the others, and knew there was a weakness here that had not come up at the Harrow home, which was why he'd needed the subterfuge there.

He had eyed the Harrow house as he moved down a fence line beyond the garage until he was halfway down the drive. Then he strode back up the driveway as if coming from the road. Now, he wanted them to see his approach, the Jehovah's Witness coming to the house to spread The Word.

This time, he entered the open garage and walked up to the door that led into the house, a mudroom just beyond, kitchen, living room. Basement was probably empty and, if he hadn't completed delivery of the message by the time he'd reached the living room, he would most likely find the children in their respective bedrooms, up a short flight of stairs.

At the Harrow house, he'd knocked on the door and been met by Harrow's pretty brunette wife in her Iowa State T-shirt, her smile wide, her lips the same color red as the shirt.

When he gave her the fictional name and shoved the Watchtower at her, she looked down, and that was her last mistake. When he pushed her inside, she'd been too startled even to scream, although her smile did disappear.

"What the hell are you doing?" she demanded.

"Delivering a message."

"What?"

The gun emerged from his jacket pocket of its own volition and answered her question, tearing through her blouse and knocking the air from her, like a shove. Even over the explosion, he heard her make the whooshing sound, then he shot her a second time, which dropped her onto her back. Dead.

He liked that she hadn't suffered.

Then the high school kid had appeared, from over left, having come the long way around from the kitchen, and tried to get the drop on the Messenger, a butcher knife raised menacingly.

The young man lost his chance, though, when he paused to whimper at the sight of his late mother on the floor, and never saw the first slug that the gun sent him, knocking him backward a step. He barely looked up before the gun issued a second shot that hit him in the chest, and raised a pink, puffy mist as if his soul were leaving his body.

Testing the knob of the garage door, he could only hope tonight's message would be as easy to deliver.

The door whispered open, and he stepped into the dark, vacant mudroom. Bleach tickled his nostrils as he crept through to the kitchen door, edged with light; he paused to listen before he opened it. On the other side, he could hear the sound of water running, and the clatter of dishes. Someone washing up after dinner.

The knob twisted slowly in his hand, each second bringing him closer to his delivery, yet feeling no urge to rush. Thinking back to when he'd watched sports on TV, a lifetime ago, he recalled the athletes who spoke of not trying to do too much—about letting the game come to them. This was like that—the game would come to him.

Then it really did, the knob slipping from his grasp as someone opened the door.

Framed in angelic light, the twelve-year-old boy was a five-foot replica of his blond father. His blue eyes widened with shock as he saw the Messenger.

Saw the Messenger and the barrel of the revolver whose snout bore a black hole big enough to swallow the boy up—and it did. The shot hit the child in the chest, knocking him back slightly before he slumped to the floor. His mother, still at the sink, up to her elbows in dishwater, spun when she heard the report, flicking water and suds.

Agape, she seemed to scream but either it was silent or inaudible over the second shot, which struck her in the sternum and shook her as if she were the child, a naughty child, and she slid down the counter as if carried by overflow from the sink.

One more shot to each party as he crossed the room ended any doubt about whether their wounds were fatal, and he was on to the family room. He found the stunned daughter sitting on the carpet, staring blankly at the wall that separated her from the kitchen as if she had seen through it and understood why her mother and brother weren't coming in. On a large flat-screen TV against the far wall, a happy cartoon child with pastel hair was dancing and singing.

Slowly, she turned toward the Messenger, her wide, uncomprehending eyes settling on the big revolver; her eyes tightened just a little, as if she were trying to make out something in a haze. She didn't scream, didn't raise a hand, just sat there numbly as the killer raised the gun and squeezed the trigger.

Two in the chest straightened her this way and

that and then she sank slowly to her left, tipping in slow motion, her eyes still on the gun, but no light in them now, glassy, as dead as the dolls on a nearby shelf.

As dead as the eyes of his own child.

When the little girl settled onto the floor, her lifeless hand stretched toward the kitchen and her mother, and—despite the open eyes—she seemed to be napping peacefully he walked out.

A terrible thing, but it had to be done.

Justice could not prevail without the sacrifice of innocents. If he had learned anything in this life, it was that.

In the kitchen, he withdrew the compact garden shears, knelt prayerfully, and, in one crunching, almost bloodless stroke, removed the mother's wedding ring and the finger it adorned. This time he had brought his own plastic baggie, and needn't steal one from the deceased homemaker.

THREE
The Road

Chapter Twelve

At 10:45 P.M., J.C. Harrow—in front of a rambling one-story stucco home in Placida, Florida—was lit by spots mounted atop a *Crime Scene!* bus. Maury Hathaway had his camera on sticks with the teleprompter below the lens. Nancy Hughes stood nearby with the boom, though Harrow held a microphone with the UBC logo on it, more for show than necessity; the sound person's headset allowed her to communicate with the crew in the production half of the semi nearby.

Next to cameraman Hathaway, perched atop the wooden box (an "apple box," in the trade), a widescreen monitor allowed Harrow to see himself standing there in HD glory, his gray suit crisp, his white shirt open at the throat, but despite expert make-up, he could see the tiredness in his face, and the additional white working into his dark brown hair. To him, he appeared far more than a mere year older than when the show had premiered last season.

He had already been on briefly, at the top of the hour, to give a general introduction to tonight's show before tossing the baton to Carlos Moreno, who'd guided the first forty-five minutes of the program through four other crimes, each segment hosted by another *Crime Seen!* reporter. With the exception of Moreno, all of these were canned, even the segment-host wraparounds pre-recorded.

"On-air feed!" Hughes announced.

The picture on the monitor switched to a commercial in progress, followed by the familiar *Crime Seen!* title card, over which was suddenly stamped a severe stenciled *Killer TV* logo—tinny audio, piped on set, made the mysterious, synthesizer-heavy theme seem a little silly to Harrow.

Carmen Garcia's voice, a confident contralto, spoke over the title card: "Tonight we debut *Crime Seen!*'s *Killer TV* segment . . ."

A publicity shot of Harrow filled the screen.

". . . with host J.C. Harrow on the road in Placida, Florida. . . ."

Helicopter shots of quiet little Placida by day rolled across the monitor.

And now Carmen filled the screen, her attractive office-worker demeanor replaced by the glamorous aura of a star worthy of a *TV Guide* feature article (see this week's issue). She wore a black suit with a white silk blouse, unbuttoned just enough. Her dark hair was perfectly coiffed, and her makeup looked invisible (thank you, Hair and Makeup Department).

Positioned in front of the *Crime Seen!* semi-trailer, a *Killer TV* logo prominent to her one side, she spoke into her own UBC handheld microphone: "This quiet village was the scene of a tragedy that our forensics investigators have tied to the similarly tragic crime out of which *Crime Seen!* itself emerged."

Under that had played file footage from Des Moines Channel 8 of police outside the Harrow home on that terrible night. The host glanced away as Carmen's voice continued.

An assistant director, also with a headset, had a pointing finger held upward, like a starting gun, waiting as Carmen said, "And now, here is your host, J.C. Harrow. . . ."

The AD's pointing finger aimed itself at Harrow.

"For there to be a war on crime," Harrow said, invoking the catchphrase he'd made famous on *Crime Seen!*, "we must *all* be warriors. . . . Ladies and gentlemen, good evening."

Last year, he had worked hard, with the help of many behind the scenes, to combine a serious, almost grave demeanor with a confident, somewhat affable vocal tone.

"I know there are a lot of expectations about what's been happening this summer, and what we'll be doing with our new *Killer TV* segment this fall."

Looking right through the camera, Harrow said, "Public response has been mostly favorable, from snail mail to blogs to Twitter . . . and we thank you for that. But there's been criticism too."

Harrow turned left, where Arroyo's camera (and another prompter) waited, providing a tighter shot. "I've been accused of exploiting the deaths of my wife and son . . . out of a desire for fame, or in a misguided effort to keep my loved ones 'alive.'"

In Harrow's earpiece, director Stu Phillips in New York whispered: *"Make them wait for it, J.C."*

Finally Harrow said, "You may be right." His smile was sad—that it was intentionally so made it no less real. "And I can guarantee my wife *would* be offended, if I turned this into a media circus."

In cameraman Arroyo's ear, director Phillips said, *"Go in tighter, Leon . . . nice and tight. . . ."*

"On the other hand, I believe Ellen would support me—*does* support me—in bringing our son's murderer to justice. She would encourage me to do everything in my power to do that—and David would feel the same, where his mom was concerned."

His eyes were tear-filled. Though he was reading the words, words he had only co-scripted, the emotion was genuine.

"And until we have their killer or killers, I promise you this—I will not speak to you of my family again."

Harrow turned back to Hathaway's camera position, who was ready with an even tighter close-up.

"I understand that some of you may find what we're doing distasteful, and if we offend you, turn us off, switch the channel . . . but as you do, ask yourself—would you do any less for *your* family?"

The monitor revealed that the director in New York had cut away to a pre-recorded wide shot of the ranch-style home at night with lovely palm trees and a full moon touched by dark smoky clouds providing a picturesque, vaguely film noir effect.

Over this image Harrow was saying, "Carmen, could you bring us up to speed?"

Back on camera at the semi-trailer, Carmen said, "Thank you, J.C. Over the summer, our *Crime Seen!* team has been very busy following leads."

Dingle was waiting with hand-held to follow her up the stairs of the trailer and inside. A pan of the lab revealed bustling activity within, staged but convincing (Carmen had spent much of the previous afternoon rehearsing her forensics stars, much to their dismay).

Nearest was Michael Pall, sitting at a computer monitor. The diminutive DNA scientist wore a white lab coat with his name on the left breast over the UBC logo set within a magnifying glass (Harrow had put his foot down, and the *Killer TV* logo was conspicuously MIA). Under the lab coat, Pall wore a light blue button-down dress shirt and a darker blue tie with a geometric pattern.

Carmen guided Pall down a path of easy questions concerning the DNA of the corn leaf found at the Ferguson crime scene. They were not on prompter, but the exchange was very much canned.

"Does that mean we know where the killer is from?"

"No," Pall said, "that's too big an assumption. But we're making progress."

"How so?"

"We know where in Kansas that particular corn seed was sold. It will help us narrow down where the killer might have traveled."

"Anything else?"

Pall gestured toward a table on the other side of

the lab, where Billy Choi sat at a computer screen displaying two bullets side by side. Under his UBC-insignia lab coat, Choi wore a navy blue T-shirt emblazoned with a huge badge and the words NYPD HOCKEY.

After introducing Choi as the resident firearms expert, Carmen said, "What's the story of these bullets, Billy?"

Playing to the camera, Choi said, "These two slugs represent evidence developed using NIBIN."

"NIBIN?"

"National Integrated Ballistics Information Network."

"Which is?"

To Harrow, the pair seemed to be competing for the camera, trading smiles, but the audience probably thought they were just flirting a little.

Choi was saying, "NIBIN's an imaging system and database of firearms-related evidence developed by the FBI and the ATF in partnership. Each had their own ballistics imaging programs—Drugfire at the FBI and IBIS at ATF—but NIBIN allows the two to communicate, and share information."

"What have you learned using this technology?"

Choi pointed at the bullets on the screen, and the camera moved in, Harrow's monitor filled now with the two bullets. "The bullet on the right came out of Stella Ferguson—from a nine-millimeter automatic, a completely different type of bullet than the one used in the murders at the Harrow home."

"Does that mean different perpetrators in these two cases?"

"No, just that a different weapon was used. May

or may not be the same killer, but there are significant similarities in the crimes . . . Still, the weapons don't match."

"To the layperson," Carmen said, "these bullets look the same."

"Actually, they're not."

As Dingle's shot widened, Choi moved to another monitor, where a picture of a third bullet was waiting. "This slug came from Ellen Harrow. It's bigger, the striations completely different."

Looking at a bullet pried from his wife's chest, televised or otherwise, sent acid rushing into Harrow's stomach, and, involuntarily, he pictured his wife and son on the floor back in their home.

What was the son of a bitch who did it thinking, if he was watching this?

"What about the bullets on the other monitor?" Carmen was asking. "You said you had a match for one in the Ferguson murders—but not the Harrow case?"

"No," Choi said. "This is new—that comes from a double murder in Rolla, North Dakota, two years ago."

"Where has that led you?"

"Check back next week," Choi said, delivering a scripted line very naturally.

The show was running smoothly, and Harrow was of course pleased.

But he also knew that by serializing this investigation on live TV, he was giving the killer a tutorial on what evidence they were finding, and how close they were coming to him. Of all the risks they were taking, this was the worst—instead of closing in on the killer, they might well drive him to ground, and never track the bastard down.

Carmen turned to camera and asked, "J.C., why didn't the police in Florida pick up on this connection?"

Back on, Harrow said, "Carmen, they did run the bullets through NIBIN, but Rolette County in North Dakota—like many rural areas—hasn't widely participated in the program. Only recently, through the state crime lab in Bismarck, did the information get into the database. The match we found has only been available for the last few weeks."

"J.C.," Carmen said casually, but scripted, "I understand you interviewed the surviving member of the Ferguson household."

"Yes," Harrow replied, framed against the stucco home in the moonlight, "this afternoon I spoke with Placida city marshal Ray Ferguson, here in his home."

Microphone lowered, Harrow watched the monitor.

In a two-shot, sunlight filtering in sheer-curtained windows in the background, Harrow was seated in a straight-back chair facing a sofa where Ferguson sat.

Paunchier and generally older-looking than Harrow—though possibly as much as five years younger—Ferguson wore boots, jeans, and a blue denim shirt with a gold badge embroidered over the left breast. Jowly, with empty blue eyes and a wide nose, he had thin, bloodless lips over a strong chin.

"Marshal Ferguson, we're sorry for your loss."

"Thank you, sir," Ferguson said, with a tiny nod. His baritone was soft spoken, with a touch of drawl. "I consented to this, Mr. Harrow, because I know you suffered such yourself."

"Marshal Ferguson, would you tell us about that night, almost a year ago to the day?"

Ferguson had been expecting the questions, but the words hit him like tiny punches. His eyes glazed over.

"Marshal, I apologize for my bluntness. But I have to ask."

He nodded. "Well, after work, I came home, and the lights weren't on. Which surprised me, 'cause it was well after dark. Stella's car was in the driveway, and that was when I first got spooked, really spooked. Just knew something was wrong."

"Go on."

"Rest of the block was quiet, but what really shook me was that the lights, in the other houses? They were all on. I'd kinda hoped that somehow it was . . . you know . . . a power outage or some damn thing."

As he watched the monitor, Harrow winced when a close cut to the marshal's trembling hands in his lap underscored the man's misery. His own hands began to tremble, and he marveled that he'd been able to summon his inner cop enough to conduct this interview.

"I just ran into the house," Ferguson was saying. "Or anyway I did after I got the door unlocked, which was another thing—Stella never locked the door when she knew I was coming home."

Neither had Ellen.

"I suppose," the marshal said, "he locked up after himself, to keep somebody from discovering what he'd done too soon. Of course, he'd have known I'd have a key. Do you suppose he wanted me to find them, Mr. Harrow? Did he do the same to you?"

"Please go on, sir."

"Sorry," Ferguson said. "Anyway, I went in, and there they were . . . all dead. All lying in the entryway, like they were there to . . . greet me. But it wasn't . . . wasn't me, was it?"

"Then you called the sheriff's office."

"Yes, and they arrived within minutes. Coroner told me that Stella and the kids'd only been dead for about an hour. If I'd got home earlier that night . . . ? Maybe they would still be alive."

"Marshal, that kind of speculation doesn't do any good. Did you get home at your regular time?"

"Right around. Not much to marshaling in Placida, Mr. Harrow."

"Nothing unusual that day?"

"No. On the way home, though, I did have a traffic stop. Not that that's unusual."

Sitting forward, Harrow asked, "Did you tell the detectives about it?"

"Oh yeah," Ferguson said. "Perfectly routine. Guy was a salesman from Tampa, just passing through. Sheriff's office and state patrol both did an extensive investigation into the guy. It was nothing."

Live again, Harrow brought up his mic and said, "We interviewed Marshal Ferguson for an hour, and, thanks to his years as a trained investigator himself, he shared with us several puzzle pieces that for now we must withhold . . . because we know that our audience very likely includes the perpetrator of these crimes. Carmen, I understand you have more to share now, with our team. . . ."

And as the image on the monitor showed Carmen back in the mobile crime lab, where she was introducing the rest of the superstar criminalists, Harrow lowered his mic. The show's sign-off would follow Carmen's last mini-segment, and would be handled by Moreno, back in LA.

But Harrow's on-air claim of Ferguson providing puzzle pieces hadn't been TV hype.

In the Ferguson living room, the marshal—late in the interview—had frowned and said, "You know, Mr. Harrow, there *was* this one thing."

"Yes, Mr. Ferguson?"

"While I had that first guy pulled over, another vehicle, a pickup truck, was coming from the direction of my house . . . and it slowed way down, and the guy gave me, you know, the old hairy eyeball as he went by."

"You made eye contact?"

"Oh, yeah. Impossible not to. He knew he'd caught my attention."

"Did you tell the detectives about the guy eye-balling you in the pick-up?"

"No, sir, I don't believe so. I forgot all about it till just now."

"Did you get a plate?"

"No, damn it. Couldn't even tell you the state. Don't even know for sure what the make was. But it was blue—light blue."

"Sounds like you got a look at the driver."

"Yeah, I saw him, all right. That SOB was trying

to tell me something with his eyes. Like he was sending a goddamn message. Sorry. Didn't mean to curse on TV."

"That's okay. Could you recognize him?"

"You bet your ass I could. Sorry." The marshal sighed. "You know, in my day, I wrote more than my share of traffic tickets, ran down kids for doin' the kinda shit kids do, even investigated a burglary or two."

"Yes, sir?"

"But this is the first homicide I was ever involved with—my own wife and kids."

"It might have been him, your eyeball pick-up truck?"

Ferguson nodded, his mouth and chin tight. "You know, I can't explain why I forgot about that truck till now. God*damn* it!"

"We'll get you with an artist," Harrow said.

"Why did he *do* that, Mr. Harrow?"

"These killers all have their own tortured—"

"No, not that. Why did he have to mutilate her? Why cut off her damn . . . her *sweet* . . . finger?"

Harrow had no answer.

The interview had wrapped, and crew were tearing down as Harrow and Ferguson sat in the kitchen where Mrs. Ferguson had been killed. The two men had coffee in Styrofoam cups provided by a production assistant.

"Everybody knows your story, Mr. Harrow. While your family got shot, you were off savin' the life of the President of the United States."

"Don't tell the Secret Service," Harrow said, "but I'd trade him for them in a heartbeat."

The marshal smiled at this bleak humor. "You're better off than me, amigo. I was writin' a goddamn traffic ticket, busting the ass of some salesman for goin' forty-two in a thirty-mile zone."

"Yeah?"

"Yeah. And the goddamn murderer slowed down to watch me do it."

Chapter Thirteen

Laurene Chase liked to sit in the back of the bus.

It tweaked her sense of irony, as a black lesbian who'd managed to survive and even thrive in Waco, Texas. Right now she had the aisle seat next to Carmen Garcia by the window, with Jenny Blake and Nancy Hughes across the way, as they headed for a town in North Dakota (*were* there towns in North Dakota?) called Rolla.

She held in her hands hard copy of material Jenny Blake had downloaded about the burg of fourteen hundred or so, which covered a scant mile and a quarter. Median income was just a shade over thirty thousand, meaning nearly twenty percent of the population lived below poverty level. One statistic stood out to Laurene: seven-tenths of 1 percent of the population was African-American.

Across the aisle Jenny was pounding at the laptop keyboard as if sending repeated SOS messages from a sinking ship. The petite blonde, hair pony-tailed back, wore jeans and a white T-shirt, the letters OMG printed on the front (the back, Laurene had previously noted, read: WTF).

Laurene asked, "How's your math, Jen?"

Jenny reacted with her usual caught-in-the-headlights freeze, fingers poised over the keyboard like gripping claws. "Okay."

"Good, 'cause mine sucks. What's seven-tenths of a percent of fourteen-hundred-seventeen?"

"About ten."

Jenny had given up three whole words in the exchange. What did that make, in the three days they'd spent together on the bus, twenty-six words out of the cute little nerd?

Laurene settled back in the bus seat. So they were headed for a town with ten black people. Two-thirds of the populace was white, with nearly 30 percent Native American. Totals for Asians and Latinos were higher than blacks, with those listing their race as "other" outnumbering African-Americans three times over.

Suddenly, Waco seemed pretty damned progressive.

Sure as hell wouldn't be a police force in Rolla, which meant they'd be dealing with the Rolette County sheriff, a thought that in itself made Laurene uneasy. She kept thumbing through the information, and when she read about the last sheriff being removed from office for gross misconduct, she immediately pictured a big old redneck John Madden-looking motherhumper, sweat stains in the pits of his dirt-brown uniform shirt, nose a mass of red veins below mirrored sunglasses and a campaign hat.

Then she laughed to herself, thinking, *That's me, just another progressive from Waco.*

Laurene remembered what her mother had once said to her: *God made us each in His own image, darling child. That's why we are all completely different.* Still wasn't sure she understood that, but it often floated through her mind.

"Something funny?" Jenny asked, with just a little attitude.

Laurene, who'd been laughing to herself, held up a hand, like one of Rolla's Indians saying, *How.*

"Not laughing at you, Jen," Laurene said. "Just amused by my own dumb ass."

From her window seat, where she'd been halfnapping, Carmen Garcia looked over and asked, "Did I miss something, girls?"

Jenny, naturally, said nothing.

Next to her, the ponytail blonde, Nancy Hughes—who'd also been napping—came slowly awake and stretched.

"So," Carmen said, looking over at Laurene, "spill it. What's so funny?"

Shaking her head, Laurene said, "I was wondering how the folks in Rolla, North Dakota, are gonna react to me and Jenny here—the world's most beautiful black Amazon, and a nearly mute blond girl wearing a T-shirt sayin' *Oh My God, What The Eff?*"

Jenny looked injured, and Carmen frowned. Nancy wasn't awake enough yet to have an opinion.

Laurene made a dismissive wave. "Jen . . . guys . . . I'm not making fun of anybody."

Carmen said, "Kinda sounds like you are."

"Well, maybe myself a little. The locals see *my* fine gay black ass, they are going to shit gold bricks, and start the gold rush all over again."

That made Carmen laugh, Nancy too, and even Jenny managed a tiny smile.

"Hey," Laurene said, "we're all freaks to somebody."

"You can't just be figuring that out," Nancy said.

But the other two had given all their attention over to Laurene, who not only was Harrow's right hand, but the oldest and maybe wisest of them.

"I always lived my life the way I wanted," she said, no laughter now. "Nobody could make me believe I was wrong—even when I was."

That drew wry smiles out of Carmen and Nancy, though Jenny remained poker-faced.

"I really thought I was in charge of myself, if not my destiny—I mean, no cop thinks the world is anything but a random damn mine field. But I was in a relationship that was working, and I really thought I was the captain of that frickin' ship too. Me and Patty. That was her name."

Now it was Carmen and Nancy whose expressions had gone blank with the fear of getting too much information, while Jenny had tight eyes and a cocked head, like a dog just figuring out what those words its master had been blurting were all about.

"Since Patty died, though, I realize I wasn't the

one with the hand on the rudder. She'd been runnin' things, all along. Made me think I was in charge. Out front, leading the way." Laurene chuckled again, but this time there was no humor in it. "Leading the way? Hell, I *lost* my way."

"We all do, time to time," Nancy said, and Carmen nodded.

But Jenny said, bluntly, "I don't."

All eyes went to the petite computer guru.

"Never *had* a way," she said with a shrug.

Laurene laughed. "That's a good one, kid," she said. "First joke I ever heard you crack."

Jenny said, "Joke?"

Then the other three howled and, truth be told, Jenny was smiling herself, just a little.

They all rocked forward a little as the bus stopped. Looking past Carmen out the tinted window, Laurene made out a low, long building with a sign proclaiming they were parked by the Rolette County Sheriff's Office.

In the aisle, Laurene Chase smoothed her blouse and pants with only moderate success, after ten hours on the bus, but for a couple of pee breaks. She slipped into a black *Crime Seen!* silk jacket, retrieved her carry-on-type bag from its perch, and headed for the front of the bus, Carmen and Nancy behind her, Jenny staying on the bus, still glued to her laptop.

They walked down the few stairs and outside into bright sunshine and a cold north wind. Behind their bus was the semi that was home to the lab and the mini production studio.

"Damn," Laurene said, zipping up the jacket at the chill. "Wasn't it just summer?"

"Not convinced it's *ever* summer up here," Carmen said, shivering as she stepped down, a hand trying vainly to keep her hair intact.

Blond Nancy, still wearing only a T-shirt and jeans and seemingly impervious to the windy North Dakota welcome, walked off toward the semi to collect her gear.

"Tough kid," Laurene said, nodding toward the sound woman.

"Crew," Carmen said with a shrug. "Different breed."

The street was two-lane with curb parking, the buildings mostly one-story, a gas station across and down the only real sign of life, as cars pulled in and out. A parking lot to the right of the sheriff's office revealed two cruisers and a four by four bearing the department logo.

From the semi, bulky Maury Hathaway emerged, lugging his camera, Nancy Hughes and Billy Choi tagging after. Hathaway, like Nancy, wore only a T-shirt, this one with a Phish logo, and jeans—in his fifties, he remained a teenager. Choi, his hair "Werewolves of London" perfect despite the wind, wore a black leather jacket over a black tee and black slacks.

Laurene gathered the camera crew plus Carmen and Choi trailing behind them, and left them grouped on the sidewalk like a parade that got sidetracked as she went in through the double glass doors. The meeting had been set up by Harrow via phone—all Laurene knew was the sheriff's name, Jason Fox.

A tall, broad-shouldered Native American in uniform with sheriff's badge loomed over a long counter. His hard brown eyes under a helmet of raven-black hair looked past Laurene at the group gathered beyond the glass doors.

So much for the redneck musclehead she'd pictured. Maybe the sheriff who got thrown out of office had looked like that.

"Sheriff Fox? Laurene Chase with *Crime Seen!*"

"Been expecting you." His eyes went past her again. "Didn't expect that kind of entourage, though."

"Not really an entourage, Sheriff—that's actually a very pared-down TV crew, plus a forensics expert working with us. I'm a crime scene analyst myself—on leave from the Waco P.D."

He clearly liked the sound of that, his thin mouth even turning up at the corners enough to qualify as a smile. "Okay. You can let 'em in."

She did, and soon they'd all shaken hands and made introductions, after which Sheriff Fox said, "Shall we move into my office? It'll be snug, but you should all make it."

The pebble-glass door had to be left open so that Hathaway could shoot from there. Otherwise the modest office accommodated them, but just— nothing fancy, a metal desk, computer desk next to it, file cabinet in a corner. Walls were spotted with diplomas, commendations, and some colorful outdoor pictures of sheriff and deputies in wooded areas.

The sheriff sat himself behind his desk, signaling for Laurene and Carmen to take the two seats across. Choi leaned against the file cabinet while Nancy ran the boom from the close-quarters sidelines. A file folder sat before the sheriff on the neat desk like a meal he was contemplating.

Laurene asked the sheriff for permission to start rolling and got it.

She asked, "Sheriff Fox, what can you tell us?"

Fox flipped open the file folder. "Burl Hanson was county comptroller."

Not law enforcement, she thought, *but another public servant. . . .*

"He came home from work and found something terrible."

Chapter Fourteen

Two years before

Nola Hanson was a typical mother, convinced her daughter Katie was no typical child. And she had typically big dreams for her daughter Katie— Dr. Hanson, Katherine Hanson (Attorney at Law), Governor Hanson, Senator Hanson, even *President* Hanson. Ever since Hillary, all the doors were open now, weren't they?

On the other hand, *Doctor* Hanson did have a real ring to it. . . .

As for eight-year-old Katie, her biggest ambition was doing well at tomorrow night's softball game.

"You're *sure* he'll be there?" the child asked for the fifth or sixth time.

The girl's mother was at the stove, stirring chicken noodle soup. Patient with her blond, pigtailed interrogator, Nola said, "Your father's working late today, so he can be sure not to miss an inning of the game tomorrow."

Tall for her age, and slender, Katie slipped onto a diner-type stool opposite her mother at the kitchen island, and displayed a big grin made memorable by a missing front tooth, the new one about a quarter of the way in. Mother and daughter shared hair color and the same lively blue eyes. Nola, in her mid-thirties, had kept on a few pounds after giving birth to Katie, but Burl, her husband, not only never complained, he seemed fully in favor of the additional curves.

"I like my women with some meat on the bone," he'd kidded her.

"Women?" she'd kidded back, one eyebrow arching.

"*Woman*," he corrected.

"No problem. I like my *men* big and stupid."

This little exchange had become a running joke with them, and seen endless repetition and variation over the years.

Burl was comptroller for Rolette County, having worked his way up from the entry-level accounting position he'd landed out of college. Nola and Burl were alumni of North Dakota State, Bisons through and through—Burl even insisted on owning a green car (the school's colors were green and gold).

Some good-natured guff had come Nola's way from her sorority sisters when she'd started dating the accounting major, but when she retorted, "CPAs do it with a long pencil," the carping had turned to laughter, and maybe envy.

The couple married just after graduation. Burl took the job out here, one interstate exit past the middle of nowhere, and Nola signed on at the Rolla Public Library. At first, their lives were about as boring as Nola's sorority sisters predicted. Slowly, however, things changed—they both earned promotions, Nola first, rising to head librarian with a speed that dismayed some of her co-workers.

And though she wasn't exactly overseeing the Library of Congress, the Rolla branch brought its own challenges, and she took pride in having the best public collections of both fiction and non-fiction (for a town Rolla's size) in the state.

Burl's rise had been slower, his path blocked by more than a couple geriatric librarians. Still, his progress had been steady, and they always considered themselves both happy and blessed—at least until Katie came along and showed them what happiness was really about. The gifted little girl became the center of their universe, and her accomplishments in school gave Nola and Burl more pride than anything in their respective careers.

Everything was working out even better than Nola could ever have hoped. Both she and Burl came from broken families, and making their house a home was a shared goal. When her female friends would whine over petty arguments with their husbands, Nola (to her slight embarrassment and major pleasure) couldn't report a single spat. She and Burl were simply on the same page, and Katie had only made life better. Nola made no apologies for her good luck.

Ladling soup into a bowl, Nola asked, "Washed your hands?"

Her daughter leaned toward the waiting bowl on the counter and said, "Smells *good. . . .*"

"Don't change the subject. Straight to the bathroom and wash them."

Defeated, Katie climbed down and trotted off toward the first-floor bathroom.

"Soap too!" Nola called.

If getting Katie to wash up was the biggest dilemma of the day, Nola knew she didn't have anything to complain about.

A potentially touchy subject had come up earlier—what Katie wanted for her birthday. The girl said she'd settle for nothing less than a little brother or a puppy. Katie didn't really seem to care which, though Burl would probably be happy to hear that Katie, given a choice, was leaning toward the canine option. . . .

Smiling to herself, setting the bowl of soup on the counter where Katie would sit, Nola was surprised to see the doorknob turning across the kitchen, on the door off the garage.

A glance up at the clock said it was only 6:45, and she didn't expect Burl for another hour, at least. Which was why she was serving Katie her dinner now.

Pleased to have Burl home, she half turned to the door and said, "*You're* early! How was your—"

She stopped mid-sentence, frozen at the sight of a strange man at the threshold of her kitchen. Middle-aged, a little chunky. Tennis shoes, blue jeans, and a blue jacket. Blue baseball cap pulled low almost over his eyes.

Pistol in his right hand.

Though physically petrified, Nola was mentally racing, thoughts streaking through her mind:

Katie was still in the bathroom, good.

Nearest knife in the block on the counter behind her.

Soup hot enough to throw at this intruder and burn him?

What then, the knife?

No getting to the phone for 911, too far away.

Duck behind the counter of the island, but what then? Fight or flight?

The presence of Katie in the house made the decision easy.

Nola shouted, "*Katie—run!*"

Then, snarling, she grabbed the pan of soup— maybe it wasn't hot enough but it was metal and she could swing at him—and moved toward the intruder and the pistol barked.

Like a hard punch, it knocked Nola back, and she felt her balance slipping. The counter's edge was right there, but when she reached for it, it seemed to move away and she found herself on the floor, tile cool against her flesh.

To her surprise, there was no pain. She knew she had been shot, from the noise echoing in the airy kitchen to the spreading warmth in her chest, but she couldn't get over the lack of pain. Everything just felt numb. Something smelled bitter— cordite. Burl was a hunter.

She tried to yell again, for Katie to run, but nothing came. She coughed and realized she was spitting up blood. The man stood over her now, his eyes on her but unconcerned, as if he were looking at spilled milk and not a dying woman.

Nola tried to recognize him, couldn't, then tried to understand why this stranger had just walked into her house and shot her.

Should have locked the door, a voice in her head said.

Too late now, wasn't it?

Spilled milk.

Sending thoughts to Katie to run, to hide, to get out of the house, was all she could manage for her daughter—a sad desperate attempt at telepathy. She tried to talk, to ask this man why he had done this thing, but her efforts were only rewarded with more coughing.

She struggled to focus on his face again, but her vision blurred.

Was she about to die? Was Katie about to die? Was the price of her happy life these terrible last agonized moments?

He raised the pistol again, and the last thing she saw was the flash.

Katie's hands were under the warm water when she heard her mother yell for her to run, but that made no sense—her mommy *never* wanted her to run in the house. . . .

A moment later, she heard what sounded like one of the M-80s the bigger kids had been shooting off last summer, on the Fourth of July, when both her parents warned her about the dangers of firecrackers. They'd finally relented and let her hold a sparkler that her dad lit.

But this bang had been so loud, she jumped, water from the sink spraying the front of her when she pulled her hands back, making a mess Mommy wouldn't like.

Katie was scared now. Something was going on in the kitchen, something not normal, something wrong, but she had no idea what. She crept closer to the open door.

A second M-80 exploded in the kitchen, and Katie jumped again, her hand stifling a scream. She tiptoed into the hallway, and looked out to the kitchen, where her mother's feet were sticking out, on the floor! Rest of her hidden by the kitchen's large island.

Standing over Mommy was a tall man who seemed to be pointing down, maybe with his hand, maybe with something *in* his hand; but from here, the man's body blocked the object and Katie couldn't see.

But she did see a stranger, and she of course understood that a stranger meant danger, and she grasped now that Mommy yelling for her to run was because *this* stranger meant danger. . . .

As the man turned slowly in her direction, Katie turned and sprinted down the hall to her bedroom and ducked inside, closing the door as quietly as she could.

Had he seen her?

She looked for a place to hide—there were really only two choices: the closet and under her bed. When they played hide and seek, her mommy always looked in the closet first. Under the bed was her best choice. More than once, Mommy had failed to find her there.

She dropped to her knees, breath coming in ragged gasps now, tears running down her cheeks, though she was barely aware of that; then she shimmied under the bed, and tried not to move.

Quiet as a mouse, that was something her grandma would say. *Quiet as a mouse.*

She knew of better hiding places in the house, but that would mean trying to get past the stranger, and she knew if he saw her, she was in trouble.

Under the bed would have to do.

The springs her roof now, Katie prayed to God that the man wouldn't find her, and that her daddy would come home. She hoped her mommy was all right. Mommy was on the floor and maybe the man had hit her. But Mommy would be all right. She had to be! Katie would be all right too, if she just stayed quiet as a mouse. This was as far as her mind could take her.

Daddy, she thought. *Please come home . . . please. . . .*

When she heard the bedroom door open, she again clamped a hand over her mouth to keep the fright in. Fear gripped her now; she was shaking, nearly uncontrollably. The door was behind her, to her left. She could hear the man coming in—he was not rushing. It was the same way Daddy checked on her when he thought she was asleep, but wasn't.

Only this wasn't Daddy.

The closet was to her right and soon she could see the man's black shoes under the edge of where the bedspread hung down.

He opened the louvered doors one at a time, and poked around in there, among her toys on the floor and the neat hanging clothes. When he shut the closet up, her breath caught in her throat and maybe, maybe, a tiny sound came out.

She was sure he would look under the bed next, that his stranger's face would be inches from hers; but he didn't. Instead, he walked around the bed, circling behind her and crossing the room to her desk and the small table where she kept her snow globe collection.

When he stopped before the table, his feet still in view under the bedspread hem, she felt something that wasn't fear—something that, had she been older, might have been described as a sense of violation.

Her snow globe collection was her most cherished possession, and the stranger was looking at them, maybe even handling them. She felt her face redden but made herself stay silent, knowing that his finding her, and touching her, could be far worse than him touching her toys.

Please, Daddy, please come home, she prayed.

Then the stranger's feet turned again—was he walking out of the room? Without finding her? A hopeful wave washed over her, but still she stayed quiet as a mouse. Then couldn't see his feet, couldn't hear him, didn't know *where* he was. . . .

Cold dry hands grabbed her ankles, and yanked.

The scream, the pure animal cry that escaped from her, seemed to echo off the walls, and engulf her whole world. She grabbed at the carpeting, but the nap gave her nothing to hold onto and anyway he was too strong, dragging her.

"*Mommy!*"

Once he had her out, he took her by the arm and brought her to a standing position, but the sudden force caused her to stumble and fall. He bent down close, his face a blank mask, his eyes staring right through her.

As he pulled her to her feet again, not roughly, not gently, Katie wondered if it was possible that this man wasn't a human at all. Adults didn't look at kids the same way they did other adults, but they did have life in their eyes, and this stranger did not.

As he swept her to her feet, Katie thrashed and kicked, but the stranger was too strong.

"*Mommy! Mommy!*"

Her throat burned, the tears streaming now, her breath uneven as she tried to fight and scream at the same time, the shrill sound of her cries hurting her own ears.

Then the stranger dragged her into the kitchen and set her on the floor, almost gingerly, next to her mother.

Katie saw two little holes in her mother's chest, Mommy, with blood on her mouth, staring wide-eyed at the ceiling, her eyes without life, like the stranger's.

"*Mommy!*" Katie shrieked one last time, and she tried to shake her mother back to life, to no avail.

Katie looked up at the stranger, who was pointing something at her now—a gun. The ones her daddy had were bigger, but this was like the ones on TV. It looked like a big black squirt gun.

Beyond the gun, the man's face remained blank as he aimed.

Katie's eyes widened and her tears stopped and even her fear fled. Then she said something. She didn't know why she said it, but she said it: "Now I lay me down to sleep. . . ."

A flash filled her vision, and she fell backward into darkness. Her last thought—would Mommy be waiting for her, in Heaven?—ended when her head touched the floor.

It was all the Messenger could do to get out to the truck before he broke down. He was weeping as he drove away from the house where his most recent message had just been delivered.

"Got too close," he whispered. "Got too close."

In town, he made sure he was obeying the speed limit as he slowly scanned the darkening business district for a parking lot.

Finally, he saw a city park, down a block on a side street, which he turned onto, coming around on the far side, near a ball diamond.

No one was around.

He locked the pistol in the glove compartment, and got out of the truck. He'd walked only a few steps when he felt the bile rising in his throat. He had only a second to check for passersby before the vomiting doubled him over.

This had been bad. This had been the worst one.

The only thing that allowed him to carry out his missions was knowing that those who received his messages were just the delivery system—symbols, *not* people. That had gone blooey at the Hanson house. The little girl had nearly touched the inside part of him. Nearly? No, she *had* touched him.

He stood, wiping his mouth, and shook his head. It could never be like this again. He would have to be sharper, smarter. He couldn't risk this sort of thing again. He might not be able to do what had to be done.

The little girl's hysterical screaming rang in his ears, and he felt more coming up. He bent over just in time as he retched again.

Wasn't supposed to be like this. All his work, all the time he had put in, couldn't all be undone this easily, could it? That screaming little girl . . .

He looked up and down the quiet street. Nothing moved. Silence, blessed silence in this park. A block over, a dog barked. Somewhere he heard the revving of a car motor in a garage, someone obviously working on it.

His life had been like this once. Blessedly silent, boring even, until they *ruined* it. . . .

He couldn't stop delivering messages until someone made it better, until someone heard his pleas for help.

If it took delivering a hundred more messages to make the world pay attention, so be it. But he could *not* have another one like tonight. No more like tonight.

He was good at this, he knew that. Efficient. Not cruel. But tonight he had found out he still needed to improve, to become even more efficient.

As he climbed back into the truck, his stomach

settled. On the long drive home he would lay the groundwork for the next message. He would redouble his efforts to know everything about the recipients beforehand. When he delivered the next message, and the one after that and the one after that, he would be more detached, more untouchable.

Tonight could never happen again.

The snow and the rain did not stop the postman on his appointed rounds, right? Or dogs or even screaming little girls.

Chapter Fifteen

Laurene met the sheriff's gaze. "Mr. Hanson found something terrible, all right—his family dead."

"Yes. Wife and daughter, both shot twice in the chest. You already know that your bullets from Florida match ours."

"We understand Mr. Hanson took his own life."

"Yes. Killed himself a week after the murders. Snapped. Hanged himself."

Why, she wondered, *was this killer punishing these men? Public servants coming home to slaughtered love ones? Or were* fathers *being punished?*

She asked, "Who did the crime scene analysis at the Hanson home?"

"State BCI. We don't have the tools for that kind of investigation."

"What did they find?"

Fox held up a sheaf of photos. "You'll want to look at these. Autopsy got us the bullets."

"You think the photos should be helpful . . . ?"

"Not my area, Ms. Chase. They're crime scene photos, and maybe they'll mean more to you."

"What did you get from the photos, Sheriff? And from being on the scene?"

He thought for a moment. Then: "Guy was real careful. No fingerprints, no witnesses, and he collected the shell casings from the automatic. Only evidence they gathered were some tire tracks that didn't match either of the Hanson vehicles."

"Do you have those results?"

The sheriff nodded. "You take the photos and the tire marks information info too—these are dupes. When we're finished here, I'll request the BCI e-mail their files to you."

"Thank you, Sheriff," Laurene said, passing the folder of pictures to Carmen, who began thumbing through. The tire mark evidence Laurene gave to Choi.

"I'll get started on these," Choi said, glancing at the several sheets. The tool mark and firearms expert squeezed past the cameraman in the doorway, and was gone.

Turning back to Fox, Laurene asked, "Who interviewed the neighbors?"

"I did—but 'neighbors' overstates it. Neighbors are few and far between out that way. Nearest one's almost a quarter of a mile away."

Another similarity to the Harrow case, Laurene noted.

"What time of day did the crime take place?"

She knew the answer, of course—actually, she

knew a lot of the answers. This was part of the *Killer TV* process: getting somebody like the sheriff here to deliver the exposition. Still, she liked getting this kind of stuff from the source.

The sheriff said, "Just before seven p.m."

"Were the not-so-next-door neighbors home?"

"Yeah, only they didn't hear anything. You wouldn't expect them to—windy night, even for around here. Anyway, they could have missed the sound even if they'd been closer."

Laurene asked Carmen, "Do you have any questions?"

"Actually, yes." Carmen withdrew two photos from the folder, showing them to Fox.

One was a picture of the daughter's room, where nothing appeared out of place—bed made, stuffed animals piled near pillows. A small table to the right of the bed was home to a considerable collection of snow globes, Disney characters mostly, whose familiar faces and forms were turned toward the bed. A desk held a computer, and, above it, shelves displayed the spines of DVDs and books, all neatly arranged. The second picture was a closeup of the table with the snow globe collection.

Fox looked at the photos with eyes that indicated he was well beyond seeing anything in these much-viewed crime scene shots.

Carmen asked, "Did you dust that room for prints?"

"Why, no."

"How about the state crime lab? Were you there when they processed the scene?"

"I was. They didn't consider the bedroom part of the crime scene."

"So they didn't check the Winnie the Pooh snow globe for fingerprints?"

Perplexed, the sheriff said, "Nobody thought the killer went in that room—nothing was out of place."

Carmen leaned in and tapped the closeup shot of the snow globes. "Except Winnie the Pooh," she said.

"Be damned," Fox said, and shook his head and grimaced, handing the closeup picture to Laurene.

Laurene looked at the photo. The snow globes all faced the same direction, except one—Winnie the Pooh had his back to the bed.

"He picked that one up," Laurene said.

"Well, someone did," Fox said. "We'll see if we can find out who."

"If the whole family has been dead for almost two years," Laurene asked, "where's the snow globe now?"

"No idea," Fox admitted glumly. "But I am damned sure going to find out."

To Carmen, Laurene said, "Hell of a catch, girl. That's *two* for you. Maybe it's time you joined the crime scene team and I took over as host."

Carmen smiled, chagrined. "I'm happy doing what I do."

Everyone on the *Crime Seen!* team was aware that all of this had been caught on camera. Funny, Laurene thought, how the knowledge that they were putting on a show as well as chasing a killer colored her perceptions.

Fox said, "I should mention there's a new family living in the house now. You want to go out there?"

After a moment's consideration, Laurene said, "Let us run with what you've given us for right now. If we need to visit the scene, we'll go out later."

"But you will call me if you go?"

"Absolutely, Sheriff. You'd be a big help. Hey, you've *been* a big help. Thank you."

"No problem. Who wouldn't want this thing cracked? Now, can I ask a question . . . ?"

"Of course."

"Is this the same bastard who killed J.C. Harrow's family?"

Laurene locked eyes with the man. "Can't be sure . . . but it's very damn likely the 'same bastard' who took out the Ferguson mom and kids in Florida."

Fox sighed. "You're covering a lot of hunting ground."

"Yes. But we are closing in. We know to a near certainty that he's targeting only the families of civil servants."

The dark brown eyes flared. "*Why* in hell?"

"Pretty soon, Sheriff . . . we'll ask *him.*"

After their good-byes, Laurene, Carmen, and the camera crew caught up with Jenny and Choi in the lab.

Choi took the ball: "First, the tires are so worn, he coulda replaced them by now."

Laurene just gave him a look.

"Tire size 275/70R18, is very popular for light trucks and SUVs. This particular one's manufactured by Michelin, and is the standard tire on the Ford F-150 pickup."

"Does that help us?"

"Oh, sure," Choi said, his smile mirthless. "Thanks to declining sales over the last five years? Leaves us only about four million F-150s, plus whatever vehicles bought them as aftermarket tires."

"So, then, that was sarcasm."

"I been saying you aren't dumb, Laurene. Ask anybody."

She sighed. "Keep digging, Billy. See if you can do something to make this a more manageable number."

His eyebrows went up. "For instance . . . ?"

"Start with Kansas. That's where our errant Florida corn leaf came from—make it Fords sold in Kansas in the last, say, ten years."

Choi smirked. "That's still going to be a bunch."

"But a smaller bunch," Laurene said. "Didn't Marshal Ferguson say he saw a blue pickup the night his family was killed?"

Choi snapped his fingers. "Right! That *will* help narrow it down."

"Go," Laurene said.

Practically bouncing, Choi moved back to his computer, and his fingers were soon flying over the keyboard.

Jenny gave Laurene a glance, which was enough to summon the African-American crime scene analyst to the petite blonde's side.

Looking up like a little girl about to show Mommy her latest drawing, Jenny said, "Sheriff said Mr. Hanson was the county comptroller?"

"That's right."

Laurene liked where this was headed already—Harrow had told her Jenny was smart; now Laurene was seeing just how quick the girl really was.

"I checked on shooting deaths involving the families of public servants in the last ten years."

"And?"

"Ten years ago, a member of the board of supervisors in McCracken County in Kentucky found out his wife was having an affair. He shot her and their three kids, her lover, and himself."

"Jesus," Carmen whispered.

Laurene could only think that it must be nice, being able to still be surprised by the evil that people could visit on each other. She'd been at it long enough that such revelations rarely made an emotional blip.

Jenny was saying, "Nine years ago, zero killings of that nature. Every year ever since? At least two, sometimes three separate instances."

Carmen gasped—Laurene hoped it wasn't just for the camera—but this news *was* news worth gasping over.

Laurene said, "That's like . . . twenty something."

"Oh, you *can* do math."

It did not seem to be sarcasm—Jenny was no Billy Choi.

Jenny was saying, "Twenty-two, so far."

Carmen, still stunned, asked, "How . . . how is that possible?"

"Killing strangers," Laurene said, "is easy. So is getting away with it."

From his computer, Choi called, "You mostly get killed by people you know!"

"Eighty percent of the time," Jenny said.

"What *I* want to know," Laurene said, shaking her head, "is how in the hell this SOB could carry out *twenty-two* such acts, murdering . . . *how* many?"

"Fifty-three women and children," Jenny said. "Twenty-two mothers and thirty-one children. Eighteen boys, thirteen girls."

The lab fell silent. Only the faint mechanical hum of sound and camera and computers could be discerned.

Finally Laurene asked, "How did he kill fifty-three people . . . and no one caught on?"

Jenny shrugged. "Killings may not all be his. But to answer your question? Small jurisdictions with limited police presence, spread across the country."

Choi left his computer. "You know, in sleepy little Davenport, Iowa, they've had over two dozen bank robberies in the last ten years."

They all looked at Choi expectantly, waiting for the other shoe to drop.

"I mean, you didn't hear *shit* about twenty-one of them. Those other three though, they all happened in 2004 when George Bush and John Kerry were campaigning in town at the same time. *That* got the attention of the national media, made CNN and MSNBC, and *still* generates a kajillion hits on Google."

"What are you saying?" Carmen asked, suddenly defensive. "That this is somehow the *media's* fault?"

"No, not all," Choi said.

Laurene said, "I think what Billy boy is saying is that this is a really big country, and it takes something completely off the charts to catch our attention . . . and he's right. Our unsub has been operating below the radar. Hell, until fifteen minutes ago, we thought he was going exclusively after law enforcement . . . and, Carmen, before you found that leaf thing? We didn't even know this monster was *out* there."

Carmen said, "So . . . this guy we're looking for . . . he's killed fifty-some people?"

"Could be," Laurene said. "Most likely not, though. We're only reviewing the stats in the most superficial way, at this point. But we *do* know he's killed three in Florida, and two in North Dakota. It's also possible, because of the MO, that he killed Harrow's family, as well. Which makes at least seven." Turning to Jenny, she asked, "When was the most recent one?"

"Three days ago."

Carmen said hollowly, "The night of our first segment on *Crime Seen!* . . ."

They all exchanged grave glances.

Laurene asked, "Where, Jen?"

"Socorro, New Mexico—family of George Reid, accountant with Socorro County. Gunned down."

Laurene drew in a deep breath, let it out. "All right. You take Socorro, Jen—really dig in. See if the mom is missing a finger. Billy, take the truck tires.

Carmen, you and I will interview the Hansons' neighbors one more time, and *maybe* someone will remember *something*. First though, I gotta call the boss."

Chapter Sixteen

Riding the other *Crime Seen!* bus, J.C. Harrow got out his cell phone by the second ring.

"It's Laurene."

"What have you got?" he asked. She wouldn't be calling just to be sociable.

She filled him in on the startling discovery Jenny Blake had made—twenty-two separate attacks in the past decade that matched their killer's MO!

He said, "We have no idea how many might be related to our cases?"

"No," Laurene said. "But I'm betting the number isn't zero."

"Well, there's only one way to find out. We'll have to look into all of them. Check to see how many of the murdered mothers were missing a wedding ring."

Laurene's pause seemed endless to Harrow.

Finally she asked, "J.C.—with this revelation . . .

aren't we going to have to turn this investigation over to the Feds?"

He desperately wanted to say no, but they both knew the answer to the question. Christ knew how many lives were at stake here. . . .

"Of course, turn over what we have . . . but first, make copies of everything, and tell Jenny to e-mail me the list of all the crimes."

"So we're not backing off?"

"Hell, no. We are, however, going to let the Feds know what we think *may* be going on, and they can investigate or not, their choice, their pace. In the meantime, we're full speed ahead."

"That is good to hear," Laurene said. "Where do you want to start?"

"Your team will gather what you can there, and I'll start on the Socorro killings. Makes sense, 'cause I'm just outside of town."

"You are?" she said, surprise in her voice. She hadn't mentioned these latest killings, specifically. "You're on top of those killings, then? The, uh . . ."

"Reid family," Harrow finished.

"What are you, J.C., a frickin' witch? How in the hell did you know that?"

"I got a phone call late last night."

"From?"

"Kate Pierson with the New Mexico state crime lab. Know her, Laurene?"

"No. Why'd she call you?"

"She's an old friend."

"No, J.C. *Why* did she call you?"

"Missing wedding-ring finger. And get this—

gun in the Reid killings was the same three fifty-seven used at my house."

An even longer pause from Laurene.

"We *are* on the right track," she said softly.

His voice was soft but had a tremor that threatened eruption. "I'm closer than I've ever been."

"You know, J.C., if you strangle him on TV, the ratings will be great, but you might find yourself hosting the San Quentin Follies next season."

Her grim humor made him laugh.

"I take your point, Laurene, and I do apologize for not filling you in sooner."

"Apology not accepted. I'm supposed to be your number two."

"You are. As for now, we'll play ball with the Feds, all right . . . but let's make sure *we're* the ones who find this maniac."

"It'll be us, all right," she said, and they signed off.

None of that had been caught on camera, and Harrow was glad of it. This was sensitive information.

Chris Anderson, seated across the aisle from Harrow, said, "Sir? We're pullin' up to the sheriff's office."

Harrow looked at his watch—just after 10 A.M. They'd already been on the road since finishing the show on Monday, and had driven all night, after Harrow got the call from Kate Pierson.

"Good," Harrow said. "Let's go."

Soon Harrow found himself standing on a bright, sunny street in front of a new two-story county administration building with old-fashioned mission styling, a facility that housed both the sheriff's office and the county's other departments.

Up and down the street, pedestrians passing each other smiled, spoke, waved. Modest traffic moved smoothly along, and Harrow felt he'd stepped into some sort of Southwestern Norman Rockwell time warp. Or he would have if they hadn't been here to investigate a triple homicide by the serial killer they were chasing. . . .

Automatic doors whispered open, and Harrow entered the modern, efficient-looking office building that hid behind the mission facade. At a round modern light-wood desk to the left of the atrium lobby, a young uniformed deputy manned a guest sign-in book.

The kid—who had a butch haircut and a well-scrubbed fresh-out-of-the-academy look—was reading something on his computer screen.

"Help you?" he asked automatically, barely glancing.

"Son," Harrow said gently, "if you want to grow up to be a policeman, you're going to have to learn to be more observant."

Now the kid looked up and saw before him Harrow with his posse of Anderson, DNA expert Michael Pall, Arroyo with camera, and Ingram with boom mike.

"Here to see Sheriff Tomasa," Harrow said.

Agape, the deputy managed a nod. Then: "May I tell him who's calling and why?"

"J.C. Harrow and crew from *Crime Seen!* Called ahead."

Before long, the sheriff was there in the lobby,

coming over to them with his hand extended to Harrow.

"Mr. Harrow," he said, and they shook hands. "Roberto Tomasa. You spoke to my secretary on the phone."

"Yes, sir. I know this is short notice."

Harrow made the introductions and more hand-shaking followed, quick, perfunctory. The sheriff was burly, about forty, with an easy smile and a steel grip. His face had more pockmarks than old cement, and his nose may have had a shape once, but not for a long time. He had a bushy, droopy, damn near bandito mustache, giving his face the impression of a frown even as he grinned at Harrow, moving everyone to a discreet corner of the lobby.

"Normally we wouldn't have much to say to a TV crew," Tomasa said, "especially at so early a stage of the investigation."

"I understand," Harrow said.

"You were a sheriff yourself, weren't you? Retired?"

"Yes. Was at the state crime lab, after that."

Mischief danced in the sheriff's eyes. "Also saved the President."

"Guilty."

White teeth flashed under the droopy black mustache. "Tell me why I should receive you in my office," he said—no anger or bitterness in his tone.

"Weren't you expecting us?"

"My secretary gave me your message, you were coming. That's not an appointment, Mr. Harrow. And it sure isn't an invitation."

"Kate Pierson—"

"Is with the state crime lab. Not on my payroll. Doesn't represent the Socorro County Sheriff's office."

"Uh oh," Anderson murmured.

That drew a glance from Tomasa, but Harrow spoke up, locking eyes with the man. "Sheriff, we're not here to step on any toes."

"Good."

"But I do think we can help you."

"Kind as your offer is, Mr. Harrow, we have handled murders in Socorro County before."

Harrow kept his tone easy-going, but his rhetoric amped up. "Sheriff, you know as well as I do that if this *is* a serial killer, you need all the help you can get."

"The FBI, for example."

"Yes, but they aren't here. We are. I am. And if we're up against who and what I think we are, we can *all* use help. We now believe the same murderer may be tied to as many as fifty-some homicides over the last nine years."

That got Tomasa's attention. "That seems impossible. . . ."

"I wish it were," Harrow said. "Kate Pierson, protocol be damned, called me because the bullets from your victims match the gun the killer used at my home. Also, the mutilation of the female vic's left hand mirrors what we believe to be the killer's current evolving, devolving M.O."

Tomasa held up a hand. "Mr. Harrow, I am not unsympathetic to your feelings. But *because* you are emotionally involved in this matter, you have taken your search to an extreme . . ." He gestured toward the crew. ". . . that exceeds any accepted law enforcement conditions or ideals."

"I'm not working in law enforcement. But I am still, in my way, a public servant—like the men whose families this perpetrator targets."

"I understand your sincerity, Mr. Harrow. But I *am* working in law enforcement."

"Did you see the broadcast Friday night?"

"Yes, sir, I did."

"Then you know I've recruited some of the best people in their respective forensics fields in the country, if not the world. Do you have the budget to assemble a team like that?"

Frowning in thought, Tomasa said nothing.

"Another thing, Sheriff—some people in this country don't like to talk to the police, no matter why, no matter what, no matter when."

"That much I know," Tomasa admitted.

Harrow gave the sheriff the kind of world-weary smile law enforcement professionals often traded. "Funny thing is—a lot of those same people can't *wait* to run their mouths in front of a TV camera. Like these we have here?"

And suddenly Tomasa roared with laughter that echoed through the atrium.

"All right," the sheriff said. "You can talk to your friend Pierson and see the bullets and whatever else you want, with my blessing . . . but I need from you one thing."

"Name it."

"You must talk to one of Reid's neighbors."

"Well, no problem," Harrow said.

"You say that now," Tomasa said slyly, the bandito quality slipping through the droopy mustache, "only because you haven't met *Archie Gershon* yet."

Chapter Seventeen

Prone in a ditch under hot sun, next to a narrow gravel lane that wound its way up to the one-story rambling white clapboard of one Archibald Gershon, Harrow understood why Sheriff Roberto Tomasa had seemed both eager and amused to have the *Crime Scene!* host handle interviewing the recluse.

Gershon lived on the property next to murder victims the Reids, and the sheriff had figured the old man may well have seen something.

"Archie's known to keep track of what goes on in and around his property," the sheriff had said.

"How do you know anything about the man, if he never steps off that parcel?"

"I didn't say he never stepped off that parcel—he comes to town once a month. Him and me usually share a beer and some talk. No, it's just anybody stepping foot *on* his parcel that's a problem."

They had left the sheriff's office in two vehicles—
Harrow and Tomasa in the departmental Tahoe,
trailed by the *Crime Seen!* bus with Pall, Anderson,
Arroyo, Ingram, and their driver (other staff members having been dropped at their motel).

Right now they were pulling up to the foot of the
place, to large red hand-painted letters on weathered white-painted wood near the gate: TRESPASSERS
WILL BE SHOT! SURVIVORS WILL BE SHOT TWICE!

Harrow frowned. "You just let him get away with
shooting at anybody who comes near his place?"

"My predecessor hauled him in, three times. But
in this part of the world, people value their privacy. Not a judge or jury around here woulda gave
him so much as a fine. Anyway, there haven't been
any incidents lately."

"*Nobody's* welcome?"

"The only person who's been up here in the last
ten years who didn't draw gunfire was the Direct
TV installation guy . . . The coot does love his TV."

"Unless he has a dog," Harrow said, with a dry
chuckle, "it's probably his only company."

In the ditch now, it didn't seem so amusing.

And Gershon was true to his word, or anyway
true to his sign: when Tomasa's SUV had pulled
up to the gate, a bullet punctured a tire, and a second one took out part of the red and blue light on
the roof. That's when Tomasa shoved the Tahoe
into park, and suggested they vacate the vehicle.

Harrow had rolled out the passenger side, hit the
gravel hard, then continued on, dropping down
into the drainage ditch next to the road. With the
open driver's side door for cover, Tomasa got to

the back of the SUV, then ducked behind the Tahoe, all the while gesturing for the bus to back off.

Then, just after a third round pierced the So-corro County shield on the driver's door, Tomasa came around the vehicle and dove into the ditch next to Harrow.

"Man of his word," Harrow said. "Sign *said* he'd shoot. I'm just glad he's as good at it as he is."

"You picked up on that, huh?" the sheriff said with a rumpled grin. "Yeah, most people think ol' Arch misses them. Truth is, he could pick off a gnat's eyelash at two hundred yards."

"Not every crazy survivalist," Harrow said, "shoots like that."

"He's no survivalist," Tomasa said. "And I wouldn't bet on crazy, either. He just doesn't like company."

"Who *is* this character?"

"Late at night, in certain bars around town, you may hear how Archie was one of the boys on the grassy knoll."

Harrow gave the sheriff a look.

"Just passing it along, Mr. Harrow. Don't claim it's gospel."

They heard a vehicle door slam—the bus's, out in the country road below the Tahoe at the gate—and watched as Pall and Anderson jumped out, followed by Maury Hathaway, lugging his Sony cam. Soon the three men were hunkered down in the ditch with the *Crime Seen!* host and the sheriff.

"What the hell are you doing?" Harrow said. "Bullets are flying. You should've stayed put."

Veteran cameraman Hathaway said, "Didn't get the memo."

Young Anderson said, "We're fine. That guy's a good shot. He's just trying to scare us."

"Really?" Harrow asked. "What if he missed?"

Hathaway said, "We'll stay put unless you say otherwise. I wouldn't risk my head *or* my camera."

A fourth bullet kicked up dirt by the edge of the ditch.

Tomasa yelled up toward the house: "Goddamn it, Archie, *stop* that! You known damn well it's Sheriff Tomasa!"

As if the preceding bullets had been so much friendly conversation, a rough-edged voice called down, *"I know who you are, Roberto!"*

"I thought we were friends!" Tomasa yelled.

"We are—that's why you're alive . . . now get the hell off my property!"

"I just come to talk!"

"Be in town next week, Roberto! We can talk then."

"I need to talk today!"

"If I wanted to talk to anybody out here, today? I wouldn'ta put up that sign. You do read English, don't you, Roberto?"

Tomasa, sighing, turned to the little group in the ditch. "Hard-headed old bastard." To the house, he called, "You don't have to talk to *me*, Archie!"

"I know I don't!"

"No—that's not it! I brought someone *else* to talk to you!"

"Maybe you read English, but doesn't seem like you understand the spoken word."

The spoken word? Harrow thought. What kind of erudite hermit lived up that hill?

"Somebody come a long ways to talk to you, Arch!"

"I don't want to talk to anybody today, Roberto. Already jawed long enough!"

Jawed long enough? Was this guy Gabby Hayes or Alistair Cooke?

Then, to punctuate his point, the old man fired a round over their heads.

"Maybe this is more trouble than it's worth," Tomasa said. "Chances are he didn't see a damn thing."

"We're here," Harrow said with a shrug. "My suit already needs dry cleaning, and probably some mending. So how about you let me try?"

"Up to you. Just don't raise your head too high— he's liable to separate you from it."

"He could probably part my hair, if he wanted." Then, toward the house, he yelled, "Mr. Gershon, this is J.C. Harrow! I'd like to come up and speak with you!"

Silence.

"Mr. Gershon, my name is—"

"I heard you!"

"I'm with a TV show called—"

"I know what the show's called! And I don't believe for an instant J.C. Harrow's in a ditch at the bottom of my hill! I don't think the Fonz or Sergeant. Bilko or Gil Grissom is, either!"

". . . You got a scope on that rifle?"

Gershon said nothing.

"Take a look at that bus on the road outside your drive! Name of the show's painted all over it!"

They waited several long, tense moments, peeking over the lip of the ditch like kids watching a ball game over the centerfield fence.

Finally, the door of the house opened, and a string bean in camouflage T-shirt, jeans, and tennies stepped out onto a cement stoop four steps up. Gershon was old, all right, with long, lank silver hair to prove it. He held a model 597 Remington rimfire rifle with a scope—Harrow had one at home, damn good gun.

The king of the hill sighted down through the scope.

Realizing that the man was trying to get a better look and probably not getting ready to fire, Harrow pushed himself to his feet.

"What the hell are you doing?" Tomasa demanded.

With uncharacteristic energy, from down in the ditch, Southern boy Anderson said, "Come on, sir—you know better!"

"Boss!" Pall yelled, overlapping the young chemist. "Get *down*—"

But Harrow stayed on his feet—his calling card was his face, the proof of his words his famous appearance. He stepped back up onto the grassy slope—the place was not fenced off, despite the gated gravel drive—and gave Gershon a good look and a clean shot . . . if that was what he was looking for.

"Be a son of a bitch! You are *him!"*

Harrow just shrugged elaborately with open arms.

"Come on up!"

"What about my crew? And the sheriff?"

"No. Just you!"

Harrow took a few steps up the slope—the grass was cut, not shaggy with weeds.

Pall whispered: "What do you want us to do, boss?"

Without turning or even halting his climb, Harrow said, "Stay out of range of that Remington. Probably ought to keep low and ease back to the bus."

Anderson said, "What about you, sir?"

Moving upward but not quickly, looking up at the skinny figure with the rifle, Harrow said softly, "I'll be fine. Sheriff, can I tell Mr. Gershon if he cooperates, there'll be no charges for the gunplay?"

Tomasa said, "If you come back with your head attached, Mr. Harrow? We'll let it slide."

"I'll hold you to that."

Harrow went on up the hillside, cutting over and stopping in a circle of gravel in front of the well-tended, unpretentious, if weathered, house. A '98 Chevy Silverado pickup in the turnaround was showroom clean. Still, everything about the place said *stay away*. Bushes with long thorns scratched at windows and crowded the narrow stoop. The front screen was closed, the inside door open, a mangy hound visible at the screen, his nose working, his growl barely audible.

So he does have a dog for a friend, Harrow thought.

Up on the stoop, Gershon held the rifle easy in his hands. The old boy wore no glasses, his gray eyes bright if suspicious, his skin leathered from life in the sun, the angles in his face suggesting an American Indian in his ancestry, the lank, silver hair lifting a little in the breeze. He was slender but hard and sharp, like boards positioned at angles on an obstacle course.

"Never miss your show," he said, genial but low-key, rifle lowered now but ready when need be.

"Never miss a shot, either, do you?"

Gershon smiled—his teeth were mildly yellowed but his own; he was sturdy-looking for a guy his age, which was easily seventy. "If you mean, could I have hit if you if I liked? You know I could. I ain't prone to missing."

"You're going to have to make up your mind, Mr. Gershon."

"How's that?"

"Are you a crazy old coot out of *Li'l Abner*, or are you a smart, seasoned veteran of wars unknown who chooses to live apart from the human race?"

". . . You know why I like your show, Mr. Harrow?"

"No."

"You ain't no . . . you're no phony. No wannabe. You and your people have helped put bad guys away, and I can admire that."

"We try," Harrow said.

Gershon stepped down the few concrete steps and offered a hand, which Harrow shook. The grip was firm but didn't show off.

"How pissed off is Roberto?"

"How pissed off do you think? You shot at his vehicle. Blew out a tire, popped his cherry top, and put a hole in the door. That'll cost the county money, and he's got to explain it."

"He knows who's to blame," Gershon grumbled.

"We're friendly, you know. No secret that I value my privacy."

Harrow lifted his eyebrows. "I appreciate that desire, Mr. Gershon. Public service was bad enough, but now I'm *really* in the fishbowl. You mind if I call you 'Archie'?"

The breeze riffled the long wispy silver hair. "Not if I can call you 'J.C.' Where was it you sheriffed? Idaho? Ohio?"

"Iowa. Story County. Just north of Des Moines. Good farmland there. Good people too."

"Not sure there is such an animal."

"What?"

"As 'good people.'"

Harrow shook his head. "Not all people are bad. You said yourself, you like how my show puts bad guys away. That suggests good people getting help."

His host thought about that momentarily. "I'm going to smoke. You want one?"

"Sure."

Gershon leaned the rifle against the stoop, fished a pack of smokes and a lighter from a pants pocket, and lit up. Then he passed the lighter and cigarettes to Harrow, who joined in.

"Sheriff Tomasa, for example," Harrow said. "He's one of the good people. The good guys. Don't you think, Archie?"

"Better than most."

"I like him too. What about your neighbor— George Reid? Was he good people?"

"That's why you're here, of course—the killings."

"You know it is. Reid a good neighbor?"

Gershon grinned. "Why, you suppose if you asked him that he'd've said *I* was? No, we weren't really neighborly. He was just the stranger who lived over there . . ." He pointed west. ". . . and did me the favor of minding his own business."

Harrow looked toward where the sun was lowering, about to drop behind the hills for the night. "He had kids, Archie."

"Yes, he did. They were never any trouble to me either."

"Whoever did this killed Reid's kids."

"I know. World's a shithole, and it can suck a kid down fastest of all."

For a shithole, the world looked beautiful right now, dusk settling in on the recluse's perch with gentle tones of blue and gray.

"Archie, you see anything that night? Hear anything?"

"If I had, don't you think I'd've told Roberto?"

"No."

"Why, because I'm a nasty old hermit? A misanthrope who's given up on the world and everything in it?"

"No. You love that old hound dog, for instance. And he's part of the world."

"You think you got a bead on me, J.C.?"

"I think you're hiding in plain sight, Archie. I think you're waiting to see which catches up with you, first—people who come around to kill you, or just the darkness that eventually swallows us all."

He stared a long time at Harrow, who could see

the shadows of approaching night washing over the old man, and they just stood there smoking.

Finally, Archibald Gershon said, "Why don't you come in for a beer?"

"Thought you'd never ask."

The living room was large and knotty pine, lined with built-in shelves holding volumes of as many varieties as a well-stocked college bookstore—novels, both popular and literary from many decades, non-fiction works on politics and world history, philosophy, poetry, engineering.

Where there weren't book shelves in the living room, gun racks displayed a collection of fircarms a crazy cult might envy. A very comfortable-looking, well-worn brown leather lounger on a braided rug on the bare wood floor faced a big flat-screen television, fifty-something inch easy, as if it were an altar. A table by the chair had beer cans and a fat satellite TV guide, a nine millimeter Browning, and a John D. MacDonald novel cracked open face down.

With the exception of the beer cans, however, the place was tidy, and the kitchen—which opened onto the big library/TV area—had a Formica table dating to *I Love Lucy* days, where they sat and had Schlitz from the can, very cold. The hound curled up under the table at its master's feet—when Harrow came in, it hadn't even growled, sensing Gershon's approval of their guest.

"Breeze was out of the west that night," Gershon said, after a particularly deep swig of Schlitz, "and carried the shots over here—it was like they were in my own yard."

"No question it was gunshots—not a vehicle backfiring, kids playing with fireworks . . . ?"

Gershon gave him a look. "I've heard plenty of guns in my lifetime, J.C."

"Enough to identify them by sound?"

"This was a handgun. Loud. I'd say a .357."

"You do know your guns."

Gershon twitched a smile. "You've already gathered you aren't the only one retired from public service."

Harrow had already suspected that it wasn't company that Gershon feared so much as *The* Company. As in CIA.

"When I heard those shots," he was saying, "I already knew it was too late to do any good. I'm not heartless, J.C.—I knew there were kids over there. But there was no saving anybody."

Harrow nodded.

"Still, I grabbed up the Remington and got outside."

"Could you see the perp leaving? Did you take a shot at him?"

The old boy shook his head, the silver locks swinging. "I meddled in other people's affairs a long time ago—I try not to do it anymore."

Harrow said nothing.

"Come on, J.C. Think it through. He'd killed who he'd come to kill, by the time I heard those shots. If I'd gone over there, they'd be dead anyway. If I shot the guy, who knows who he is or he's working for? No. I have enough on my plate just keeping my own ass alive."

"Why do you bother, Archie? Keeping your ass alive, if the world is such a shithole?"

"Why, J.C.—if I was dead? Something terrible would happen."

"What?"

He grinned. "I'd miss your show."

Harrow grinned back at him. "Okay, Archie. You didn't take a shot. But what did you see through that scope of yours?"

He swigged more beer. "You're right—I did watch as the guy drove off."

"What direction?"

"East."

"So, then . . . he drove right by here."

Gershon swigged again.

"What did you see, Archie?"

"Late model Ford F-150."

Harrow tried not to show any reaction. "Color?"

"Blue—light blue."

Another hit.

Still, Harrow remained impassive. "See the driver?"

"Not really. Probably a man. That's about all I got."

"What makes you say it's a man, then?

Gershon shrugged. "Just didn't feel like a woman. Loud gun like that mag, truck like that. . . . No, I think it was a man, all right."

"What else did you get, Archie?"

Gershon took another gulp of beer.

"Come on, Archie—what is it you've been trying to decide whether or not to share?"

". . . You want the license number?"

Harrow just looked at him.

"Oklahoma plates," he said, and gave the number to Harrow, who wrote it down in his mini-notebook.

Harrow shook his head. "You memorized the number?"

"Sometimes having a good memory comes in handy. Other times you'd trade it for being able to forget."

"And sometimes," Harrow said, "memory is all you have."

"Truth in that," the old man said.

Harrow finished his beer, then stood. "Look, Archie—I've got to go run this plate. You got anything else for me?"

"I don't think so."

But Harrow couldn't quite let go. "Why didn't you tell anyone? Just call your friend Roberto?"

"No phone."

"It's just . . . Archie, goddamn it—somebody might have caught this bastard, if you'd just notified the police."

"If that's all, J.C., I got shows to watch, and books to read."

Harrow shook his head. "None of this means anything to you?"

"You lost your family, didn't you?"

". . . Yeah."

"Ever want to cash it in after that?"

Harrow sighed. "I could use another smoke."

The old man provided one, and the two went back outside where dusk had deepened to purple evening.

"I might want to cash it in," Harrow said, "but I can't think that way. I have to stop this son of a bitch before he does this sick thing again, and again."

"See, that's why I like you on TV, J.C. Why other people like you on TV."

"Huh?"

"You don't give a shit about being a star or having your fifteen minutes of whatever-the-hell. You're the only person on television with an unselfish motive for being there."

"Oh, I have a selfish motive, Archie. I want justice for my family."

"Not revenge?"

"Semantics."

Gershon chuckled dryly, letting smoke swirl out. "People think *I'm* crazier than a shithouse rat, living out here. I survived things I never should have, and that survival's so ingrained in me, I couldn't ever punch my own ticket. So, here I sit on this goddamned hill just waiting to die."

"Or for someone to come kill you?"

"That's just one way of dying." He looked out into the gathering darkness. "What those 'good' people do out there to each other, that doesn't mean squat to me anymore. Yet I'm still here. Waiting."

Harrow stubbed out the cigarette under his heel, but before he turned to go, he asked, "Were you in Dallas in 1963, Archie?"

". . . Don't believe everything you hear."

"I don't," Harrow said. "But I do pay attention."

Bestowing his guest a tight smile, Gershon said, "I will tell you one thing—I was in the Dominican Republic in 1961."

"Trujillo?"

"You know your history. If a man knows his history, he might keep from repeating it . . . not that anybody in charge of this country for the last twenty years ever *got* that." The breeze blew at his hair again, and the old man shivered, possibly with the cold.

Harrow sighed. "Been a lot of blood spilled in a lot of places."

"I said you knew your history."

"Whoever spilled that blood next door, Archie, has got to be stopped."

"Don't disagree. But it's your job, not mine."

"It is at that . . . and I should get to doing it."

"You should," Gershon said. "But if you ever want to stop back and shoot the shit again, chances are I won't shoot at you. And if I do, I won't likely hit you."

Harrow gave up a lopsided grin. "Thanks for that much. And thanks for the license plate number. That should put you in solid with your pal Roberto. And I'll get my network to pay for the damage to his vehicle."

"And they say TV stars are just a bunch of phonies."

Then, laughing at his own joke, the old man turned around and went into the house and joined his hound, his TV, his lounger, his books, and his guns.

Chapter Eighteen

For tonight's show, Carmen Garcia—chicly businesslike in black slacks and a gray silk blouse, her dark hair pulled up in a tight bun—was about to do the live segment intro. This would be followed by a long walking shot sans teleprompter—she'd memorized a full page of script—and Carmen could not remember ever feeling more nervous. She prayed it didn't show, or else her meteoric rise might be quickly followed by the same kind of fall. . . .

As the assistant director counted down to the second, Carmen sent herself a mixed signal: *Stay calm . . . and energy up!*

"I'm Carmen Garcia. Welcome to *Killer TV* on the road with *Crime Seen!*"

Hathaway, on Steadicam this time, followed Carmen down the institutional hallway, as did Nancy Hughes with her boom.

"We're on our way to a conference room at the

Rolla, North Dakota, sheriff's office, where our team's set up shop. We are investigating the two-year-old murders of Nola and Katie Hanson—wife and daughter of then–county comptroller Burl Hanson, who later took his own life, becoming the killer's third victim."

Hathaway followed her in as she moved along and around the big table dominating the room. Behind her, easels held bulletin boards arrayed with crime scene photos from the Hanson house (the most explicit had come down for the broadcast).

Cameraman Phil Dingle was already in the room, capturing tighter one- and two-shots of the others at the table—Laurene Chase poring over more crime scene photos, Jenny Blake hunkered over her laptop, Billy Choi sitting before a computer as well. Both Hathaway and Dingle's shots were being uploaded by the satellite truck for director Stu Phillips back in LA to work his (and his staff's) magic.

Carmen stopped next to Choi. "Bullets from the Ferguson home in Placida, Florida, match bullets from the Hanson murders here in Rolla. Firearms and tool mark examiner Billy Choi has been working on this evidence. . . . Billy?"

The firearms expert with the perfect hair wore the now-familiar *Crime Seen!* lab coat over an open-collar blue shirt and navy slacks.

"Carmen, using NIBIN . . ." A pop-up defined NIBIN for new viewers. ". . . we'd already matched the bullets from the two crime scenes. But look at the slides of the two—the striations are a perfect match. These bullets were fired from a vintage Browning nine-millimeter automatic."

"You can be certain of the make of the weapon?"

"Oh yes—the striations are made by the rifling in the barrel. Glocks, Sig Sauers, and the like have barrels struck on a mandrel, with no rifling. The Browning's rifling gives us a way to identify it. The killer may have picked up the shell casings . . . but we can still get a match through the bullets themselves."

"But this is a different gun than the one used in the murders at the Harrow home?"

"It is," Choi admitted. "The Harrow murders and, we now know, at least one other set of murders were committed with a .357 revolver."

"And what's next?"

"Because of Jenny's discovery, I'll be looking for matches among several other gun attacks across the United States."

"Thank you, Billy."

Carmen turned to Jenny and asked, "What *was* the discovery you made?"

Her name and area of expertise superimposed at the bottom of the screen, Jenny wore not her usual T-shirt and jeans, but dress slacks and a silky blouse, her blonde hair tied back in a loose ponytail. In real life, she rarely wore makeup, but this was television and she was mildly glamorized, still looking painfully shy . . . but steady.

By punching some keys on her computer, Jenny brought up a map of the United States with red stars scattered around. "These mark different towns where attacks may be related to those we've been investigating."

Dingle got in close on the map, showing the audience the twenty-two different towns where attacks on the families of civil servants had occurred over the last nine years.

Jenny and Carmen went on explaining the theory, as scripted, while halfway across the country, in the office of Sheriff Roberto Tomasa, the rest of the team—Harrow, Pall, and Anderson—sat before a monitor studying the map as they waited for Carmen to throw the show to them.

Till now, these attacks had been a list of names, addresses, and dates on a page. Now, displayed on a map, they started to carry weight, graphically indicating the possible extent of the killer's carnage, and his travels. Texas, Nevada, California, Nebraska, Colorado, Kansas, Missouri, Michigan, Arkansas, Pennsylvania, Ohio—the red stars seemed to be everywhere. All this, plus the Iowa, Florida, North Dakota, and New Mexico murders.

Chris Anderson could only shake his head in frustration that these statistics made feeling the true weight of the tragedy so elusive.

At twenty-seven, the blond, boy-band handsome chemist had himself pegged as the youngest member of the team, with the possible exception of computer cutie Jenny Blake, and perhaps segment host Carmen Garcia (although she wasn't, technically, a member of the team).

Turning to Pall, Anderson asked, "We could use a print-out of that map, don'tcha think, Michael?"

"I do," the short, muscular Pall said.

"Sheriff?" Anderson said, turning to Sheriff Tomasa, who stood off to one side, waiting for Harrow to interview him during the upcoming segment.

"Yes, son?"

"Can you get someone to get me a fold-out map of the United States?"

Tomasa glanced at Harrow, to see if he had time to honor this request, and the host nodded. Then the sheriff made a quick cell phone call to one of his deputies.

Harrow called over to Anderson: "What is it, Chris?"

"I don't know yet, sir, not for sure," Anderson said, voice lazy, eyes alert. "There's somethin' about all those towns, but I can't quite put it together. . . ."

Sound man Ingram was counting down, and they all turned their attention to the show at hand.

Harrow introduced a short segment that included, from the bottom of the gravel drive, pieces of his encounter with Archie Gershon. The audio from Hathaway's camera hadn't picked up anything worth using, so Harrow had prerecorded a voiceover explanation, saying that the recluse had given them a significant lead—the license number of the perp's vehicle.

Back on camera, Harrow said, "Meet Michael Pall, one of the premier scientists in law enforcement."

Pall's thick black comma of hair hung Superman-style, his black glasses giving him the right professorial look, a white shirt and dark tie peaking from beneath his *Crime Seen!* lab coat. The sleeves of the white jacket seemed stretched to the limit by the compact man's muscles.

Pall was, Anderson knew, a zealot about his workouts. Even with their hours mostly spent on the bus, in the semi-situated lab or in a motel, Pall always seemed to find a place and the time to lift weights. The guy was a good twenty years older than Anderson, but had more energy than a crate of Red Bull and no apparent need for sleep.

"So, Dr. Pall," Harrow was saying, "what can you tell us about the license number Mr. Gershon gave us?"

Looking at Harrow and not the camera—as he'd been taught in the crash course in TV technique the network had provided—Pall said, "Oklahoma plate registered to a Honda Accord owned by a seventy-year-old woman in a little town called Clinton."

"Probably not our suspect," Harrow said.

"No, but when the Oklahoma Highway Patrol got to her house, they found the license plate on her Fusion was actually a Kansas plate, and the woman hadn't noticed the switch."

"She hadn't noticed that her car had a license plate from a different state?"

Pall shrugged. "The OHP discovered that the only plate that had been switched was the rear, and it had just escaped her attention."

"Was that the plate from the truck Gershon saw?"

"No—the Kansas plate was registered to a Dodge van belonging to an out-of-work female bartender in Pratt."

"And the license plate on that van?"

"We haven't found it yet," Pall said. "The bartender's ex-boyfriend said she packed up her stuff and hit the road to find work. No forwarding address, no nothing."

Off-camera, a deputy came in and handed Anderson a fold-out map of the country. The chemist continued to listen while he quietly unfolded the map and compared it to the list of crime scenes.

Harrow was asking Pall, "But she was driving the van when she left?"

"She was."

Anderson got a Sharpie out of his pocket, then started marking the different towns around the country where attacks had occurred.

Harrow said, "Mr. Gershon said our suspect was likely a man."

Pall nodded. "We have two puzzle pieces. That they don't fit together doesn't mean that we're not closer to solving the puzzle."

Anderson looked up at the boss. Even though Harrow knew all this before they went on the air, and the dialogue had been loosely scripted (no prompter, but essentially canned), the host still looked gravely disappointed.

Was that just good acting? Anderson wondered.

Turning to the young chemist, who rose from his chair, Harrow introduced him to the viewing audience.

Anderson tried to keep his breathing even as he did his best to ignore the black hole in the center of the camera. He was also conscious of the hovering boom mike, but managed not to look up at it.

"Chris, have we had any luck matching the tire marks from this crime to the ones Billy Choi sent you from North Dakota?"

"They don't match—at least not completely."

Harrow appeared confused (for the sake of the

TV audience, anyway). "What do you mean, 'not completely'? Either they match or they don't, right?"

Harrow had set this up for Anderson to look good, and the young man appreciated it.

"The tires in North Dakota were nearly bald, Mr. Harrow. Though the tires here in New Mexico show *some* wear, they're nowhere near the same age as the Dakota tires."

"So they *don't* match."

"That's right, sir—they have the same tread design, which means they're the same brand, Michelin, and they're the same size, 275/70R18. It's possible that the suspect has changed out the old tires for new ones on the same vehicle."

"Are there other possibilities?"

"Sure. There could be two separate suspects, who both own light pickups that have the same brand tires—one worn, one fairly new. But if you believe that . . . and remember we have two separate gun matches . . . then the killer in North Dakota killed a public servant's family in Florida, and a different killer murdered the families of George Reid here . . . and yours, Mr. Harrow, in Iowa."

"That would make one hell of a coincidence."

"Yes, sir, it would. Particularly since forensics evidence indicates the same gardening implement was used in the removal of the wedding-ring fingers of both Mrs. Ferguson and Mrs. Reid. Distinctive characteristics of one garden-shear blade, and plant DNA, make that conclusive."

"Thanks, Chris," Harrow said, moving slightly to let Arroyo get the sheriff into the shot, so the boss could interview him.

With his part finished, Anderson dropped back into the chair, Sharpie in hand, as he went back to the list and the map.

He *had* something—he didn't know what—but he had something.

Chapter Nineteen

In his dreary, dusty living room, sitting on the edge of his seat, the Messenger watched *Crime Seen!* intently. When it had gone off the air with J.C. Harrow's familiar "war on crime" homily, the man of the house kicked back in the aged Barcalounger and smiled.

Finally!

After years of planning and delivering his messages, and fearing that these fools could never stop him, he finally had someone's car—someone who could make everything all right.

Despite a slow start, J.C. Harrow seemed to be the one who could and would put the pieces together . . . though it did take plenty of help. No matter by what process, however, at last the Messenger's signals were coming through. Maybe the help Harrow was receiving from his much-vaunted team was the key to making sure the world eventually understood completely.

He had watched the young woman who co-hosted with special interest. *What* was her name? Carmen Something. He would rewind the tape and get it.

She might prove just the one to help him deliver his next and, he hoped, *final* message.

His sighed and allowed himself a relieved smile. After all these years, the end was in sight. He had to clean the house, and there was planning to do, one more trip to make, one more message to deliver. . . .

After all, company was coming.

Chapter Twenty

The *Crime Seen!* viewer tip line had received calls about every single blue Ford F-150 in the United States—or at least so it seemed to Jenny Blake.

As the team's computer expert, she was the beneficiary of this sort of grunt work, tracking down the vehicles in tips and running checks on them. Funny how they'd all been hired as "superstar" forensics experts, with the media playing that up, the Internet too. But none of the *Killer TV* team had any underlings to pass off work to.

The chemist, Chris Anderson, had said it best: "We got a great starting line-up, but no bench!"

Still, she wasn't complaining, though the tip line stuff tended to come to her, and while the team was obviously making progress, she was feeling a very small part of that. She wanted to do more.

Her drive to succeed, to please, and her loyalty to Harrow and his cause, kept her going. The Wyoming crime lab had provided her plenty of tough cases, but never a challenge this great.

At least being with new people gave her a new chance to overcome her shyness. So far she hadn't been able to take much advantage of the new start; if anything, she felt more isolated, living on the road with strangers.

The rest of the team, though they all seemed nice enough, were obviously out of their comfort zones as well. Everybody seemed vaguely on edge, not only because of the life on the road—motel, work, eat, ride the bus, motel, work, eat, ride the bus—but because of the complicated job at hand.

And not the least of the complications was having the leader of the team so emotionally vested in the case, not that Harrow had slipped up in any way or shown the emotions that must have been churning beneath the surface.

Jenny knew all about such emotions.

With the bus rolling south now, heading for Pratt, Kansas, where the halved team could reunite, she had a little quiet time in the back by herself. Today, she wore a PETA T-shirt and her usual jeans with canvas tennis shoes, her normal work clothes at both the Wyoming crime lab and on the bus. The only time she wore anything else was on those painful Friday broadcast nights, when they dressed her up like a Barbie doll.

This bus was set up with only a dozen regular seats up front, six rows of two seats on either side, and another half dozen in back, beyond the restroom. Behind the front seats was a work area with a pair of compact desks and bolted chairs. Before you got to the bathroom were two facing chaise lounges, windows blacked out, the lounges mostly used for catching naps. They were equipped with seat belts, but Jenny didn't have hers on as she sat back there in the dark, her computer on her lap providing the necessary light.

She knew she shouldn't be bitching. The tip line stuff *was* culled before she got it—PAs back in LA were battling under Everest-sized piles of mail, e-mail, text messages, and phone calls, an onslaught that had begun right after the first show.

When *Crime Seen!* made the connection that Harrow was former law enforcement and Ferguson current—implying the families of lawmen might be targets—the tip lines exploded with everything from actual leads to communiqués insisting the *Killer TV* team investigate the death of all family members of every former or current law enforcement official that had not died in their sleep at 101 or over, and in the sight of a dozen eyewitnesses.

After the second show, when the victimology moved from strictly law enforcement to public servants in general, the deaths of every fedcral, state, and local government employee and their families going back a quarter century seemed to have been dredged up.

Those tips joined the sea of information flowing into the show. The show's staff, from showrunner Nicole Strickland to the lowliest PA, believed that everyone in America knew *someone* whose death could somehow be tied to the murders of the families of Harrow and Ray Ferguson.

Six degrees of J.C. Harrow, Billy Choi put it.

The vehicle tips had been forwarded to Jenny in the field, because she was right on the front lines, if she got a hit. Tons of other messages and questions were being sifted through thoroughly at UBC in LA.

As for the rest of the team, Billy Choi and the cameraman Maury Hathaway were riding in the trailer of the semi behind them, Choi working in the lab, Hathaway picking up "B roll" of Billy, whatever that was. Billy roll, maybe?

On the bus, in the rows beyond the restroom, Carmen Garcia was going over notes from the previous show while lanky Laurene Chase sat across the aisle, her overhead light out, arms folded, catching a nap. Way in back, Nancy Hughes was in a little puddle of illumination, lost in a sudoku puzzle.

Jenny continued running down dead leads on the pickup, knowing that once she got through them, next up would be running down the tips on the missing bartender's van.

That van was the reason they were headed for Pratt, Kansas. Though the trail was a week old, this would be the closest they'd been to the killer. The missing van had generated nearly as many viewer tips as the myriad F-150s. Police departments in Oklahoma, Kansas, and surrounding states were searching for both vehicles, but no one was having any luck finding either.

Feeling overwhelmed, Jenny yawned, set her laptop aside, rose, and went into the bathroom. She locked the door and looked at her face in the tiny mirror over the minuscule sink. The toilet was normal size, seeming an oversized fixture in this tiny closet—a full-sized chair in a dollhouse.

She had to rest a knee on the stool's lid just to study her face in the postage-stamp mirror, which was just large enough to show her how limp her blonde hair was looking. She had scrubbed the yucky makeup off after the show and not worn any since, making it easy (she knew) to see the black circles under her red-filigreed eyes. Not normally a vain person, she nonetheless recoiled from her image— she looked like a homeless person with the flu.

She grabbed the rim of the stainless steel sink and tried to wrestle it free of its mooring as she yelled, "*Goddamn son of a bitch shit!*"

The string of epithets, which included various forms of the fabled *F* bomb, continued for a good ten to fifteen seconds, after which—muscles sore, chest heaving, a sheen of sweat on her forehead and upper lip—she stood staring at the sick homeless person in the mirror for a good minute more, trembling.

After taking in a deep breath through her nose, she let it out through her mouth. She repeated the action three more times, splashed a little cool water on her face, and used a paper towel to dry off. Feeling much better, she stepped out of the bathroom, into the aisle of the bus at her agape co-workers.

Jenny gulped. "I, uh, figured the engine noise would cover that."

Still wide-eyed and open-mouthed, the trio shook their heads in unintended unison.

She forced a smile. "Hey, girl's gotta let off steam sometime, right?"

Laurene said, "If you want to borrow my Midol, just say so, sugar."

That made Jenny and the other two women laugh, and the computer expert returned to the chaise lounge area, where Carmen, Laurene, and Nancy joined her.

Perching across from Jenny, sitting Indian-style, Laurene said, "We *have* been going at it a little hard."

Next to Jenny, Carmen said, "You think? Trying to stop a serial killer while putting on a weekly network show?"

Nancy, next to Laurene now, said, "Goes way beyond 'let's put on a show in the barn.'"

"All *righty*, then," Laurene said, doing a Jim Carrey impression so dated Jenny barely understood it. "Time for a girl's night out!"

"You wish," Carmen said.

Laurene patted the air. "No, no, for real. We'll get to Pratt fairly early, right?"

Nobody argued the point. They had, in fact, left Rolla yesterday and driven ten hours to Omaha, Nebraska, where they'd spent the night. That left today's trip of about six hours. They would meet up with Harrow's group, compare notes, then call it a day.

"Once we finish work," Laurene said, "look out Pratt!"

Carmen and Nancy whooped and clapped, but Jenny sat silently.

Finally Laurene asked her, "Are you in?"

"I'm pretty swamped. All these tip-line . . . tips."

"Don't you know girls just want to have fun?"

This, too, was a reference that only rang distantly for Jenny. "We can *do* that?"

"What?"

"Have fun?"

"Hell yeah!"

". . . In Pratt, Kansas?"

This got some unintended laughs, though Jenny nonetheless felt like she'd been vindicated, and Laurene had the expression of a wiseass who'd just been topped.

Laurene leaned forward, looking straight at Jenny. "I suppose you've got something else planned tonight. And I don't mean tip-line tips."

"Well . . ."

"Got a date, maybe? With that cute chemist with the nice buns, maybe? Or our well-seasoned firearms man with the guns." Laurene made like a muscle man.

"No!" Jenny's cheeks were burning.

"Didn't think so. You know what I think? I think it's time we got that bony ass of yours out of them jeans and into a dress."

Jenny shook her head, nervous now, fear rising. "No! I don't even *own* a dress."

Next to Jenny, Carmen said, "You know, I've got the cutest little black dress—you would look *so* hot in it."

"I don't think so."

Nancy said, "We've all seen the looks our Southern-fried Beach Boy sneaks at you."

"What? Who?"

Laurene said, "The cute *chemist*. Talk about chemistry! I don't even dig men, but he's worth looking at, coming *and* going."

"He was never looking at me," Jenny insisted.

"He sneaks peeks all the time, sugar."

"Why would he do that?"

Carmen said, "Looking to hook up."

"Hook up what? I'm wireless."

The laughter of the other girls took a while to die down, before Jenny removed her blank expression and let a smile form.

"*Got* you," she said. "I'm quiet, not . . . inexperienced."

She guessed they didn't know she used to fish for child molesters online, and that she knew a lot more than she let on, much of it disgusting and revolting.

They sat and chatted the rest of the way to Pratt, Jenny feeling more at home with these strangers— these new acquaintances—than she had with her co-workers back in Wyoming.

Maybe here, on this bus, with these women, she could find the freedom to be herself, not the Jenny that she was always expected to be back home. Out here, she was Jenny Blake, computer guru.

Whoever the hell *that* was.

Chapter Twenty-one

Now they were on his trail for real.

Still, he'd had to practically *spoon-feed* them, to get them this close. Using the same gun in New Mexico that he'd used at Harrow's seemed at the time heavy-handed, too obvious a clue; but the so-called super-star *Killer TV* team had proved only slightly better at deciphering his messages than the myriad police departments and state police around the country, where he'd made deliveries over the years.

The gun had told them it was him. Trading license plates along his route gave them the road map they needed to get close. That damn female bartender in Pratt driving off into the night threw a slight monkey wrench into his plans.

But they would have to figure that one out for themselves. He could deliver messages to help them understand, but he could not simply hand himself over on a silver platter—they had to earn it.

Didn't they know nothing was free in this life?

The license plate he'd placed on the bartender's van in exchange for the original was from his hometown, but most certainly wasn't his own plate. Hell, it didn't even belong to the monster who'd turned him into the Messenger!

No, it came from the dark blue Ford F-150 of that yahoo down the street with the dog that wouldn't shut its yap. He'd asked the guy to keep his dog quiet, but the thoughtless asshole had laughed at him and told him to buzz off.

Would have been sweet to see how the yahoo liked it when the *Crime Seen!* team, the Kansas State Police, the FBI, and God only knew what other law enforcement agencies crawled up his hiney, thinking he was the one delivering messages. Would have been a hoot to watch, from just up the street. He'd have been laughing his ass off at how close they'd come to him while striking out.

If he'd been feeling *really* cocky, he'd have driven to the grocery store for a quart of milk while all those cops were right on his block tearing the yahoo's house to hell and gone. Could have driven right through all the cars, parked haphazardly on the street, their lights blinking, so consumed with the yahoo that they'd never have even seen the real Messenger among them.

Parked in his own F-150 now, eyes closed as he leaned back, daydreaming about getting even with the yahoo with the dog, the Messenger felt the thing between his legs quiver.

The thing had been dead for so long, he barely

recognized the sensation. The feeling was both familiar and wonderful and gave him a second or two of hope before he came back to reality.

The bartender with the van had disappeared—a message that never got properly delivered, and if the stupid bitch turned up within the three and a half days until the show, maybe the asshole and his dog would *still* get their due.

Otherwise, it was just another dashed hope, just like every other goddamned hope he'd ever clung to in his life.

Hope—sometimes he thought he hated that word more than any other. Hope represented not only everything that he could never have, now or in the future, but also the loss of his dreams for the futures of those he'd loved most.

The mere thought turned his knuckles white as he caught himself practically strangling the steering wheel. He fought back the rage, though it still coursed through him, barely controlled. His hope (that word again) was that he'd keep the rage in check, at least until his target arrived.

He figured the *Crime Seen!* team would be spending most of their time this week in the place where the trail went cold—that meant Pratt, Kansas, which was where he was now. Pratt, known as "The Gateway to the Great Plains," was famous for having two water towers that didn't feature the town's name, instead bearing the legends HOT and COLD. Ha ha.

The *Killer TV* team wasn't here yet, but they'd be on their way. He and his Ford were in a corner of the parking lot of one of Pratt's seven motels, which—along with the police department—were all he had to cover. Sooner or later, Harrow and his cronies would show up in their big obnoxious tour buses plus that semi-trailer rig, not only advertising the show, but pinpointing their location.

This team was so accustomed to being the hunters, never occurred to them that they might be the prey. That gave him a huge advantage. They'd be so busy searching for him, they wouldn't see him right in front of them. Like a snake in the rocks, he would strike before they even knew he was there.

And there'd be no rattle of warning, either. . . .

The Messenger was at the police department when, an hour later, the first *Crime Seen!* bus arrived. He was right there, coming out the glass double doors of the brick police department when the big stupid vehicle rolled up and parked right in front. Having gone inside, just another citizen using a public bathroom, he'd come out at the perfect time. He stood frozen, mesmerized by his good fortune, staring as the door of the bus swung slowly open.

J.C. Harrow himself stepped down, jeans, navy blue sports coat, white button-down shirt open at the throat. He had dark glasses on against the afternoon sun as he crossed the sidewalk, as square-jawed and ruggedly handsome as the hero in an old western.

Breaking out his first genuine smile in a long while, the Messenger held the PD station's door open as Harrow passed him and went on into the building, the reality show host even granting the Messenger a nod of thanks.

Thinks he's *the star of this show*, the Messenger thought with inner glee.

As Harrow strode to the front desk, the Messenger watched through the glass and savored the moment. Then he held the door for the blond pretty-boy chemist and the muscle-bound dwarf DNA "expert" too. The chemist thanked him in a cornpone drawl; the dwarf relinquished a crisp nod. After that, some crew members were coming from the bus, and they could open their own goddamn door.

He strolled back to his truck, whistling, a long-abandoned habit from his old life, back when he was still alive.

Would have been nice to see *her*—his next message—but there was no reason to push his luck. Harrow had given him a nod, and the Messenger would replay that moment at least once an hour for every hour of every day of the rest of his life.

Chapter Twenty-two

Following Anderson and the boss into the Pratt PD, Michael Pall had to wonder if the guy who'd held the door for them had been giving him the hairy eyeball. This was not an uncommon thought for him, and wouldn't have been even before his face and form had been broadcast all across the nation on a top-ten TV show.

He was a handsome guy, in his own considered opinion, and physically fit just didn't cover it. So gay guys gave him looks, and straight guys envious glances. But also sons of bitches who thought he was short. They gave him looks too, and laughed to themselves, and there wasn't a damn thing he could do about it, except break them apart in his mind.

The attractive fortyish blonde woman in uniform behind the bulletproof glass of her booth gave them a big goofy smile as the trio trooped in, Arroyo and Ingram trailing, capturing the whole entrance on camera and boom. The only way into the PD proper was through a single door to the right of the booth where the receptionist oversaw the compact lobby.

A phone was the only way to communicate with the booth, and the boss picked it up and said, "Good afternoon."

The woman, who wore a headset, said something only Harrow could pick up, and he replied, "Yes, ma'am. We're here to see Chief Walker, that's right."

She made a call they couldn't hear, then said something to Harrow that took a while.

"Sure," he said into the phone. He turned to Pall and Anderson. "Chief's expecting us. But before she buzzes us through, there's an admission price to pay."

Anderson frowned. "What's that, sir?"

"She wants our autographs."

The reception officer, who had a nice smile, passed a torn-off half sheet of report paper with a pen clipped on through the small slot under her window. Her name was Sandra, and they all signed the thing with the felt-tip Harrow carried for such occasions.

Pall wondered for a moment if she'd only asked Harrow for his autograph, and the boss was just being nice to him and Chris, to make them feel important too.

Not that Pall didn't already have people coming up wanting autographs. Though he'd only been on camera twice, Pall seemed to spend half his days now, signing napkins in restaurants, magazines in drugstores, even a towel in a motel swimming pool when a fan had interrupted him doing laps a couple of days ago.

Whole thing felt weird to Pall, but for now he just followed Harrow's lead and was always polite, tried to remember to smile, and never talked down to the fans. Seemed to be working.

He was unaware that the scientist side of him was at war with the bodybuilder—the scientist preferring to keep to himself and his colleagues, the bodybuilder wanting to look good and attract admiration, particularly from strangers. What he did know was this: being thrust into the public eye sometimes made him feel like an ant on the sidewalk looking up to see a kid with a magnifying glass.

Police Chief Alton Walker was a lanky fifty or so, with a hawk face and short white hair gone bald at the crown; he stood ramrod straight, and had a steel grip handshake, eye contact, and a smile ready for every introduction. Pall at once liked the man. The chief wore the same dark blue uniform as his officers, except for polished gold stars riding both shoulders, as if to say Walker might be chief, but was still a working cop.

Harrow had just finished the introductions when the phone buzzed and the chief excused himself, and was on for only a moment. When he hung up, he told Harrow, "Looks like the rest of your team's arrived."

Soon Garcia, Blake, Chase, and Choi were tramping in with their camera crew, and a second round of introductions was made. Walker wanted to get a uniform to bring in more chairs, but his quarters were cramped enough and—except for Harrow and his second-in-command, Laurene—everyone else stood.

"Been watching the show," Walker said, behind his desk in his chair now.

"Thanks," Harrow said.

"Don't jump the gun, J.C.—I didn't say I *liked* it."

Harrow just smiled. "No, sir, you didn't. But you *have* agreed to cooperate, and that's all that counts."

Before an uncomfortable silence could settle in, Walker grinned and raised a hand, admitting, "That was just a bad joke. The wife and me watch the show religiously."

Choi said, "You mean you TiVo it till Sunday morning?"

The chief laughed at that, and so did everybody else, a little. Harrow glanced back at his resident smart-ass as if to say, *You got away with that, but don't push it.*

Pall wasn't surprised the chief had something "funny" prepared to offer, since the police they contacted all knew they'd be on camera and human nature made them want to look clever and smart for the show. Usually this meant a little awkwardness at the top of an interview, but that soon went away and everybody—sometimes even the team itself—forgot they were being recorded for Friday night, if not posterity.

Walker got his long frame adjusted in the chair, and his attitude shifted as well. "Hell of a thing you've uncovered. If this fella is a serial killer of the proportions you say, this one goes in the history books."

"We want *him* to be history," Harrow said. "The books can wait."

"I hear you," Walker said with a grave nod. "What kind of progress are you making . . . and how can we help?"

Pall listened as the boss brought the chief up to speed. He glanced over to see Anderson still studying a section of the folded U.S. map he'd been poring over since the show last week, like a frat boy studying a centerfold. Actually, this was about the fourth map the kid had attacked with a Sharpie. Pall hoped Anderson was at least halfway paying attention. . . .

Harrow was saying, "We followed the trail of license plates from Socorro, up the road to Albuquerque, then east on I-forty to Clinton, Oklahoma, then north on one eighty-three to two eighty-one to, well, here."

Walker nodded. "Trail's end of *that* hunt. Let's hope it's the whole damn deal."

"Would be nice," Harrow said, nodding. "Of course, no one has had any luck with the bartender—"

"Valerie Jenkins," Walker supplied.

"Yes, Valerie Jenkins. Your department talked to her ex-boyfriend, I understand."

"We did. Fact, I accompanied the detective who took the interview."

"Anything come of it?"

"Nothing much," the chief said. "The guy she

dumped, Clayton Marxsen, is devastated. Said she left him cold. He never saw it coming, though others say it was her MO with guys, to up and leave."

"She isn't buried in Marxsen's backyard, is she?"

"I've been at this thirty years, Mr. Harrow—"

"J.C."

"Thirty years, J.C. *You* did this job—how's *your* bullshit detector?"

"Still working just fine. But I've run into some good actors along the way . . . long before I moved to California."

The chief smiled at that, then said, "If Marxsen is faking, he's the best I've seen. Guy looks like hell. He's let the apartment go to shit, there's pizza boxes around, more fast-food wrappers than a dumpster back of Mickey Dee's, bottles, ashtrays full of butts. Guy looks like the real miserable run-out-on deal to me."

"You said he wasn't her first ride at the rodeo."

"No, but there's no other guy in the picture right now that we've been able to find. We interviewed Valerie's friends and co-workers at the bar where she got let go, and no one said anything about her fooling around, despite her rep from past days. Fact, to a man and woman, they were all surprised that Val left Clayton. I couldn't even find anybody who had any idea where she might have been thinking of splitting."

Laurene said, "This isn't the kind of case where a disappearance doesn't get an investigator thinking."

"No, ma'am, it isn't," the chief said.

"Like . . . maybe our suspect took her out."

"On a date?" Choi asked. "Or just *out*?"

Silence draped the room briefly.

"Either way," Walker said, "we haven't found the van."

"Doesn't feel right," Harrow said. "He switched other plates and didn't have any contact with the owners at all—why her?"

"Maybe," Laurene said, "she caught him in the act."

Pall said, "He's too careful to get caught like that. He's committed murders all over the country, for nearly a decade, and you could fit all the evidence we have in a drinking glass. He's not going to get caught switching license plates."

Laurene cocked an eyebrow and asked Pall, "You trying to *profile* this son of a bitch?"

Like all of them, Laurene believed in evidence, hard science—that was the team Harrow had put together, which notably lacked a profiler. The forensic sciences were Pall's mantra as well—fingerprints, footprints, tire tracks, tool marks, DNA, chemistry, computer forensics, and firearms examining, these were the tools of their trade.

"I understand your desire to catch this guy with hard science," Pall said, choosing his words carefully, Laurene being his other boss, and the camera rolling. "But, Laurene, we have to use *all* the tools we have at our disposal . . . and profiling is one of them."

"All right," she conceded. "But have you had the training?"

"Yes," Pall said flatly. "It's not a specialty, but what I said about using all the tools also goes for acquiring as many as I can. I've taken seminars with the best in the field."

"Okay," Harrow said. "Take a run at our man."

"He's a loner," Pall said.

Laurene rolled her eyes. "*He was a quiet loner,*" she said.

"I know, I know," Pall said, patting the air. "But this guy really *is*. They're not *all* loners, you know. Look at BTK. He was married for thirty-three years, had two kids and killed ten people without anybody even considering him a suspect. John Wayne Gacy was active with the Chamber of Commerce—in Waterloo, *Iowa*, boss."

He had Harrow's attention. All of their attention.

"This guy though? He travels extensively, probably days at a time, in the case of the Placida murders. These are not targets of convenience—he's picked them out and planned them. The victims are family members of a male civil servant. He didn't just happen to be in Florida and open a phone book. He struck when the male wasn't home in every case. That tells us several things."

Carmen asked, "For instance?"

But it was Laurene who quickly answered: "Males weren't the targets."

Pall said, "Good."

"He maintained surveillance on them," Harrow added. "Somehow he's chosen these particular families and scouted them well enough to know when he could expect to *not* run into the male."

"Exactly," Pall said.

Wincing in thought, Choi said, "It's not just that

the male isn't the target—the killer wants to *avoid* that confrontation. He's a chickenshit." He looked at the camera. "If you don't want to bleep that, I'll start over. . . . He's a coward. He doesn't think he can take the male, no matter *who* that male might be, so avoids him."

Pall said, "That's my theory as well."

Harrow asked, "Then, why the families of civil servants?"

Glances were passed around the chief's office like a game of keep-away.

Carmen said, "He hates the government?"

"Join the club," Choi said.

Chief Walker pitched in: "Then why not just kill the civil servant?"

Carmen mulled that momentarily. "Like Billy said, he's a coward."

"I'm not so sure," Laurene said, shaking her head. "Maybe he is, maybe he isn't . . . but even if he *is* afraid of the male, it's more than that. He wants his victims to suffer."

Jenny Blake spoke up, surprising everyone, including herself: "The victims don't suffer. He takes them out with killing shots."

"But they aren't his *real* victims," Laurene said with an awful smile. "His *real* victims, his primary intended victims, are the males. The survivors. That suicide in the Hanson case? It may represent our killer's greatest triumph."

The chief asked, "What kind of sick shit *is* this?"

They all considered the crude, profound question for several seconds.

Finally, Harrow—who had reason to know—tapped his own chest and said, "He wants us to suffer. Like he suffers."

"*He's* suffering?" Jenny asked.

Grabbing onto this new insight, Harrow said, "Somehow he feels the government has made him suffer . . . and he wants the 'government' to suffer just as deeply. An individual like me represents the government—stands in for the government."

The chief asked, "What could make him feel like he's suffering as much as people who have lost their wives and children?"

"Maybe he lost his," Harrow said.

The room fell silent and still.

Then Harrow said, "He's someone who thinks the government took away his own wife and family." He looked around at his people, one at a time. "We need to start looking for someone who fits *that* profile."

Glancing up from his map, Anderson said, "Someone who fits that profile . . . *and* who probably lives in Kansas."

"That's why we're here," Laurene said, pointing to the floor. "The trail ran out in Kansas."

Anderson moved to the chief's desk and spread the map of the United States out on it, big black dots from the Sharpie showing the scattering of towns where attacks on families of civil servants had occurred.

"What do you see?" the blond chemist asked.

They all stood over the map looking down.

"Easy," Choi said. "Bunch of black dots."

"Try connecting them," Anderson said.

His voice soft and dry, Harrow asked, "If you do . . . what picture does it make?"

"Several, sir. I tried spokes, I tried grids, I tried all kinds of stuff—then I got it."

They watched as he drew a big circle that connected dots in California, Texas, Placida, Florida, Pennsylvania, the upper peninsula of Michigan, Rolla, North Dakota, and Montana.

Laurene squinted, then widened her eyes. "What the *hell* . . . ?"

Anderson drew another circle, this one smaller. It connected dots in Utah, Montana, North Dakota, Minnesota, Indiana, Kentucky, Mississippi, and Texas.

"Oh," Pall said. "*I* get it."

Garcia was frowning. "Well, I wish you'd tell me, then. . . ."

The next smaller circle included Harrow's town, South Dakota, Colorado, Oklahoma, and southern Illinois.

The next circle included Lincoln, Nebraska; Blue Rapids, Kansas; Garden City, Kansas; and North Platte, Nebraska.

"Chris, you earned your pay today," Harrow said, then asked the others, "Does anyone remember Luke John Helder?"

Pall said, "The dippy Minnesota kid with the pipe bombs."

"Right," Harrow said.

"I've heard of that," Laurene said. "I just don't remember the details."

Pall explicated: "Kid was a student at the University of Wisconsin-Stout. He planted eighteen pipe bombs in the Midwest in the spring of 2002. When he was caught, he confessed he'd set the bombs to make the pattern of a smiley face across a map of the United States."

"Right," Harrow said. "Only *this* son of a bitch is making a *target*."

"That's what I believe," Anderson said, bobbing his blond head.

"Okay," Jenny said. "Then where's the bull's-eye?"

Anderson said, "Could be anywhere within this. . . ." He traced the last loop, which still left them with a 250-mile-by-250-mile circle. It wasn't perfectly symmetrical like some of the other circles. They had a considerable area to deal with.

Laurene asked, "You think that's where he lives, somewhere in that circle?"

"Might be," Harrow said. "Might be where the people are he holds responsible for his suffering. Could be both. Either way, we need to find him. Jenny, forget the vehicle stuff—concentrate on this. Find out where the center of the bull's-eye is."

"Right away," she said.

"Rest of us need to find any clues we can that'll lead us to that center point." Harrow took a deep breath. He let it out. "We're getting close, people. Our subject doesn't think we can stop him. Let's track him down and prove him wrong."

Choi asked, "Has it occurred to anybody that we're in the bull's-eye right now? Not dead-center maybe, but inside it, anyway?"

Harrow said, "Yes it has, Billy."

"Okay, then," Choi said. "So before we break our arms patting Chris on the back, could we keep in mind we're in the middle of serial killer's target?"

Chapter Twenty-three

"Girls Night Out" had been cancelled, or anyway postponed, after Chris Anderson's "target" breakthrough; but Carmen Garcia nonetheless did not get back to her motel room till after midnight. The team had worked through the afternoon and well into the evening—coming up with nothing worth bragging about—followed by a long dinner break at a Mexican restaurant recommended by Chief Walker, who seemed to be J.C.'s new best friend.

The Tex-Mex turned out to be delicious, though Carmen didn't dare eat nearly as much as she'd have liked. Now that she was on-air talent, Carmen waged a never-ending, round-the-clock battle against gaining an ounce. She was spending far more time working out now, trailing Pall and mimicking the weightlifter's regimen to some extent. Extra effort was spent on grooming, as well, and she occasionally rode in the hair/makeup Winnebago so that the girls could experiment and refine her look.

No longer a T-shirt and jeans girl in the public, Carmen—who attracted almost as many autograph seekers these days as Harrow himself—was careful to always wear a nice blouse and slacks or a skirt. Her Visa card might be taking a beating, but everyone seemed to look at her with admiring eyes now, even the boss, and she dug it. No longer the lowly PA, the "girl" with an office job, she was a woman with a career.

Even the seating chart at dinner seemed to reflect her newly exalted status. Harrow, of course, took the head of the table, Laurene Chase at the opposite end, the mommy and daddy chairs at the long table. Carmen, however, had gained the favored-nation status of sitting at Harrow's right hand, Chief Walker across from her. With the crew thrown in too, that made eleven.

Everybody had chatted amiably while they waited for their dinner. Carmen listened to Harrow and the chief trade war stories, which was pretty fascinating stuff, but her eyes kept shifting down the table to where Jenny Blake and Chris Anderson were seated side by side.

Normally, Carmen might have considered this a random occurrence—only after their talk on the bus today, she wondered if Jenny hadn't quietly orchestrated the arrangement. Still waters running deep and all.

While Anderson did 90 percent of the talking, Jenny was actually engaged in conversation with him, instead of merely staring at her plate, as she so often had in the past.

After dinner, the team trooped back to the Pratt

police station and spent another four hours trying to discern whether the killer himself might be the bull's-eye's center . . . or would it be his ultimate quarry? Or was the target an entirely obscure message, so twisted in the unsub's mind that using logic or psychology to unravel its meaning was a hopeless task?

They had been at it for a while, seemingly gaining only inches at a time, when Laurene Chase floated the notion that the bull's-eye might mean nothing more than that the killer was targeting the whole country.

"Remember our ever-loving smiley face in the Helder case," she said. "Turned out it didn't mean shit, except to Helder and his sick sense of humor."

Harrow lifted his eyebrows and then set them down, as if they were a heavy load. "You have a point, Laurene—we've been trying to assign a meaning to the bull's-eye when what it means to the *killer* is the key."

"I think," Pall said, "he's trying to tell us something—or, at least, *show* us something."

Harrow's eyes slitted. "Go on."

"We have twenty-some crimes here. If we assume the ones that fit Anderson's theory and line up roughly with the circles of the bull's-eye, that's still a lot of crimes . . . and a lot of time."

Pall had their attention now. Nobody, not even Laurene, was quibbling about the efficacy of profiling.

"So much time," he was saying, "so much planning—I can't buy that there isn't something behind it all. Something important to the unsub, anyway—something he's trying to get across."

"Helder took time," Laurene said, "and planned. And his 'message' was just a big goofy smile."

"Granted, but Helder's crimes were a spree. He set eighteen bombs in Illinois, Iowa, and Nebraska. The last few weren't even rigged to explode. The crazier he got, the more focus he lost. Our killer has *never* lost focus—he's plotted and carried out maybe as many as four dozen murders over the course of almost a decade, and never really slipped, never started leaving clues he didn't intend to leave."

"Except," Laurene said, "for the corn leaf."

"Even that may have been intentional," Pall said with a shrug.

"No clues he didn't intend to leave," Harrow echoed, like a mantra. "That means he's used the same gun in Rolla, North Dakota, and Socorro, New Mexico, because he *wanted* us to know it was him. Why?"

Anderson said, "He's filling in the bull's-eye, sir. Finishing up. And he wants someone to recognize his work. Goin' out of his way to make his message more clear."

"Whatever the hell it is," Laurene muttered.

"Meaning no joke, Chris, you might be on target," Pall said. "What's the point of going to all the trouble of creating this great big target, if no one recognizes it? It's a ten-year performance art piece, remember . . . and if there's no audience, why do it?"

The group stared at the broad-shouldered scientist.

"Granted it's a *psychotic* performance art piece," he said, offering an open palm.

Choi said, "Performance art's by definition psychotic."

Laurene said, "The Manhattan Art Council's opinion heard."

That got a chuckle from the entire team, even Choi.

Harrow, smiling, pushed his chair back and rose. "We're getting punchy. Been a long day. Nothing wrong with our thinking that some sleep won't cure."

On the bus ride back to the motel, Carmen sat with Jenny Blake. The cute little computer guru smiled when Carmen joined her—the kid was starting to loosen up. A little.

"So—you and Chris," Carmen said, as the bus door closed and the driver slipped the vehicle into gear. "What's the story?"

Even in the near dark of the bus interior, Carmen could see Jenny's smile had faded.

"Story?"

"At dinner. You two were talking."

"So?"

"So . . . I want to hear *everything*—and don't tell me you were talking business."

Jenny glanced around. Choi and cameraman Hathaway were in back on the chaise lounges. Audio gal Nancy Hughes was in her usual seat near the front, apparently asleep. Laurene sat across the aisle and—even though Jenny didn't seem to notice—Carmen was sure Harrow's number two was only resting, and not asleep.

"We just talked," Jenny said. "You know."

"I don't know."

Jenny shrugged. "Stuff about where he grew up. Some stuff about where I grew up."

"He seemed to be doing most of the talking."

She nodded. "I like to listen to him."

"Really?"

Another nod. "Like the sound of his voice. He's quiet, and I'm kind of quiet, too . . ."

"No kidding."

". . . and he's got that lilt, you know—that Southern thing?"

"Also big blue eyes."

Jenny smiled again. She might have been blushing, but it was hard to tell in the dim lighting.

"Also big blue eyes," she admitted.

Their parting words, as they stepped down off the bus, covered Carmen inviting Jenny to come over to her room, if she wanted to talk some more. Jenny had been noncommittal, saying she'd probably just hit the sack, but her shrug said she might be considering the offer.

Now, alone in her hotel room, Carmen let down her hair, stripped off her jacket, and plopped onto the bed, where it was all she could do to not fall asleep atop the covers.

Still things to do though. She propped herself on an elbow and set the alarm for 6 A.M.—they were leaving for the police station just before eight tomorrow, but she needed time to get ready first, both personal and work prep.

She climbed off the bed, tugged her cell phone out of the pocket of the jacket she'd removed, then attached the charger cord and plugged it into an outlet in the bathroom.

Some people washed the day off, some people showered before facing the world come the morning, some did both. Carmen fell into the middle group, but she did scrub off her makeup and comb out her hair before bed.

She also kicked off the clothes from a very long day and snuggled into the Ozomatli T-shirt and gym shorts that she slept in. She'd just turned the bed back and was getting ready to slide in between cool sheets when she heard a knock on the door.

A smile tickled her lips.

So Jenny had changed her mind!

Tired as she was, Carmen considered herself the little blonde's (self-appointed) fairy godmother, and she was eager to talk with Jenny . . . if Jenny wanted to talk to her.

So certain was she that it was Jenny knocking, Carmen didn't think to check the peephole before jerking the door open.

When the portal was filled with a middle-aged man in a blue baseball cap, a Kansas Jayhawks sweatshirt, and jeans, Carmen was too stunned to move. But she noticed right away that he held something in his right hand.

He was smiling at her and neither spoke for an endless second, then Carmen knew the thing in his hand was a Taser. Before she could slam the door or scream or even think, the two little metal javelins fired, and she felt their sting as they bit into her chest.

She had only enough time to grunt from shock

before her body rocked spasmodically and she melted to the floor in a puddle, aware only that he'd stepped over her and shut them in together before everything in her world spun wildly into a black vortex that sucked her in too.

FOUR
The Message

Chapter Twenty-four

Billy Choi noticed first.

"Carmen isn't usually late," he pointed out to Harrow, as they were loading the buses to go to the Pratt PD. "Matter of fact, she's usually the one complaining *I'm* late."

Shrugging, Harrow said, "Probably just running behind. Why don't you go see if you can hurry her up?"

"Turnabout fair play and all that? Sure, boss."

Choi took off for the motel entrance. He was a professional, as far as it went, but he'd read enough *Penthouse* letters to harbor the hope that the gorgeous Carmen might answer the door wearing only a towel.

He clipped through the lobby, then down a long hall that intersected with a cross hallway. He turned right and strode down toward the last door on the right, Carmen's. He spent the entire walk letting a sheer nightie stand in for the towel in his developing fantasy.

At the door, Choi knocked.

Ten seconds, and nothing.

He knocked again.

Still nothing.

He tried a third time, this effort harder than before, and waited . . . and *still* nothing. For the first time, Choi wondered if something might be wrong. Maybe Carmen was sick—Mexican food didn't agree with everybody, after all, and that Tex-Mex fare had been rich.

This time, when he rapped on the door, any *Penthouse* fantasy long since flown, he shouted, "Carmen!"

Again, there was no answer.

Genuinely worried, Choi got out his cell phone and punched in Harrow's number.

"Billy? Waiting for you two."

"Something's not right here, boss. I've knocked on the door till my knuckles are red, but I can't get her to answer."

"Be right there."

As he waited, Choi kept knocking, and by now he would have settled for Carmen answering in a nun's habit, which was definitely not a fantasy of his. Eventually, the guy across the way stuck his head out and complained.

Choi just snarled, "Go away," at the portly man, who pulled his head back in his shell.

But more knocking only earned him further disappointment.

Finally, Harrow showed up, an assistant motel

manager—a squat fortyish woman with brown hair, very red lipstick, and a white blouse over navy blue slacks—trailing him, having to work to keep up.

"She doesn't answer," Choi told them.

The manager stepped forward and knocked.

"Oh, yeah," Choi said to her. "Knocking. I hadn't thought to try that."

"Billy," Harrow cautioned.

She kept rapping, getting no answer of course, but she was also running a pass keycard through the lock.

The woman opened the door, but Harrow held up a hand.

"Remember," he told the assistant manager. "This may be a police matter, and I need to check it first."

"You bet, Mr. Harrow," she said, obviously impressed with her guest.

So, Choi thought, *J.C. had played the celebrity card. Good. Whatever it took. . . .*

Harrow looked around the motel room and the bathroom. Choi followed, while the manager remained silhouetted in the doorway.

The room was vacant, the night-table lamp on.

"Where's the bedspread?" Choi asked.

"Gone," Harrow said.

"Something to wrap somebody up in, maybe?"

Harrow's silence was confirmation.

Checking the bathroom himself, Choi spotted her cell phone plugged into the electrical socket. "Cell's here, boss."

Harrow peeked in.

Choi said, "She'd never leave the room without that phone."

"Not voluntarily," Harrow agreed.

"Unless she stepped out for some ice or pop or something, and . . . ran into something."

Or someone.

Neither man could say it out loud, but both thought it.

"What happened here?" Harrow said. He was calm, but it was a cop calm, edged with steel.

Choi had a thorough look-around, particularly on the floor, and noticed something near the door. On one knee, he bent as close to the carpet as he could and discerned a small spot.

Dark.

Nearly maroon, as it dried.

"Blood," Choi said.

Harrow knelt beside him, and they both studied the drop, no bigger than the diameter of a good-sized sewing needle.

"Good catch," Harrow said.

Always nice to get a compliment from the boss, but Choi didn't feel like celebrating.

On his feet again, Harrow said to the assistant manager, "Call the police—tell them that J.C. Harrow's group has a missing person here at the motel, and we think it's an abduction."

The woman's eyes were big and her mouth hung open, but she remained motionless.

"Go," Harrow said.

The woman swallowed, nodded, and trundled off down the hall like a reluctant tank moving into battle.

Harrow got out his cell and punched a speed-dial number.

"Laurene?" he asked.

Choi could not hear her response.

Harrow told her, "Carmen's been taken. Bring your crime scene kit to her room, now."

He told Laurene to send the rest of the team ahead to the PD to keep working the serial killer case. This was likely the same unsub, and they needed to find him.

When Harrow got off the phone, Choi asked, "You really think it's him? You think it's our bull's-eye guy?"

Harrow sighed. "We're in a town with less than seven thousand people, and other than the police chief and a few other cops, we don't know anybody here. Carmen didn't know anybody. Yet it looks like someone got her to open the door, Tasered her, then abducted her."

"Taser?" Choi asked.

"One drop of blood, and only one drop of blood—what do you think would cause a wound that wouldn't bleed any more than that?"

Choi lifted an eyebrow. "Taser."

Harrow made another call, this one to Chief Walker. He explained the situation, told the chief what they were doing, and clicked off.

"How's the chief feel about us getting involved?" Choi asked. "I mean, this isn't *our* crime scene. . . ."

"He's up for the help. He'd have to wait for the state crime lab to come down, do what we're doing, and then maybe wait a month for the results. Right now, we're Walker's favorite visitors."

Laurene came up to the open doorway at a trot.

"What the hell happened?" she asked, as she set

down her big metal crime scene case in the hall, just outside.

Harrow pointed out the stain on the carpet and explained what they figured had happened.

Laurene's upper lip curled nastily. "She just opened the door, and let this asshole take her? What does she think peepholes are for?"

"She's not a police professional, Laurene. We're all housed in this motel like a bunch of kids on their way to the big game. She thought it was one of us."

"Gonna have to have a talk with the girl."

Choi said, "Really think that'll be necessary?"

Harrow said, "Cut the crap, boys and girls. You are our two crime scene analysts. Go over the scene fast. The cops are on their way."

Laurene's eyes widened. "And they're fine with us taking over their crime scene?"

"I've cleared it with Chief Walker. Anyway, if there's evidence, I want us to be the ones that find it."

"*That* I get," Laurene said.

As she went to work, Billy said to Harrow, "You don't need two of us to process this small a scene."

"Get the security video for the motel, and any business around here that has it. Then grab one of these cops who are about to show up, and have him drive you to the PD. Get the chief to set you up in a room and find something on that video we can use to track this son of a bitch."

That didn't require a reply, and Choi didn't offer one, just tore down the corridor the moment Harrow was done. Choi found the dowdy assistant manager in the office off the check-in, hanging up the phone.

"Police are on their way," she said.

"Good. How many security cameras do you have?"

The woman had to think about that, then she ticked them off on her fingers. "Parking lot out front, lot on the side, lobby . . . then there's three where the two main halls intersect. Six altogether."

"Tape or disc?" Choi asked.

"Disc," the manager said.

"May I have them?"

"Shouldn't I save them for the police?"

"We're working with Chief Walker's blessing, ma'am, and every second counts."

The woman fetched the discs and soon was handing them to Choi.

"Was there a night manager last night?"

"Yes—Ann Ford."

"She wouldn't be here now, would she?"

The manager shook her head. "Went home when I came on."

"Did she mention seeing anything or anyone unusual?"

Another head shake.

"A male, who wasn't a guest, who may have asked after Ms. Garcia?"

"No, but that girl Ann spends most of her time with her nose buried in some romance book or other. You know, those Harlequin things, where a strong man drags off a willing woman?"

Choi didn't bother with a reply—he just took the discs as three cops strode into the lobby like a small army, Chief Walker out in front.

When he saw Choi, the chief asked, "Where's your boss?

"Harrow's at Carmen Garcia's room—one forty. I've got the security video." Choi had a question he'd saved up for the chief: "What other businesses around here would have security cameras?"

Walker needed only a second or two to think. "Convenience store across the street. Bank two blocks down, on the left—ATM camera and the parking lots."

"All right," Choi said. "I'm going to want to gather any other video, and then'll want space at your facility to go over them. Somebody to assist, and clear the way for me, would be great."

Turning to an officer, Walker said, "Jake, go with Mr. Choi here. Make sure the convenience store and the bank cooperate. If they want warrants, have them call me."

The blond patrolman stood six-two and looked like he had just stepped out of a recruiting poster for the Aryan Nation. "Yes, sir. I saw Mr. Choi on TV, sir."

"Good for you," the chief said patiently.

Choi shut his eyes momentarily, and managed to suppress any remark.

Chapter Twenty-five

Forty-some minutes later, Choi was set up in a dark room in the Pratt Police Department with a DVD player hooked up to an old tube TV. While most of his team was down the hall, working their own specialties, he was subjected to your classic Dirty Job But Somebody's Gotta Do It: going through security video, grainy washed-out footage, looking for even a single frame that showed something it shouldn't, something *off*, a person in the wrong place, a car that looked out of place, *any* damn thing.

Mounted where it met the cross corridor, the camera on the hall from the lobby should reveal anyone coming in that way. Ten rooms were on each side to the left, and ten more to the right. Other cameras gave views of that same corridor in either direction.

Choi started with the hallway with Carmen's doorway. He would fast-forward until he saw someone, then would slow down, back up, and look from just before the person entered until they went into their room. Shortly after midnight on the video, his teammates made their appearances—Jenny went into her room, Anderson into his, and even Choi himself. The last one to enter a room, at the far end, was Carmen . . . then nothing.

He fast-forwarded as slowly as possible—unlike the old VHS, DVDs skipped frames rather than skimming over them. Finally, nearly half an hour after Carmen had closed her door, someone came down the hall.

Choi sat up.

With the person's back to the camera, all Choi could make out was a sweatshirt and jeans and a ball cap.

Choi's cell seemed to leap into his hand; but he didn't hit any of the numbers just yet. Instead, he watched as the ball cap–wearing man—at least that much seemed clear, that this was indeed a male— fairly swaggered down the hall, in a gait with purpose and no hesitation.

Someone who knew where he was going. . . .

Ball Cap stopped just short of Carmen's room, and knocked. A pause while he waited. Then, he lifted the front of the sweatshirt slightly and withdrew from his waistband what, from this angle and distance, appeared to be a gun . . . but Choi already knew it wasn't.

When Carmen finally opened the door, Choi somehow managed not to yell, *No!* at the screen.

Instead, he merely watched in mute rage as the

Taser fired, and he caught just a glimpse of Carmen before she tumbled back into her room.

The man went in after her, his face still not visible as he slipped in and shut the door.

After a minute or so, the door opened, and he stepped out with a human-sized shape wrapped in the bedspread over his shoulder, like a carpet hauler making a delivery. The door to the side parking lot was right there, couldn't have been handier, and the guy disappeared through it.

Choi hadn't seen anything that would help them identify Carmen's attacker—all he had accomplished was to confirm that Carmen had indeed been abducted.

He hoped Jenny could work some of her computer voodoo and enhance the picture enough that they'd be able to ID the guy; but he frankly didn't hold out much hope, from what he'd seen so far.

He gave Harrow a call, and reported.

"So it's a kidnapping," Harrow said.

"Yeah. Where does that leave us with the FBI?"

". . . I'll work on that. Keep at that footage. Maybe you've seen enough to make him on the convenience store or bank video."

"Still some motel vid to check, too. Anyway, I'm on it, boss."

He pocketed his cell and changed discs to check the hallway coming from the lobby. Without a key card, the front door would be the only way the guy could get in at that hour.

He fast-forwarded to just short of the time the

man came around the corner into Carmen's hall-way. This camera provided a view from the inter-section with the cross-corridor straight to the front door.

The man came in, head down, glanced for a sec-ond toward the front desk to his left, then kept com-ing right at camera, seemingly aware of its presence and not wanting to give it a good look.

How did he know the camera was there?

Had Ball Cap been in a motel of the same chain, laid out identically, or had he been in this particu-lar motel before? Was he a local? A non-local who had cased the place?

When the man disappeared from the shot, Choi reran the disc twice before he decided he hadn't missed anything. The next disc was the main park-ing lot, but there was nothing to see. The abductor had probably parked on the side and walked around, staying close to the building. Otherwise, he would have to carry Carmen's body to the front, and that was unlikely.

This camera, from above the entrance, swept back and forth across the parking lot and revealed no sign of movement after the team's buses emptied and they'd all come inside.

The camera on the side of the building was mounted above the door too, and similarly swept back and forth. Choi synced up the time for when the kidnapper and his package should have popped out the door, but the investigator saw nothing. Pro-blem with the camera was that it showed the lot and nothing of the sidewalk next to the building, aimed just a few degrees too high.

"Shit," Choi said.

He kept the video rolling, hoping the guy would come out and cross the parking lot to one of the vehicles . . .

. . . but he never did.

Choi was just about to give up when the camera swept left and caught the roof of a vehicle sliding by to the right.

"*There*," he said, pointing to the right as if that would make the camera move faster.

Painfully slow, the camera finally swept back to the right, Choi expecting the truck to be long gone. To his surprised delight, the truck sat at the motel entrance, its tail to camera.

Better to be lucky than smart, he thought.

A car passing on the street had forced the truck to wait, and those few seconds were Christmas to Choi.

The truck was obviously a Ford F-150, gray on the washed-out security video, and the license plate stared right back at him, as did a sticker on the back window. From here, nothing was clear enough to make out, but he felt Jenny Blake and her laptop would see this stuff just fine.

He dialed Harrow, who answered on the second ring.

"I think we've got the son of a bitch," Choi said, then he explained.

"Get Jenny on it," Harrow said. "Anderson's been going over the map some more—he thinks whatever the target's center indicates, it'll be within Smith County. Probably a town called Lebanon—about a hundred seventy miles north of here, straight up US 281."

"How soon we leaving?"

"That's up to Jenny. Get her on this. Once she's got what she needs at the PD, we're on our way."

"You got it, boss."

Soon, after Jenny Blake had loaded the contents of not only that disc onto her laptop, but all the rest—including the convenience store and bank footage—she told Choi they were set to go.

"Already?"

"Yup. I'll do the work on the road. You found a good image, Billy. Shouldn't take long."

Within half an hour, both buses and the semi-trailer crime lab were rolling up the highway toward Lebanon, Kansas, where three hundred people normally lived. When *Crime Seen!* showed up, they would add twenty-some to the population of the town, which would represent more growth than the place had seen in a decade.

The team rode in the trailer-cum-crime lab, each working in his or her own way on finding Carmen Garcia. Though the search for her kidnapper and that of the serial killer were almost certainly one in the same, the team was now centered upon getting Carmen back.

No camera or audio personnel were in the crime lab, the camera teams having been ushered to the bus by Harrow. The lab was now off limits for them. The TV show was a secondary concern at present (really, it always had been); but now they were trying to save one of their own, and didn't care to cater to camera crews underfoot.

In the lab, Harrow sat them down right away, and

stood in their midst, working them like an actor doing theater in the round.

"We have a kidnapping," he said, "and that means FBI."

Laurene asked, "Have we called them?"

"Chief Walker will be doing that. I asked him to give us, well . . . what they used to call in old western movies, a head start."

Chris Anderson was frowning. "Why?"

"Because if we waited for the FBI, we would be stuck back there, Chris, as material witnesses to that crime. We aren't law enforcement, and we aren't required to deal with the FBI until or unless they catch up with us."

Laurene said dryly, "So keep an eye on caller ID."

Harrow nodded. "We'll cooperate with them, of course. But right now I think we have a better shot at this bastard than they do."

Pall said, "No wonder you didn't let the cameras record this."

"Michael, would you suggest we wait back there, and turn this over to the FBI?"

"No. Make that, *hell no*. I never had any use for those stuffed shirts."

Coming from the well-dressed, fairly formal-of-speech Pall, this was pretty amusing. But nobody laughed or even smiled. Or, for that matter, objected.

"We will of course cooperate fully," Harrow went on. "The originals of the security-cam discs are back with Chief Walker—the federal investigators will have access to the same evidence as we do. If anyone feels I'm overstepping, or putting the team in any legal jeopardy, say so now. And I won't try to stop anyone who feels that calling the FBI right now is the thing to do."

No one did.

They had been on the road for just over an hour now. Jenny Blake was working on enhancing the crappy quality of the security video from the motel. Choi was next to her, at a computer station, checking convenience-store video, Laurene nearby going through bank cam footage. Anderson was at another computer researching Lebanon itself, and Pall was testing the blood from the motel room to make sure it really was Carmen's. Having seen the security video, Choi already had no doubt.

Harrow was on the phone, and his half of the conversation with network president Dennis Byrnes served as a soundtrack for their labor.

"That's right, Dennis," Harrow said. "Abducted. Kidnapped, yes."

A long pause was followed by the chipmunk sound of someone speaking quickly on the other end of a nearby cell.

Exasperated, Harrow said, "I don't *know* what the network's liability is to her family, Dennis. I'm sure it will be less, if you let us do our work, and get her back alive."

Another pause.

"Ask the lawyers, Dennis . . . What? I haven't really *thought* about it. Dennis, I have to get back to it."

And Harrow clicked off and said, "Jesus."

Choi asked, "What?"

"Byrnes wanted to know if I thought this would make 'good TV.'"

Nobody said anything for a long time.

"You know what would be a good twist?" Choi asked. "The killer throwing Dennis Byrnes off the rooftop of UBC."

"Bad taste, Billy," Harrow said.

Laurene said, "But a good idea."

"Oh *shit*," Jenny said, and they all turned her way.

"What?" Harrow asked.

"Got the license number."

"And?"

"It's registered to Herman A. Gibbons of Lebanon, Kansas."

Choi swung a fist, saying, "We've *got* him!"

But Jenny's face registered confusion, not jubilation.

"What?" Choi asked.

"When I got the name from the DMV," Jenny said, "I Googled the guy."

"And?" Harrow asked.

The little computer expert met her boss's gaze. "Herman A. Gibbons? He's the Smith County sheriff."

Chapter Twenty-six

Company was coming.

Wouldn't be long now. They wouldn't make it today, maybe not even tomorrow, but Friday for sure.

They could even do the show live from his house. That would be something—all those messages he had delivered would be worth it. And he had *just* the bait. . . .

Leaned back in his frayed old lounge chair, the Messenger looked over at the couch where the TV girl lay on her back, duct tape over her mouth and binding her hands behind her back. She had awoken earlier, but homemade chloroform had put her back to sleep.

He took no pleasure in putting her through this. He hadn't anticipated how uncomfortable this would make him, prolonged dealing with somebody up close and personal. Usually, delivering a message, it had been get in and get out. He'd mostly been able to avoid even viewing his targets as people at all, just dots on the big target he was making.

This was different. This was unsettling.

He expected her to be waking up soon. He'd had her for nearly sixteen hours now. Even in just the T-shirt and shorts, without makeup, she was still pretty.

In some ways, she reminded him of Cathy. Reminded him of what it was like to have a life, a wife, a family. The thing between his legs was twitching quite a bit now, and it felt good, but made him feel guilty. He was not about hurting people or humiliating them, not at all. He wasn't that kind of person.

Suddenly he became aware of tears trailing down his cheeks. This was no time to give in to weakness. It was weakness, after all, his inability to protect his family from men who were stronger or more powerful than he was, that had put him in this situation. *His* weakness, not Cathy's. Never Cathy's.

The woman on the sofa awakened, slowly, looking around, not sure what had happened to her or where she was. He didn't rush it. They had some time left—no need to be harsh.

He watched as she got used to her shabby new surroundings, took them in. When she finally looked over at him, he tried to smile, a sort of comforting, welcoming smile. But her face became a mask of fear and confusion and something else . . . hate? She didn't need to hate him. He didn't hate her.

Under the tape, her mouth tried to scream, but the sound was a muffled nothing, as she thrashed around on the sofa.

The thing twitched. *Stop it*, he told it.

Rising, smoothing his pants to keep that thing down and in its place, and moving to her side, he made cooing sounds, hoping to soothe her; but for no good reason, the closer he got, the more she thrashed and muffle-screamed.

Finally, as if to a naughty puppy, he said, "Now, honey, you have got to settle down."

She glared at him. Big brown eyes, terrified and hateful and pretty.

"Look, tell you what—if you settle down, I'll help you into the bathroom. You must need to you-know-what, by now."

She continued to glare at him.

"Or . . ." He made a show of shrugging. ". . . you can go right where you are. Doesn't matter to me one way or the other." He turned away and folded his arms, and his chin went up, a disapproving parent.

She responded, as best she could, through the tape, not screaming, but a sort of pitiful plea now.

He turned back to her.

Her eyes were still wide, but something in them had softened.

"All right," he said. "Bathroom it is."

He unbound her feet, and, when she didn't try to kick him or anything, he helped her up, then led her to the tiny bathroom. At the door, she implored him with her eyes.

"Sorry," he said. "Can't untie you. I promise not to look."

She frowned.

"Sorry, honeybun, that's as good as I can do. We

can always take you back to the couch, and you can piddle yourself."

The bathroom had faded green windowless walls, gray bubbled ceiling that was once white, rust stains in the sink, tub, and toilet. He wasn't proud of it by any means.

"Ain't much to look at," he admitted when he saw the concern in her eyes. "But she'll do the trick."

He lined her up in front of the toilet, then—keeping his eyes on hers—he squatted a little and gently drew down her shorts. It twitched, and he told it, *Stop that!* When he got her situated on the stool he walked out and closed the door. Nothing in there for her to cause trouble with.

He listened at the door, heard tinkling, then no tinkling, and went back in, maintained eye contact as he pulled her up, then her shorts. He flushed the john. When they were back in the living room, he let her sit on the couch instead of recline.

"Thirsty?" he asked.

She swallowed. Then nodded.

He opened a cooler next to his chair, withdrew a can of Diet Coke for her, which he opened, then inserted a straw.

He crossed the room to her, and said, "This is your brand, isn't it?"

She seemed momentarily surprised.

She shouldn't have been, he thought—thanks to Facebook and MySpace, she'd supplied him a goodly portion of information about herself. Just because he lived in a crummy house didn't mean he couldn't use a computer.

He got his pocketknife out. "Hold still."

Her eyes widened, but she froze. He made a tiny slit in the tape where her lips met. He was very careful when he did it, just as he was careful in every aspect of his life now. If he'd been careful back then, when he had a life with Cathy, maybe things would be different now.

He stuck the straw through the slit, then held the can up, saying, "Drink."

She did.

"You're going to have to lie down again, after this," he said. "And you'll have to take another little nap."

She looked terrified.

"No, go ahead and drink—it's okay."

She drank but still looked scared.

"It's just that I've still got a lot to do. Your friends will be here soon, and everything has to be ready."

Her eyes widened.

He looked at her gravely. "Company's coming."

Chapter Twenty-seven

When Jenny Blake announced the F-150's license plate belonged to the county sheriff, Harrow immediately suspected another switch.

He asked the computer expert, "What kind of vehicle is the plate registered to?"

Eyes on the screen, she reported, "A 2007 Chevy Tahoe."

"Which," Harrow said, "doesn't look remotely like an F-150."

Pall said, "He switched again."

This news draped the mobile lab in glum silence. They all knew, too well, that the other license plate switches had led exactly nowhere.

Oh, in each case a trail had been left for the team to follow, but in the long run these searches had revealed no ties to the actual crimes.

This one, however, felt different.

Harrow said, "Certainly this being the sheriff's

vehicle can't be a random occurrence. Must be a vehicle of choice."

Pall said, "None of the other license plates appear to've been chosen for a particular reason."

Anderson chimed in: "Just from cars registered to folks who lived along the trail."

"A trail," Pall pointed out, "that the killer wanted us to follow."

Laurene said, "*Think* about it—nothing this guy does is random."

"Right," Pall said. "He's a planner, a schemer. All the other plates belong to people who couldn't possibly be our suspect."

"Then in that respect," Harrow said, "none were random choices. The killer has *wanted* us on his trail, wanted us to keep coming, and not get bogged down in the red herrings the license plates might provide. Why?"

Laurene said, "With just a little study, the killer *could* have picked license plates belonging to people who might've served as reasonable suspects, if only for a few hours."

"Right," Harrow said. "Still, in this instance, when he had the chance to throw us off the track, to cover his scent? What did he do?"

Pall said, "Just the opposite."

That made Harrow very wary of what awaited them at the end of this road. And now that the killer almost certainly had Carmen, Harrow's worry deepened.

"Shouldn't we call the Smith County sheriff?" Laurene asked. "This Gibbons? And let him know we're on our way?"

Harrow considered. If the killer had chosen to switch plates with the sheriff on purpose, there had to be a reason for it. The unsub would also have to assume that Harrow and the team would be talking to Gibbons ASAP, if only to rule him out as a suspect.

"No," Harrow said, firm. "Let's roll into town unannounced and play it by ear."

Laurene frowned. "Why?"

Harrow explained his reasoning.

"Sounds like a plan to me," Choi said. "We've been eating this bastard's dust for too long."

Pall agreed: "Might not be much, but it could just be something our guy doesn't expect."

"*Anything* would help at this point," Anderson said. "He's been leading us around the whole darn time."

Choi glared at the blond. "Could you goddamn it *curse* once in a while? You're driving me bat-shit."

Jenny asked, "*Where* is he leading us?"

Harrow said, "Well, to Lebanon. Beyond that, we don't want to go there . . . because if the unsub stays in charge, Carmen could wind up dead. And maybe the rest of us too."

"Let me check something," Jenny said, and her fingers flew on the laptop keyboard, stopping occasionally, then flying some more. "Here's an interesting stat—Settler Feed field corn KS1422 is sold in twenty-three counties in Kansas, one of which is Smith County."

"Lebanon's in Smith County," Harrow said. "Did the unsub leave it on purpose, back in Florida? Or did he actually make a slip?"

Jenny shrugged. "Does it matter?"

Silence, but for the semi's engine and rolling wheels, draped the little lab.

Finally, Harrow said, "We can't exactly be subtle with two buses and a big rig, meaning when we rumble into town, everybody will know. Jenny, find me a rental car and a place to pick it up, well outside of town. I want to go in unannounced, and anonymous."

Choi asked, "What about the TV show?"

Anderson said, "Hell with the TV show."

Everybody clapped.

Everybody except Jenny, that is, who was again busy tapping the keyboard. "Renting the car is easy," she said. "Assuming you have a credit card. . . ."

Harrow smiled. "I have a credit card, all right— for my expenses, on UBC's dime."

This elicited more applause.

Harrow got out his wallet and passed Jenny the AMEX black card.

"Never seen one of these before," she said.

"I hadn't either," he said.

Laurene came over for a look. "You wanna inspire me to catch bad guys? Some new Jimmy Choos would do the trick."

Harrow said, "When we catch this guy, Laurene, and bring Carmen back safe and sound, I'll put your shoes on my own damn card."

Suddenly embarrassed by her flip remark, Laurene said, "We'll get her back, boss. Carmen's a smart, tough kid. And you've got yourself a good team here."

"I know I do," he told her, and them. "I know we

came together under the umbrella, even the cloud, of this *Killer TV* concept. You know I've always viewed that as a means to an end. But finding the bastard that took my family away is not as important as getting Carmen back. I don't mean to embarrass you, but . . . *you're* my family now. And she's part of that family. Game faces *on*, children."

The team members, nodding, seemed every bit as determined as their leader.

"Nearest place to rent a car's Topeka," Jenny said. "Round trip, about three hundred miles out of our way."

"Unacceptable."

"What can we do?"

Harrow thought for a moment. "Rent the car," he said. "Tell me when you have it ready, and find me a town between here and Lebanon, where we can pick it up."

Jenny shook her head. "No way to get the car there."

"You rent the car, I'll get it to the drop point."

She frowned, but said, "Okay."

"I need ten minutes," he said.

Sensing that Harrow wanted to be alone, Laurene took over, giving the others fresh assignments.

At the far end of the lab, away from everyone, Harrow sat at a work station and rotated his head. Next, he put his elbows in front of him, closed his eyes, and leaned forward until his forehead rested in his hands.

He didn't sleep when he did this—the exercise was actually closer to meditation—but it gave him a chance to center himself, and to find that place within where he could focus and set aside frustration, exhaustion, anger, any issue that kept him from concentrating on what was at hand.

Critics of *Crime Seen!* and its new segment had already started howling, even after just two episodes. Despite a good number of positive reviews, Harrow ignored those and concentrated on the pans.

Some said he was exploiting the deaths of his family. He'd expected that—those voices had been there even during the first season. Others said the show suffered from a slow pace, because they had not yet captured, or even identified, the serial killer. After only two shows!

If Harrow thought there'd been pressure when he was sheriff, or at the DCI, this TV life was many times worse—about six million times worse, actually, and growing (if the overnight ratings were to be believed).

At times he wondered if some part of him needed this, if some dark secret place craved the celebrity, if he was, in fact, somehow profiting from his own misfortune. For years, he'd fought the battle of whether or not the deaths of Ellen and David were his fault.

He even found himself singing the familiar guilty survivor's song: if only he'd *been* there. . . .

His job had been to serve and protect. He had served the public well that day, protecting the President of the United States, but not his own family.

And now who was he serving—the public? The show? His own interest in justice? Revenge? *Who was he protecting?* Certainly not Carmen. The cast, the crew, and his team had become close to him, a chance to start over, and here he was putting his second family in harm's way.

What the hell good was he doing?

He was trying to stop a madman, yes, but now that they had information, he could just step aside and let law enforcement do its job. He and his people were, in fact, actively avoiding the FBI at the moment, playing off the limitations of distance and personnel the federal field offices faced.

No, he'd *had* to push it, had to do it *himself*, with the help of the team, of course. . . . Yet what had he accomplished? The abduction of one of their own.

But these emotions roiling within him had to be set aside, contained, compartmentalized until this was done, until Carmen was safe. He took a deep breath, held it, and waited for everything to subside, then let the breath out slowly.

When he sat back and opened his eyes, Jenny was standing there, a small sheaf of hard copy in hand.

"Got it," she said.

"The car or the drop point?"

"Both." She removed a sheet from atop the pile. "Russell, Kansas—it's at the intersection of this road and Interstate seventy, running west from Topeka."

"What's all the paperwork?"

"Rental contract."

"You did good, Jenny," he said, taking the papers.

Then, on his cell, he called Dennis Byrnes and explained what he needed.

"What makes you think I can make that happen?" Byrnes asked.

"Dennis, you're president of a major television network. What can't you do?"

"Control the talent."

"Then make the 'talent' happy. Does UBC have a Topeka, Kansas, affiliate?"

"No."

"Well, you employ freelance crew all over the world. You must use *somebody* out of Topeka. Hire him or her to drive the car to Russell."

"You're lucky your ratings are on the rise. . . ."

"Dennis, I'll owe you one."

"I know you will," Byrnes said, and hung up.

Twenty minutes later, Byrnes's assistant called with the details for picking up the car.

And when they got to Russell, everything went well. Harrow accepted the keys to a Chrysler 300, and he and Choi jumped in to lead the parade toward Lebanon.

In a hamlet called Downs, twenty-two miles south of Lebanon, the team pulled into a little diner-cum-truckstop that would serve as their staging area.

The diner was a retro affair, checkerboard tile floor, fixtures done up in black, red, and metallic silver, shiny and bright. Maybe ten late afternoon diners—truckers taking breaks, and farmers who had knocked off early for a cup of coffee—were scattered around the joint, all gawking for a second when the entire *Killer TV* team trudged in, from stars to PAs, camera and sound personnel as well.

Harrow figured—or anyway *hoped*—the reaction was due more to the size of the group than who they were. Famous people really turned heads in this part of the world; but once that second or two of recognition was over, locals tended to remember their manners, and go back to minding their own business.

Harrow recalled why he'd always loved the Midwest, and it reinforced his belief that, eventually, he would move back.

The diner manager opened up a closed-off area for them, and the booths and tables were soon filled. Harrow gathered the forensics team at a table, and included cameraman Hathaway and audio gal Hughes. The other camera and audio personnel had been given permission by Harrow and the diner management to go out and gather B roll.

Over coffee, Harrow said, "All right, gang—Laurene, Billy, and I will go into town in the rental. The rest of you will wait for our call and then join us."

Pall, Jenny, and Anderson were clearly disappointed.

"Look," Harrow said, "this is not personal. Billy and Laurene have the most experience, if things go sideways—that's the only reason they're going. Besides, you three are strong in the lab. I don't want you in the field with me, when at any moment we might need you there."

They didn't look happy, but accepted their lot.

"What about camera?" Hathaway asked. "We *are* going to shoot this, aren't we?"

Harrow didn't want them along but knew, whether he liked it or not, trying to do this without shooting footage would be the end of their show-within-the-show. And that was something he wasn't prepared to give up yet.

Besides, he had imposed on Byrnes, and didn't have it in him to double-cross the man.

"You and Nancy go with us. Stow your gear in the trunk. Pack as light as possible."

"Roger that," Hathaway said, catching Harrow's toss of car keys.

Then the husky cameraman rose, Hughes tagging after, ponytail swinging, as they went to fetch their gear from a bus.

Harrow nodded to Choi, got up, and Choi followed him to a quiet corner. "Suppose, hypothetically, I wanted three handguns. Where would I go to get them?"

"You'd go to me."

"Good to know."

"What, no hypothetical hand grenades?"

"What?"

Choi grinned. "Just kidding."

"Round up the Kevlar vests too, before we go."

"Can do."

They went back and joined the others at the table, where baskets of burgers and fries and other traditional diner fare was being served up.

"All right," Harrow said, when everyone had eaten. "Let's get ready. Any questions?"

"*Excuse me!*"

The voice came from just behind Harrow. It belonged to a matronly lady in purple knit slacks, a purple sweatshirt, and a large red hat. She and three similarly dressed women lined up near Harrow's chair—he had to swing around a little to take them all in.

Then he rose, and said, "Ladies."

"We do apologize," the spokeswoman said, "for interrupting you."

"We were just finishing our meals. No problem."

"You are J.C. *Harrow*, aren't you? And this *is* the *Killer TV* team, isn't it?"

He smiled a little. "Guilty as charged."

"We're with the Red Hat Society. We all watch your show, and just love it."

"Thank you, ma'am."

Now the spokeswoman's features grew somber. "We were wondering—you don't think that killer you've been chasing is here in *Downs*, do you?"

He shook his head. "No reason to worry, ma'am. We're just passing through."

Their group sigh of relief amused Harrow and the rest. But he suddenly realized another problem with the size of their operation—rolling into a little town, their semi and buses all but announcing *serial killer* seemed the modern-day equivalent of shouting fire in a crowded theater.

"Well, uh . . . before you go, could we have your autographs?"

"No problem," he said. Much as he wanted to hit the road, he was not about to insult matrons in a diner in Downs, Kansas. A napkin was passed around, and everyone signed.

"Where is that nice young girl?" the woman asked. "Carmen Garcia? We just love her."

"We love her, too," Harrow said. "She'll be joining us later. Leave your address with my friends here, and we'll see you all get signed photos."

Chapter Twenty-eight

Carmen promised herself she would not cry.

She was terrified, of course, but hoped she hadn't betrayed that to the sick psycho who sat in the lounge chair across the room—just out of her sight line, at the moment. She still wore the Ozomatli T-shirt and shorts in which she'd been abducted.

At least he hadn't stripped her naked—not yet anyway. Sometimes his eyes got a weird gleam that made her queasy . . . but she didn't let herself think further along that line. . . .

The room was dark, though it was daytime, slivers of light making their way around the edges of windows where blinds were drawn tight. Not pitch black, but dark enough to give her trouble making out more than the vague outlines of scant furnishings.

She lay on her back on a ratty sofa, a spring poking her backside, hands bound behind her, her mouth taped shut. Earlier, he had let her sit up for a while, but a short time ago he had pushed her back.

When he'd moved to her, she'd been scared all the more, not realizing he was still in the room. A low coffee table had been dragged into the middle of the floor, away from the couch. On a stand in a corner sat an old tube TV, but whether it worked, she didn't know—it was either turned off or defunct.

She knew he was there now, she could *feel* him, watching her. Could feel the glittering eyes moving down her torso, stroking her legs, caressing her bare feet, then sliding their way back up to her face.

From where he sat, he could see all of her, and she could see none of him; but she knew he was there, all right. For one thing, she could hear him breathing, faint but unmistakable, like an obscene phone caller.

He spoke and she jerked.

"Do you want another drink?" he asked. His voice seemed almost soothing, concerned, yet somehow that only made it creepier.

She shook her head. She would have loved another drink, but that would only lead to her having to urinate again and suffer the indignity of him pulling down her shorts and forcing her to sit on that filthy toilet, a thought that made her want to puke.

And if she puked under the duct tape, she would choke and die. No, a repeat trip to the bathroom was something she would avoid, for as long as she could, anyway.

"You *know* this isn't personal."

He had shot her with a Taser, kidnapped her,

brought her to this hell hole, forced her to expose herself in the bathroom, and even ruined her favorite T-shirt with that damn Taser.

What could be more personal than that?

"I know you're wondering, why *you?* The others must've wondered the same thing too, I guess. Only with them, they didn't have the kind of time you do . . . to think about it? I am sorry you are uncomfortable in this prolonged way. With the others? I could just deliver my messages, and they'd be gone, and I'd be gone. Simple. Straightforward."

That he remained so calm, so blasé about the murders of so many people, chilled her even more than the kidnapping. This man could kill her and feel no more emotion about it than if he were mowing the grass or licking a stamp.

"With you," he was saying, "it's more . . . complicated."

Complicated or not, it sounded like he meant to kill her.

She had little memory after opening her motel-room door, seeing the man, who, surprisingly, had no face in her memory, then the Taser, then this sofa. The amount of time that had passed between was blank.

Even if it hadn't been long, with the sun visible around the windows, Harrow and the team *must* know something was wrong. . . .

They would be looking for her. She just had to hope she could last until they found her.

"I want you to know, Ms. Garcia, this isn't personal. I don't do this to humiliate you. I don't do this to make you feel uncomfortable. I would not strip the clothing off you and do something sexual. I am not that kind of person. Just so you know. Just so you know."

But she *didn't* know. She didn't even know if he was trying to convince her . . .

. . . or himself.

Chapter Twenty-nine

The sun was well along its westward journey, but the temperature remained warm, though a soft breeze blew in from the south when—just before five in the afternoon—Harrow and company rolled into Lebanon. Laurene Chase rode shotgun, Choi and Hathaway sandwiching Hughes in the back of the Chrysler rental.

They headed directly to the sheriff's office, where Herm Gibbons's '07 Tahoe was nowhere to be seen. Harrow parked the rental, and told his people to stay put while he went in to get the lay of the land.

A single glass door opened into a tiny vestibule that had a bulletproof window and a telephone on the wall. Straight ahead was another glass door, this one locked, its glass crisscrossed with wire.

He picked up the receiver and waited only a few seconds before a pleasant female voice said, "May I help you?"

The fiftyish woman sitting at the dispatcher's station was not unattractive, though her red hair was a shade that did not exist in nature.

"I'm looking for Sheriff Gibbons," Harrow said, not identifying himself yet.

"The sheriff isn't in—could someone else help you?"

"Do you have a detective I could speak to?"

"I'm sorry. Detective's with the sheriff. They're at a crime scene."

Something lurched in Harrow's chest. *Were they too late?*

"Where?" he blurted.

"I'm sorry, sir," the woman said, starting to sound a little cross. "We don't give out that sort of information."

Frustrated, Harrow considered trying to trade on his name, but thought better of it. When he was on the job, he'd always hated people who played the "Do you know who I *am?*" card, and he refused to become one of them now.

Had to be another way to find the sheriff, and what seemed to be Lebanon's only detective.

"Thank you for your help," he told the woman.

"Mr. Harrow?"

His eyes met the woman's. The dispatcher gave him a pursed, possibly flirtatious smile. "Sorry I couldn't be more help."

Busted, he smiled and nodded to her; and he was about to hang up when her voice in the receiver whispered in his ear.

"I wish I were allowed to say that if you were to

drive two miles out of town, on Granger Road? You'd find Sheriff Gibbons and Deputy Wilson—at the old Morton place."

Smiling through the glass at his benefactor, he asked the phone, "Not meaning to bribe a public servant, but could you accept an autographed picture as a token of thanks?"

"Not until after eleven at the Old Mill."

"The Old Mill?"

"Bar about two blocks over. It's on Granger Road too."

"Might take you up on that," Harrow said pleasantly. "Let's see how my visit with the sheriff plays out."

"I'm Janet, by the way," she said, smiling again.

"J.C."

"I know."

Back outside in the car, Laurene Chase asked, "What did he say?"

"He's not there."

"Where *is* he?" Choi asked.

Starting the car, Harrow said, "A crime scene."

"A crime scene where?"

Harrow caught Choi in the rearview. "Why, do you know the neighborhood?"

Choi smirked in the mirror. "Boss, nobody likes a smart-ass."

Thanks to the rental's GPS, Harrow quickly found Granger Road, and after driving two and a half miles on a two-lane highway into the country, he came upon the sheriff's Tahoe and a county cruiser, light bar flashing, parked on the narrow shoulder.

Pulling around the vehicles, Harrow saw the

sheriff and deputy herding sheep back into a fenced-in field.

After parking on the shoulder, Harrow turned the emergency flashers on, and they all climbed out, Hathaway and Hughes going for the trunk, lanky Laurene stretching her legs and looking amused by the sheep-herding effort, breeze lifting her corn-rows. Harrow watched Choi go over and give the officers a hand.

Looking at Hathaway, who was pantomiming turn-ing a key in a lock, Harrow shook his head.

When he got closer to the cameraman, he handed him the keys and, sotto voce, said, "Not until the gate's locked. I don't want any footage that's going to make these men look silly. We don't need any rustic comedy. Understood?"

Hathaway nodded. "I guess somebody's gotta get those sheep off the road."

"That's right. I herded cows like that back in Iowa, and nobody put it on TV."

Harrow seldom ordered Hathaway around, be-cause the senior cameraman knew his job well enough that Harrow stayed out of his face. On the other hand, when Harrow spoke, Hathaway paid heed.

Using his cell, Harrow made a quick call to Jenny Blake, reading her the number off the plate on the back of the sheriff's Tahoe.

"Let me know when you've run it," he said.

Jenny didn't bother to answer, just clicked off and got to work.

As Choi chased the last of the sheep through the gate, the deputy—balding and about fifty—

closed the gate and latched it. Choi climbed back over the fence as Harrow walked up to the sheriff.

Beefier than his associate, his brown hair full but showing signs of gray, the sheriff wore the same tan uniform shirt as his deputy. The only differences were a gold star on his collar where the deputy bore a single gold bar; also, the junior officer wore brown uniform pants where the sheriff was in blue jeans.

Harrow said, "Sheriff, I'm—"

"J.C. Harrow," the sheriff said, holding out a hand. He had brown eyes, a square jaw, and a thin-lipped straight line of a smile.

Shaking hands, Harrow said, "Your dispatcher called you."

The sheriff nodded. "Janet's a big fan of your show, and she rang me right after you left the office. I'm Herm Gibbons, by the way—Sheriff of Smith County."

"Good to meet you, Sheriff."

"Herm, please."

"Herm," Harrow repeated. "And make it 'J.C.'" He introduced Choi and Laurene, then pointed out the camera crew.

"They're free to film," Gibbons said. With a head bob toward his associate, he said, "This is Deputy Colby Wilson."

The deputy shook hands all around. To Choi, he said, "Thanks for the assist. You don't look like a country boy."

Choi said, "I'm from the wild, wild East."

"I was told you were at a crime scene," Harrow said to the sheriff. "Is this it?"

The sheriff nodded. "Some fool opened the gate on purpose."

Choi blinked. "And that's a crime?"

Gibbons grinned. "Around here it is. More serious than cow tipping, son, less so than rustling. Sheep get out in the road, they can cause an accident, since not everybody obeys the speed limit in the boonies. Doesn't really seem to be the sort of offense, though, that'd attract the host of *Crime Seen!* What *really* brings you around?"

"In Pratt last night," Harrow said, "one of our staff was abducted."

"One of your own? Damn!"

Briefly, Harrow explained.

The sheriff frowned. "Hell of a thing. How are you people holding up?"

Nods all around, and Harrow said, "We're dealing with it by going proactive."

"Good for you—that's the only way. A plus on your side? Chief Walker's a good man, and the FBI'll back him up—may take 'em a day or two to find their way to Pratt, though."

"We frankly haven't connected with the federal people yet. With our unofficial status, well . . ."

"I get it, J.C. You want to stay in the game, and those boys are likely to sideline you. Is there some way we can help? Something that makes you think your kidnapper's headed our way?"

Harrow said, "The suspect drove a Ford F-one fifty."

Deputy Wilson put in: "No shortage of those in Kansas."

"We have a license number," Harrow said, and gave it to them.

"Hell," Gibbons said, frowning, jaw dropping.

Deputy Wilson was frowning, too. "Herm—don't tell me you know who that vehicle belongs to?"

"Not the truck," Gibbons said, "but the license number—it's mine."

"Yours?" Wilson blurted. "What . . . ?"

To Harrow, the sheriff's surprise seemed genuine.

"Sheriff, we've been chasing switched plates since New Mexico. Someone is trying to draw us here. Any idea who, or why?"

The sheriff and the deputy traded a long look, but they were both shaking their heads.

"This is a quiet town," Gibbons said. "Always has been."

"And you can't think of anyone," Harrow said, "who might abduct a member of my crew? We think he's trying to draw attention to himself or perhaps some perceived problem or even injustice by a civil servant."

Gibbons shook his head again, but added, "We'll sure look into it. We'll get the state boys down here to help out too."

"I appreciate it," Harrow said.

Once again, they'd gotten close, and the trail had gone cold. Before Harrow could ask another question, his cell vibrated.

"Excuse me," he said, and stepped off a few feet and answered the call. "Harrow."

"Jenny. I hacked the Kansas DMV and ran the tag you gave me. The plate is registered to a red Ford F-150."

"Same truck as our suspect."

"The one we've been looking at is probably a 2000," Jenny said. "This one is a 2007."

"And the owner?"

"Brown," Jenny said. "Daniel T."

She gave him the address.

"Thanks, Jenny. And Jenny? Do me a favor."

"Yes, boss?"

"Don't use the term *hacked* on a cell conversation."

"Got it, boss," she said, and clicked off.

Turning back to the sheriff, Harrow could see that Gibbons, Wilson, Choi, and Laurene had moved to the rear of the Tahoe, and were looking at the plate.

Harrow walked back to join the group.

"They're not your plates, are they?" Harrow asked, looking down at the back of the sheriff's SUV.

"They're not mine," Gibbons agreed almost robotically. He seemed to be trying to figure out when they might have been stolen.

"I just got a call," Harrow said. "My computer specialist says the plates are registered to—"

"Daniel T. Brown," Gibbons said.

Wilson appeared shocked. "Brown? No shit. . . ."

Harrow felt his eyebrows raise. "How did you know that?"

Gibbons shook his head, sighed. "Dan Brown had this job before I did. He's the retired Smith County Sheriff. I know his plate number well as I know my own."

The suspect using the license plates of a retired civil servant sounded alarm bells.

Harrow said, "We need to see him right away."

Shaking his head, Gibbons said, "Not until tomorrow night, at the earliest. He's fishing in Canada—one of them backwoods places. He's supposed to be flying home tomorrow."

"Lebanon's a little small for an airport."

"He'll land in Kansas City and drive back."

Harrow did some quick thinking.

Since Brown fit the profile of the previous victims—at least in that he was a retired civil servant—Harrow was concerned that by using his plates, the killer might be sending a message that Brown and his family were the next intended victims.

On the other hand, all the other victims had been killed in their homes, poised for quick discovery by the returning male head of the house. In that sense, Brown being out of town might be a break for them.

Harrow asked Gibbons, "Is Mr. Brown married?"

"Yeah, why?"

"Does he have kids?"

"Grown, both of them." Gibbons was frowning now. "J.C., are you gonna tell me what the hell this is *about?*"

The children being grown didn't fit the profile. Odd.

Harrow said, "I'm glad to tell you all about it, but prefer to do it in your office, not on the roadside."

"We can do that," Gibbons said. "With the sheep in, I'm getting ready to go there now."

To Deputy Wilson, Gibbons said, "Colby, go tell

Mr. Riley we've got his sheep back, and we'll do what we can to find out who opened the gate."

The deputy nodded and went back to his patrol car.

Under his breath, Choi said, "Don't forget the fingerprint kit," and Harrow gave him a look.

Gibbons was turning to go too, when Harrow said, "One more question."

"Yep?"

"How old are Brown's children?"

"Lori is twenty-five, a teacher. Mark's twenty-one. He's at KU."

All the way back into town, Harrow mulled what they had learned so far.

Truth was, he didn't know if they knew more or less than when they had driven into Lebanon, and Carmen's time might well be running out.

He was starting to wonder if the killer really was making a target on the map—or did the bastard just have them running in circles?

Chapter Thirty

The sheriff's office was a reconverted downtown storefront, as the deputy explained, letting in Harrow, Laurene Chase, Maury Hathaway, and Nancy Hughes (the latter two with camera and audio gear at the ready).

"Real sheriff's office is in the county seat of Smith's Center," Wilson was saying, "but because of the tourist traffic? We need this auxiliary office here now, too."

"Tourist traffic?" Billy Choi asked. "In Lebanon, Kansas?"

The deputy was taller than he was wide, but not by much, and might have played football without a helmet as a kid or been a bad boxer, his nose like a glob of flesh-colored Play-Doh haphazardly stuck onto his face.

To Choi, the deputy said, "Friend, you're standing at the geographic center of the forty-eight contiguous United States. People come here for that."

This throwaway information, these casual words, hit Harrow like an arrow—an arrow sent by a Robin Hood–like marksman into the dead center of a target.

Laurene and Choi had stunned expressions that said they got it too.

Some people went to Hot Springs for the springs, some visited Turin to see the shroud. Others, it seemed, came to Lebanon to say that they'd been to the center of the United States.

Harrow excused himself and gathered the little group back out on the sidewalk. The host of *Crime Seen!* allowed Hathaway and Hughes to record the brief discussion between himself and two of his forensic stars.

"So we're *here*," Choi said, pointing downward. "We're at the center of target, right where he led us."

Laurene said, "I'd say he must've grown up here— heard this 'center of the United States' routine his whole life, and worked backward from there, making the map into a big, round target."

"Could be another red herring," Harrow said. "Could be too easy. . . ."

"Oh yeah," Choi said archly, "it's been way too damn easy. Especially for those fifty-some murder victims. J.C., we're here. We're at ground zero on the nutzoid map."

Harrow had no argument.

"But how," Laurene asked, "does this knowledge change anything?"

"It doesn't," Harrow said. "We proceed as before. It's just . . . Billy's right. We're here. This is the end of the journey. So we make sure it's the end of *his* journey, not Carmen's."

Choi and Laurene nodded gravely.

Sheriff Gibbons's office reminded Harrow of his own back at Story County—a few framed citations and awards on one wall, bookshelves lining another, the third consumed by a large window overlooking the downtown, where traffic was sparse in the orange glow of the setting sun. The wall behind Gibbons's desk was given over to a large Smith County Sheriff's Department logo.

The deputy had brought in a third chair to join the two facing the sheriff's large dark wooden desk. A combination phone-intercom rested on one desk corner, a computer on a separate table. Two photos in a double-frame faced the sheriff's side, wife and kids probably.

Maybe, just maybe, the next target was Gibbons and not Brown.

Harrow shook his head. Some balls on this bastard, stealing the plates off both the retired and current sheriffs.

Laurene, Choi, and Harrow took the visitor chairs, while Hathaway and Hughes camped in a corner, prepping to shoot the meeting. They'd been waiting nearly ten minutes when Sheriff Gibbons strode in.

After the sheriff sat, Harrow laid out what they knew, what they thought, including the target on the map of the United States where they were all sitting dead-center.

For his part, Gibbons took it all in, not commenting till Harrow had finished. Then he moved his head to one side, widened his eyes, and said, "Hell of a story."

"I wish it were just a story," Harrow said.

Laurene sat forward. "We're looking for a man with issues with authority. He's going to be a person who isolates himself from the community, a loner. He's probably going to have a record."

Harrow almost smiled at the way Laurene had come to embrace Michael Pall's profiling of their unsub.

"My guess," she was saying, "is he's had scrapes with the law where he's been belligerent, combative—disorderly conduct, maybe even resisting arrest. He'll be resistive to change. If he has a family, they'll kowtow to him. In that type of situation, he'd be orderly, regimented. To the community, he'd appear a strict disciplinarian."

Choi picked up: "The BTK killer, Dennis Rader, was a Cub Scout leader and supervisor in the Compliance Department of Park City."

"We know about that son of a bitch," Gibbons said, nodding. "Maniac was right here in Kansas."

"So you know the drill," Harrow said. "Can you think of anyone locally who fits that profile?"

The sheriff gave up a darkly amused smile. "Do I know somebody who fits the profile of a *serial* killer? You just saw me herding *sheep*, J.C. We've had maybe four homicides in Lebanon in as many decades. Why would my mind work along those lines?"

The sheriff's frustration indicated a temper getting frayed, and Harrow was almost relieved when his cell vibrated. He excused himself, and took the call.

"Me, boss," Jenny Blake said. "We've got something."

"So do we—Lebanon is the center-point city of the United States."

"Interesting. But I have something else—remember the fingerprint on the snow globe?"

"Sure," he said, recalling with a pang that Carmen was the one who'd noticed the object was out of place in the dead child's room.

"Finally got a hit on the print," Jenny said. "We went through enough databases, and finally found it. U.S. Army. I had to—"

"Don't tell me how," Harrow cut in. "Tell me who."

"The man's name is Gabriel Shelton."

"What do you have on him?"

"His service record lists his hometown as Lebanon, Kansas."

"Just earned your paycheck, Jenny," Harrow said, and could almost hear her smiling over the phone.

"One more thing," she said. "I've sent his service photo to your cell phone."

"Good. While I've got you, tell everybody, saddle up. I want you guys up here."

"I'll make it happen, boss."

They signed off, and Harrow returned his attention to Gibbons, saying, "Sorry for the interruption—information from one of our team."

Gibbons, his expression thoughtful, nodded.

"You've had time to mull it," Harrow said. "Come up with anybody in town your department's dealt with, who might fit our subject's profile?"

The sheriff rocked back, sighed deeply. "J.C., I've known most of these people my entire life. Some are oddballs I suppose, some are peculiar or maybe set in their ways, some may be just plain crazy . . . but none stand out as crazy in the way *you're* talking."

"How about I throw out a name?"

"All right."

"And you just tell me if you think it's even remotely possible."

"I said all right."

"Gabriel Shelton."

Gibbons's eyes widened, then tightened. He sat forward. "You think *Gabe* is your man?"

"Gabe," Laurene said. "So you know him."

Rocking back again, the sheriff shrugged and said, "Like I told you, I know most everyone in town. There's only three hundred people in Lebanon, and not even five thousand in the county. Met more than my fair share of 'em, some while I was out campaigning, others after I won the job."

Harrow asked, "Where does Gabe Shelton fall?"

"Straddles both stools," Gibbons said. "And since you're pressing me . . . some of those things you listed? Disorderly conduct, problems with authority? Both *are* on Gabe's record."

Choi said, "May we see that record?"

Harrow almost smiled. The kid had never been so polite. Maybe he was catching on to the world beyond New York.

"Normally," Gibbons said, "I'd say no—I'd insist on a court order. But I understand this is different.

You have a kidnapping on your hands, one of your own . . . and you're looking for a suspect who may be a serial killer."

This little recitation had apparently been for the sheriff's own benefit as much as Harrow and company's. Gibbons turned and typed something into his computer.

Moments later, he said, "Come around here, and see for yourself."

Gabriel Shelton's mug shot showed an unlikely candidate for the serial killer pantheon. Shelton needed a shave and a haircut, but otherwise looked nothing like a threat—curly dark hair, big blue eyes, a firm-jawed face and the general demeanor (even in a mug shot) of someone you could trust—someone who might be your next-door neighbor.

The only thing disturbing to Harrow about the face was that he'd seen it somewhere before. . . .

Harrow asked, "When was the mug shot taken?"

"Nine years ago," Gibbons said. "We haven't had much trouble from him since."

Something about the face, the eyes. . . .

Shelton's police record showed nothing until a battery charge ten years back, and another two years later. Between were three disorderly conducts and several misdemeanors, chiefly unpaid parking tickets.

For about three years, Gabe Shelton went from anonymous citizen to minor-league asshole, then became barely a blip on the cop radar . . . just a speeding ticket (thirty-seven in a twenty-five mile-per-hour school zone), a few more parking tickets, but no subsequent arrests.

After three years of terminal bad attitude disease, Gabe Shelton had gone into sudden remission.

While Laurene went over the file in detail with the sheriff, Harrow called Jenny and got her to forward Shelton's military record. Then he got Choi to show him how to bring it up on his phone.

Harrow wasn't terrible with technology, but cell phones seemed to morph on him every six months or so, and the network kept giving him complimentary new ones. When Choi got Shelton's record up, Harrow read it fast.

Born in 1957, Shelton had graduated high school in '75, gone into the service on July 14 of that year; served four years, missing Vietnam by mere months, and was granted an honorable discharge upon his separation.

Everything seemed fine in Shelton's life through his time in the Army. Which was no help. Harrow banished the phone to his pocket again.

He turned to Choi and asked, "Anything?"

Choi said, "Nothing you didn't already know."

Laurene said, "I've got Shelton's address."

This was good, if not surprising, news, and they would spring to action; but Harrow was troubled.

"There's got to be more to it," Harrow said. "This guy was living a normal life, then got pissed about something, and started turning up in a few police reports. Finally one morning he wakes up and decides to become one of the worst serial killers in American history? What made a good soldier and average citizen go so goddamn far off the rails?"

Gibbons said, "I can tell you."

They looked at the sheriff. Harrow returned to his chair. Laurene was already back in hers, as was Choi. The sheriff's expression seemed almost sheepish. He'd known something since Shelton's name had first come up, and hadn't shared it yet.

Now, softly, with the embarrassed tone of a kid caught stealing from a sibling's piggy bank, he said, "About ten years ago, Gabe's wife and kid . . . they were murdered."

The investigators traded sharp looks.

"The thing is," Gibbons said, shifting in his chair, "he always blamed my predecessor for it. Sheriff Brown?"

Harrow frowned. "He thought the *sheriff* killed his family?"

"Not that Sheriff Brown did it himself. But Gabe believed Dan was behind it, or anyway covering up . . . but he wasn't. The state police came in and looked into the murders, and said our investigation was thorough, and by the book. And they came up empty, just like us."

"It happens," Harrow said.

"Shelton couldn't accept that. That's when the trouble with the authorities started. The disorderly conducts, the battery, all that crap. Then, fast as he lost it, Gabe stopped being a pain in our ass. Just straightened up and flew right—keeps to himself, and he's been an okay citizen, far as it goes. So we stay out of his way, and he sort of seems to stay out of ours."

Laurene said to Harrow and Choi, "So he's re-creating the crime done to him, and letting other public servants, sheriffs in particular, suffer like he did."

Choi said, "I have nothing to add to that."

Neither did Harrow.

"All right, Sheriff," Harrow said, getting up. "Let's visit Mr. Shelton, and see if he's holding my team member."

Rising, Gibbons said, "Sounds like probable cause to me."

Harrow didn't point it out, but the truth was, he wasn't law enforcement anymore and didn't give a good goddamn about probable cause.

All he cared about was getting Carmen back in one breathing piece.

Chapter Thirty-one

Outside the police station, Harrow handed the rental keys off to Laurene, telling her, "Everybody into Kevlar. I'll be on the front line. You and Billy arm yourselves, but stay back unless you're needed."

"J.C., we—"

"*You* will obey orders. And one of them is to keep Hathaway and Hughes back. Tell them if they get killed we don't have a show. Understood?"

"Understood."

In the rider's seat of the Tahoe, Harrow made a quick call to Pall and told him to get directions from Laurene. They were on the move.

"How far?" Harrow asked.

Gibbons said, "Five minutes—Shelton's got a place over on the south side. It's not much."

The sheriff radioed for backup. Wilson and the deputy in the auxiliary office both said they were on their way, and two more deputies would be sent from Smith Center, ten miles to the west.

Night crept in, turning the houses of the quiet neighborhood into dark hulks with occasional glowing windows, set in yards that were shadowy voids that could hold just about anything.

Harrow recalled something an older officer had told him when he was a rookie: *Kid, this job is ninety-five percent boredom and five percent piss-your-pants fear.*

Harrow had laughed, but a look from the older officer had silenced him before adding, *It's okay to be so scared you piss yourself, long as you get the job done.*

As they slowed to park, Harrow tugged from his waistband a nine-millimeter Browning he'd gotten from Choi. He checked the clip and made sure one was in the pipe.

"Got a permit for that puppy?" Gibbons asked, looking over in the dark SUV.

"Backup's not here yet, and I'm going in," Harrow said. "You really want to see my California carry permit?"

"No," Gibbons said. "I just want my ass covered if something goes wrong."

"Covered by me having a gun, or covered by me having a permit?"

"Yes."

Even though he was tensing for action, Harrow couldn't help but grin. "You're some politician, Herm. I bet you're one hell of a sheriff."

"Second term, gettin' ready to run for a third next year. I don't mind havin' the brownie points this could earn me, if it goes right . . . but I'm gonna make damn sure those points aren't on sharp suckers getting jammed up my nethers, if it goes south."

Harrow nodded. "This goes right and we get Carmen back, Herm, you're the hero. Goes south, I'm the goat."

"We are on the same damn wavelength," Gibbons said with a cheerfully nasty smile.

The sheriff pulled to the curb and killed the lights, shut off the Tahoe, and they climbed down.

"Across the street," Gibbons whispered. "Second house from the corner."

Following the sheriff's gaze, Harrow made out a white crackerbox, the F-150 sitting in a gravel driveway on this side. House dark, truck empty.

They stayed on this side of the street and walked quietly, two guys out for an evening stroll. Each held their pistols down against a leg, out of view from the house. As they drew closer, Harrow could see a one-car garage at the end of the drive, nearly behind the house. They crossed the street, keeping the F-150 between them and the crackerbox.

At the other end of the block, a deputy from the office was approaching at a walk, his arm stiff at his side as well. Just behind him were Laurene and Choi, the camera crew on their heels. Obviously, they had followed the deputy to the scene.

Gibbons gave them a small wave to hang back.

Deputy Wilson's voice growled over Gibbons's radio. "I'm in the back with my AR-fifteen. He's not coming out this way unless he's in a bag."

His voice a hoarse whisper, Gibbons said, "Sit tight, Colby, and for Christ's sake remember he's probably got a hostage."

"Ten-four," Wilson said.

As they got to the pickup, both men ducked,

Gibbons staying at the rear, using it for cover as he trained his pistol on the house. Moving up the driver's side, Harrow stayed in a low crouch, and hesitated when he was even with the front tire.

He glanced toward the garage and saw nothing to indicate any life back there. Slowly scanning the yard between garage and house, Harrow tried to spot Wilson; but in the darkness, that was impossible.

Harrow reached up and touched the hood of the truck—cold. This vehicle hadn't moved for some time. He crept forward, and peeked around the front—nothing.

He looked back at Gibbons, who gave him a nod.

They'd never worked together, but both had sheriffed for years, and each had a good idea what the other was thinking.

With Harrow's nod, they rushed together, Gibbons from the rear of the truck, Harrow from the front. They met on the postage stamp front stoop of the dark, silent house.

Gibbons quietly opened the screen door, and the two stood for a long second listening, poised to make rude entry.

No sound from inside, no TV, no radio, and most important—and disturbing to Harrow . . .

. . . no sounds of life.

Chapter Thirty-two

Carmen was back on the couch again, but as day shifted to night, she felt more frightened than before. Late in the afternoon, when she'd finally managed to overcome her fear enough to sleep for a few minutes, he had roused her, and slit the tape that bound her hands behind her.

"Take off the shirt," he said, voice as calm as if asking the time.

She fluttered her hands at her sides, trying to get some feeling back.

"No," she said from behind the tape, and shook her head, seizing the courage to stand up to him.

Then the two prongs of the Taser touched her spine through the fabric of the T-shirt, and she felt her resolve melt.

"You *know* what this is," he said, the prongs against her. "Don't make me ask you again."

He stayed behind her as she lifted the shirt over

her head. He might be watching her back, but she moved carefully to make sure that was all he saw.

She'd wondered if it would come to this—to rape. She had played it out in her mind, and even wondered if it might be to her advantage if he tried that, because he might untie her, and hadn't he just freed her hands?

Somewhere in her mind, her own voice laughed a shrill hysterical laugh. *To her* advantage *if he tried to rape her? That was a good one. . . .*

When she had the shirt off, he said, "Drop it."

She dropped the garment.

Careful not to step around her, he handed her a blue sweatshirt.

"Put this on."

As she stood there bare-breasted, holding the sweatshirt before her, she realized it was the Kansas University one he'd been wearing when he abducted her. She held it at arm's length, disgusted by the thought. It didn't smell rank, but it did smell like *him* . . . and the thought of having that aroma so close to her flesh repulsed her.

The prongs of the Taser touched her bare back. They were cold and hard and amped her fear up another notch.

"Put it on," he said.

His voice quavered! Was he frightened? Aroused?

Finally, fear overcame revulsion, and she slipped on the sweatshirt, which was hot and scratchy against her skin. And, as she'd thought, his scent on it turned her stomach.

That was when he'd re-taped her hands, behind

her again, and put her back onto the sofa. She saw him pick up her T-shirt, then he disappeared from view. No sound of the lounger reclining, but that didn't mean he wasn't sitting in it, just out of view.

Now, with dark of night settling over the room, she couldn't tell whether he was in there with her or not. Her mouth was still taped shut, and she lay helplessly, eyes on shadows crawling across the ceiling.

When she heard a noise beyond the walls of the house, she froze. She tried not to breathe, afraid her breathing or the pounding of her heart would drown out the sound, should it occur again.

She struggled to identify what she'd heard.

Was it a footfall on a wooden step out front? The wind? Her imagination?

She strained to hear, every fiber of her being focused on listening, her only concession a fast prayer for the sound to repeat.

Then it did.

This time she was sure she'd heard something, and it did sound like feet on a wooden step outside. Then more footsteps, and she realized at least two people were out there.

Someone coming to rescue her?

Caution be damned, she rolled over, onto the floor, and her eyes sought her kidnapper in his chair.

The old lounger sat empty.

Outside, the sounds grew slightly louder. Were those muffled voices?

Through the tape, she yelled, "Help!"

The tape ate up the sound, but if Harrow or the

cops or *anybody* was out there on that porch, she needed to try to let them know she was in here . . . alive!

Crawling on her knees, hands bound behind her, she used all her energy and will power to get closer to the door, as she continued to scream into the tape.

The going was slow, and the screaming seemed to eat up all the oxygen. Her breathing became labored as she crept ever so slowly toward the door. . . .

Voices on the porch.

And even in the darkness, she could see the knob turn a little.

Then Carmen heard a distinct voice, outside.

"Hey, you kids! Get the hell away from there!"

She could hear the footsteps pound down the stairs . . .

. . . and slowly disappear.

The sounds were gone by the time the front door swung open and her abductor came in, wearing a white button-down shirt and nice black slacks.

Gazing down at her, shaking his head in disappointment, he said, "You're not going anywhere."

Though she'd vowed not to cry in front of this monster, and had been successful until now, Carmen could feel the tears welling.

"Kids," he said, with a shrug and a glance toward the door. "What are you gonna do?"

I'm going to die in this room, Carmen thought, on the floor, helpless. *I'm going to die right here. . . .*

Chapter Thirty-three

Gibbons raised a foot to kick open the door, but Harrow held up a hand.

He had an idea.

As Gibbons lowered his leg, Harrow reached out and carefully tried the knob. It turned easily, not locked.

Slowly, he swung the door all the way open. The room was pitch black and seemed to be empty.

"Flash," Harrow said.

Gibbons produced a mini MagLite and stepped into the room, shining the light around, Harrow on his heels.

Other than furniture, the living room was empty. They moved to their left, Harrow pointing his pistol down a hallway to the right while Gibbons and his flashlight checked out the tiny kitchen.

"Clear," Gibbons said.

Leading the way down the hallway, Harrow slipped into a minuscule bathroom on the right, the shower curtain drawn. Behind him, Gibbons sent the flashlight into the room even as he remained in the hall, pistol pointed toward the two rooms still ahead.

As his fingers touched the edge of the shower curtain, Harrow couldn't help but picture the image of a dead, blood-spattered Carmen sprawled there.

He let out a breath, whipped back the curtain, and peered into an empty tub.

After a relieved sigh, he said, "Clear."

Two rooms—presumably bedrooms—were opposite each other at the hall's end. Gibbons and his flash led the way, then went left and Harrow right, finding himself in a master bedroom that he could make out fairly well, thanks to night vision and moonlight seeping through windows.

The queen-size bed came out from the right wall, a tall armoire immediately to Harrow's left, a small closet beyond that. The wall to his left was bare except for a longer, low dresser with an attached mirror. Harrow tried to see the other side of the bed in the mirror, but it was all shadows. The opposite wall, painfully close to the bed, had two curtained windows with precious little moonlight filtering through.

Edging to his left, Harrow looked on the far side of the armoire—nothing. His back to the dresser and mirror, Harrow edged around, keeping track of the closet door.

No one on the far side of the bed, either.

His heart beat faster now, his breathing raspy as he squatted down, still trying to watch the closet as he peeled back the bottom of the spread and peeked under.

Nothing except for a couple pairs of shoes and slippers.

From the other room, Gibbons said, "Clear," the sound of the sheriff's voice giving Harrow a start.

It had been a while since he'd entered a house with no idea what lay inside, and he had to admit he was a little anxious—maybe more than a little, if his hammering heart was any indicator.

He rose and took two quick steps to the closet, and jerked open the door. Some clothes hung, but nothing else presented itself.

"Clear," Harrow said.

He went to the doorway where Gibbons waited.

"Gone," the sheriff said, flipping the switch for the bedroom light.

Harrow glanced at the sheriff, who was looking at something on the bed. Turning, following the sheriff's gaze, Harrow saw it too.

It had been there the whole time, but Harrow had been so intent on clearing the dark room, he'd not noticed it—folded to display two round holes from the Taser down below the logo: the T-shirt Carmen had frequently worn back when she was a P.A.—the black shirt with the white circle enclosing the letters OZO.

Gibbons asked, "That belong to your teammate?"

"It does."

"So she was here?"

Harrow looked around. "*Somebody's* been here."

He clicked the nine millimeter's safety on and tucked it back in his waistband.

Gibbons radioed, "Clear," to his deputies.

"Sheriff," Harrow said, "you have any problem with my people processing this crime scene?"

"None at all."

Using the walkie-talkie feature on his cell phone, Harrow passed along the message to Chase and Choi.

"Laurene, is the rest of the team here yet?"

"Yeah," she said. "They rolled up a couple of minutes ago."

"Good. You and Billy get your crime scene kits and work this scene. Start Billy in the kitchen—you take the master bedroom."

"You got it, boss."

"Her T-shirt's here."

"Her T-shirt?"

"Yeah."

A pause, then Laurene asked, "Any of her other clothing?"

"Not that we've found. The shirt's a message, I think. Get in here."

Laurene gave him a ten-four.

He noticed Gibbons looked as rattled as Harrow felt. "First time into an unknown house in a while, Herm?"

Gibbons nodded. "How long for you?"

"Ten or twelve years," Harrow said.

"Always a kick, huh?"

With a grim smile, Harrow said, "Safer than working traffic."

The pair went outside and let the two crime scene analysts in to do their work. Standing in the yard with Gibbons, the two deputies, and the rest of the

Killer TV team, Harrow had the empty feeling they were too late.

Though they hadn't rolled into town with the whole damn circus, their presence had still somehow been known by the bastard.

Across the yard, Deputy Wilson and the other deputy from the office were smoking and chatting. Joining them, Harrow bummed a cigarette. The smoke felt warm and calming in his chest.

The cops in the yard, the dark house, even bumming a smoke, it all reminded him too much of when Ellen and David had been taken from him. Emotions he didn't want to deal with right now were stirring within him.

His cell rang. "Harrow."

"Where are you?"

The voice, a familiar one, was a surprise—it belonged to *Crime Seen!* reporter Carlos Moreno. "J.C., where are you?"

"Lebanon, Kansas. Where are you?"

"Same place," Moreno said. "Downtown with a camera crew from the Topeka affiliate."

"What the hell are you doing here? I thought you were in Chicago on a story."

"I was till Byrnes called. He put me on the Cessna and had a camera crew meet me in Wichita. With Carmen kidnapped, he wants another reporter here."

Harrow shook his head—he should have known the network president would pull something like this. If Carmen turned up dead, the coverage would be massive in all media, and Byrnes couldn't allow

UBC to shortchange itself on its own story. Harrow felt like Byrnes was writing Carmen off.

"Beautiful human being," Harrow said, "our Dennis."

"Yeah, but he signs the checks, J.C. What's going on?"

"Just get out here, and I'll fill you in."

Harrow gave Moreno directions to the Shelton house.

In less than ten minutes, Moreno and his camera crew pulled up in a van marked with the call letters and channel number of UBC's Wichita affiliate.

Moreno got out, came over, and the two shook hands.

"Sorry about this, man," the affable reporter said.

"Not your fault."

Harrow had just finished introducing Moreno to the locals when Laurene and Choi came out.

Choi trotted up and said, "Boss—there was a jewelry box under the T-shirt. I left it for the feds, but . . . I sneaked a peek. It's full of wedding rings. Fifteen or twenty of 'em."

One of them Ellen's, Harrow thought, filled with excitement and dread.

"No fingers, though," Choi added.

In her latex-gloved right hand, Laurene bore an envelope. She ignored the sheriff and handed it to Harrow.

Harrow asked, "You're not worried about prints?"

She shook her head. "They're frickin' everywhere. He's not hiding."

Harrow accepted the envelope. In big block letters, HARROW was printed across the front. He opened the envelope and fished out a piece of paper.

Gibbons came up to him. "J.C., that's *evidence. . . .*"

With just a sideways glance, Harrow communicated with Hathaway, and the camera's eye switched from Laurene and Harrow to the sheriff.

"It's addressed to me," Harrow said.

Gibbons, realizing he was on camera and that the whole nation would be siding with Harrow and not him, wisely backed off.

The letter was printed in neat block letters not unlike the envelope. Harrow read:

Mr. Harrow,

Carmen Garcia is alive.

For the time being, she is well. I have been trying to communicate with you and others for a very long time. You are the only one who has even come close to understanding.

We need to talk. I would suggest that you come alone, but we both know that is not possible.

I will say simply if you wish to see Carmen Garcia again (alive) that you come to the address listed below.

I look forward to meeting you.

Gabriel Shelton

P.S. Your wife and son did not suffer.

Below was an address.

Working to keep his emotions in check, Harrow handed the letter to Gibbons, who read it quickly.

"My God," Gibbons said.

Harrow asked, "Recognize the address?"

The sheriff nodded numbly. Jerking a thumb toward the crackerbox behind him, Gibbons said, "Shelton bought this house after his family died. *This* address?" He held up the letter. "That's the house he lived in when his family was murdered."

My God indeed, Harrow thought.

"Ten years of this man's life," Harrow said, "have been building to this moment."

Gibbons and the rest, including the camera, just stared at him.

"Let's not disappoint him," Harrow said.

Chapter Thirty-four

While the others loaded equipment and crime scene kits back into their vehicles, Harrow made two stops. The first was Jenny Blake, about to get on her bus.

"Find me everything you can about Shelton," Harrow told her. "Find out what happened to his family, and get me everything you can about the investigation. Apparently there were *two* inquiries— local followed by state, when there were some conflict of interest concerns raised."

She frowned. "But aren't you going after Shelton now?"

"Yes. I may be in the thick of it when you come up with anything."

"But you want it anyway?"

"I could well need it. Boil it down."

"I'll try not to be verbose," she said with a perfectly straight face, then she disappeared up into the bus.

Next stop was audio expert Nancy Hughes. The blonde with the ponytail was packing up her boom mike to put in the trunk of the rental car.

He asked, "Can you rig me a special earpiece?"

"How special?"

"I need it for the usual reasons, particularly so Jenny can get to me. But for the main feed, I want to hear the sheriff and his deputies communicating."

Hughes sneaked a glance over at the Tahoe, where the sheriff was conferring with his two deputies. "You don't trust the local good old boys?"

"Our suspect has an unhappy history with local law enforcement. There'll be guns and more guns at this shindig. I just want to know who's doing what, so neither Carmen nor I wind up collateral damage."

Nodding, Hughes said, "I don't think that'll be a problem—I may need some help tapping into their radio frequency."

"Check in with Jenny on that, but try not to take up too much of her time."

"Okay. Still, J.C.—that'll be a lot of voices in your head."

He gave up half a smile. "Maybe I'm used to that kind of thing."

She grinned back, and took him by the elbow into the makeup Winnebago, where she wired him for sound and provided the earpiece.

Minutes later, when Harrow emerged, Gibbons came over. "J.C.! You want to ride shotgun with me again?"

"Sure, Herm. Particularly if it's a real shotgun."

"Ha! Come on, then."

The deputies Gibbons had summoned from Smith Center had already set up a perimeter at the Shelton house. As Gibbons drove, he radioed to reroute them to the new target, and told them to set up a much tighter perimeter there—nothing in, nothing out.

Glancing at Harrow, Gibbons said, "You know that means your cameras too."

"I'd do the same," Harrow said with a shrug.

And back in his sheriff days, he would have. But now he knew that Hathaway and Arroyo were used to working commando style, even if the crew from the Topeka affiliate wasn't. No matter how big a perimeter Gibbons set up, no matter how tight, his two principal cameramen would find a way to get the shots.

And at this point, Harrow doubted if he could even call them off if he wanted to. Hard news was in the air, and this was the *Crime Seen!* story to end all *Crime Seen!* stories . . . maybe literally.

Shifting subjects, Harrow asked the sheriff, "What exactly did happen to Shelton's family?"

He'd pitched the ball casually, lobbed it in; but there it was.

At the wheel, the square-jawed Gibbons gave him a sharp look in the darkened car. "You of all people can't be thinking of taking *his* side?"

That response blindsided Harrow.

He tried to chalk it up to Gibbons being defensive about his old boss's reputation. After all, the state police had already questioned their investigation, and found no wrongdoing.

"It's not about taking sides, Herm. It's about going in to talk to this guy, and wanting the background, so he doesn't just dismiss me out of hand."

"Fair enough," Gibbons said, feathers unruffling. "Shelton worked second shift at the radiator factory in Smith Center. It was a Friday in September, ninety-nine. He got off early that day. Gabe always claimed he took half a day off, to go home and surprise his wife and son with a weekend trip. Which always seemed like a lame-ass story to us, pardon my goddamn French."

"So what happened?"

"Which version you want?"

"How many you got?"

Gibbons sighed. "I've got to tell you, even though I believe *one* of the two versions—and it's sure as hell not Shelton's—there's really no proving either."

"Okay. Start with Shelton's."

"Gabe claimed it was a home invasion. Said that coming from work, he got passed by a speeding car heading the opposite direction. Said there were three men inside, and all of 'em were wearing black ski masks. Then when he got home, Shelton says, he found his family murdered. Shot, almost execution-style."

"And the other version?"

"It's a simple story, about as old as they come. We think, a lot of us anyway, that Shelton committed the murders himself."

"Why d'you think that?"

"For one thing, he got off early, at seven-thirty p.m., and the 911 call didn't come in until after ten.

Where was he, for all that time? Coroner placed the time of death between eight and nine."

"Where did Shelton say he was?"

Gibbons shook his head, and his smile was knowing. "You'll love this—said when he saw his family murdered, he flew into a rage, and went looking for that suspicious car he'd passed."

Harrow said nothing for a while. Having been in Shelton's place—or anyway the place Shelton claimed to have been in—he could see how the man might have raced off looking for the killers, full of rage and sorrow and revenge.

On the other hand, this was just the sort of alibi that guilty suspects made up, spur of the moment.

Harrow asked, "Did he find the car?"

The sheriff grunted a mirthless laugh. "Yeah— right where he left it: in his imagination."

The night out the Tahoe windows was washed in moonlight, the world an ivory-blue that would have been soothing in other circumstances.

"So," Harrow said, "Shelton claims he went out searching for the intruders' car—then what?"

"Said, after a while, he just pulled over, and parked. And sat there and cried."

Harrow could believe that; anyone who'd been through a similar tragedy could. But a hard-bitten law enforcement guy like Gibbons could easily shrug it off.

"Anybody see him, Herm? Sitting by the road crying? You said it yourself—Lebanon's not a very big town."

Gibbons shook his head. "Nobody came forward, and we put out the word, that's for goddamn sure.

What's more, Gabe couldn't even remember *where* he parked."

"Convenient," Harrow said, his skepticism outweighing his empathy. "Could he identify the car? Did he get the plate numbers or anything?"

"At first, all he could say was that it was a dark four-door."

"At first?"

"Yeah. When he was first interviewed, that is. Later, he said it was a dark brown Ford Crown Victoria."

"Like so many cops use, right?"

Gibbons nodded. "In the second interview, maybe an hour or so after the first? Suddenly he's sure the car was one of the two unmarked Crown Vics the county owned back then."

Which sounded as weak to Harrow as it probably had to the investigating officers. Witnesses who changed or enhanced their stories automatically slid from the witness category to the suspect list. That Shelton had gone from something so vague to something so specific—especially implicating the sheriff's department—had to raise alarm bells.

Harrow said, "Surely he'd didn't just pull that out of the air, deputies killing his family?"

"Pulled it outta his ass is where he pulled it from."

Harrow tried again: "Why would the sheriff and his people want to kill Shelton's family?"

Gibbons managed a feeble grin. "That question came up at the time too."

Again, Harrow had to try a second time: "And?"

". . . There were real estate developers or speculators or what-have-you, buying up property in that neighborhood, around then. Shelton claimed the real estate people were using sheriff's deputies as muscle—you know, to force people to sell."

"And were they?"

Gibbons frowned at his rider.

Harrow met the gaze evenly. "Chief, I have to ask."

"Yeah, I suppose you do. And I have to answer. And the answer is no."

"How'd Shelton get that idea?"

Shrugging, Gibbons said, "You ask me, he was looking to deflect the blame from himself, and the deputies were a target of convenience. After all, we were crawling all over him at that moment. He just made up the first thing that came to mind."

"No deputies ever worked for those developers?"

"I didn't say that. A lot of law enforcement guys work second jobs, and in particular do security work for this party and that one. Probably some of our boys did that kind of thing for the real-estate boys. So what?"

Out the window, Harrow could make out a neighborhood that had a few houses and several obviously derelict homes, and some vacant lots. This late at night, no lights were on—the area looked like a ghost town. Still, even in a hamlet where everyone was early-to-bed and early-to-rise, he'd expect to see a light here and there.

But there was nothing.

"Your deputies clear the neighborhood already?"

Gibbons seemed puzzled, then, after a second, got it. "Oh, no . . . this neighborhood was pretty much all bought up by those speculators. It's been sitting vacant for a while now."

"Why let it sit? If they're developers, why don't they develop it?"

"Companies that own the houses think they have a plan. Been talk for years about a new four-lane, north-south highway to connect Interstates seventy and eighty. Hasn't gone through yet, but one of these days . . ."

Harrow saw it instantly. "And the speculators feel they're sitting on a goldmine."

"I suppose."

"Are they right?"

Gibbons gave an indifferent shrug. "Not my field."

Moments later, the sheriff pulled the Tahoe to the curb, and killed the lights. The pair sat in the dark for a few seconds. A deputy leading the parade of *Crime Seen!* vehicles stopped a block farther back.

"Across the street, in the next block," Gibbons said, with a nod in that direction. "Second house."

From this distance, Harrow could barely make out the shadowy outline of the structure. "What's the plan?"

Gibbons's face was a blank mask. "Well, we're sure as hell not gonna wait for the SWAT team."

"Because the county doesn't have one?"

"Bingo. But we *do* have a sharpshooter in Colby Wilson. You met him."

Harrow nodded.

"He can pick a fly off a dog's ass," Gibbons said, "at five hundred yards."

"How often does that come up?"

The two old pros exchanged grins.

The sheriff made a radio call to make sure the perimeter was up. The deputies confirmed the neighborhood had been isolated.

"So your plan," Harrow said, "is let Colby take him out?"

"That's it."

"I have a Plan B, if you'd care to hear it."

Gibbons said nothing.

"Herm, let *me* talk to him. Let *me* bring him in."

The sheriff's eyes met Harrow's. "Are you freakin' nuts, son?"

Gibbons reminded Harrow of himself when he'd been sheriff back in Story County. If the positions were reversed, he might have said much the same thing.

"I'm asking for a reason, Herm, and it's not crazy."

Gibbons stared at him, waiting.

"That's my team member in there."

No reaction.

"The note Shelton left at his house was addressed to me. He *wants* to talk—and he wants to talk to *me*."

"*Or* he wants to kill the big-deal TV star and get his fifteen minutes."

Harrow couldn't really debate that one. "Maybe, but if he blames the sheriff's office for the deaths of his family, what do you think he'll do to my associate, if he sees one of your men?"

Gibbons considered that.

"And," Harrow went on, "if he spots Wilson targeting him with a sniper scope, what are Carmen Garcia's odds to grow old enough to see her grandchildren?"

"Not so good," Gibbons admitted.

"Herm," Harrow said, shifting in the seat, "this bastard killed my wife and son. I have killed him in my daydreams and my nightmares—trust me, you can't want him dead more than I do. But more than anything right now, outdistancing even revenge, I value Carmen's life."

Gibbons sighed. "I can understand you putting your teammate first. But you and I know, we'd be doing the world a favor to take this prick out with a head shot, and save a whole lot of money and a whole lot of grief."

"Maybe not. Maybe we want him alive. There are fifty-some murders out there, with twenty-some families attached, that need closure. He could provide that. We owe those families more than we owe the taxpayers a savings."

For a very long time, Gibbons just sat there staring out the windshield considering his options.

"All right," the sheriff said at last. "But you wear a vest and, no matter what, you don't go in that house. Otherwise, no deal."

"Fine," Harrow said, not willing to push the negotiation any further. "And I'm already wearing my Kevlar longjohns. . . ."

They got out, careful not to slam the SUV's doors, and moved to the back of the vehicle, where the sheriff got out a boldly labeled SHERIFF'S DEPT bulletproof vest, and put it on. As Gibbons was doing this, Laurene Chase and Billy Choi appeared at Harrow's side.

Laurene said, "Deputy wouldn't let the cameras any closer back there than the next block over."

She gave Harrow a raised-brow look that told

him Hathaway, Arroyo, and their audio teammates were moving in covertly.

"That's good," Harrow said. "You two hang right here."

Gibbons said, "Your boss is right—no closer than this."

"Sure about that?" Choi asked Harrow, ignoring the sheriff.

"You have your orders," Harrow said ambiguously.

Chapter Thirty-five

Together, Harrow and Gibbons crossed the street and moved up close to the first house. When they were safely into the shadows, Harrow looked back to see Laurene and Choi still beside the Tahoe, but with pistols drawn now, and obviously planning on following at a distance. They'd understood he intended them to ignore his instructions.

Gibbons withdrew his pistol and held it barrel down at his side. Harrow plucked the nine millimeter from his waistband, and the gun felt good in his grasp, an extension of his hand. He flipped the safety off and checked to make sure a bullet resided in the chamber.

The pair crept house-to-house like Kevlar-wearing, heavily armed kids playing ding-dong ditch. When they got to the corner of the cross street before Shelton's block, they hesitated, Gibbons covering Harrow as he sprinted across and then cut through the yard of the corner house, to plaster himself against its wall, chest heaving.

Then Harrow returned the favor, as Gibbons crossed the street and pressed himself to the wall next to him.

Glancing back, Harrow could see Choi and Chase mimicking their moves half a block behind.

Harrow slipped the pistol in his waistband, but at the small of his back, safety off. If need be, he could get to it, easy.

Gibbons whispered, "Sure you want to do this, son?"

"Oh yeah."

"Well, then—let's go pay a call on a freakin' maniac. . . ."

Staying in the shadows close to the abandoned house, Harrow and Gibbons crossed the yard. Now that he was closing in on his target, Harrow could see the house where he'd been invited by the killer of his family.

The old two-story home had a long wooden un-enclosed porch of the kind where a swing once had been, and had once been white, but even in the dark Harrow could see neglect had turned it dingy gray.

No lights.

That was no different from the other houses on the block, and Harrow hadn't expected to see any. No curtains either, but blinds were pulled down over windows on the second floor.

As they drew closer, Gibbons—a few steps in the lead—stopped jerkily short, and Harrow pulled up even with him.

"*Sheriff's just seen me, Mr. Harrow,*" said a voice from the porch.

Gibbons's pistol was pointing at the darkness.

Then the killer stepped from the shadows and into the moonlight, his back to the house as he gripped his human shield with an arm looped round her waist, and held an automatic pistol to her temple.

Carmen Garcia wore boxer-style shorts and a Kansas Jayhawks sweatshirt that looked way too big, like a little girl playing dress-up in the oversized sweatshirt. Her hair was disheveled, but otherwise she appeared unharmed.

Her eyes revealed fear, but—at least with Harrow and Gibbons on the scene—she seemed to be keeping it under control.

Good, Harrow thought, his eyes on her. *You're doing good. . . .*

Shelton was in white short-sleeved shirt and black jeans, as best Harrow could tell.

Pressing the pistol's snout to Carmen's left temple, his voice oddly matter of fact, Shelton said, "The sheriff disappears, or it's over right now."

Gibbons stood firm, his pistol pointed at the killer's head, only a splinter of which was visible behind Carmen.

"I can take him," Gibbons said, his voice icy.

"No," Harrow snapped. "Back off."

"I can *take* him, I said."

A head shot would mean all motor functions turned off like a switch—Harrow knew that damn well. But not much of Shelton's head was showing.

And plenty of Carmen's was.

Crouching down behind his hostage even more, Shelton yelled, "Gibbons needs to back off *now!*"

"You miss and kill my associate, Herm," Harrow said softly, his tone just as frigid as the sheriff's, "then you and I are going to have a real problem. You agreed that I could talk to this man—let me do it."

Slowly, with obvious reluctance, Gibbons lowered his weapon, and his stance relaxed.

Gruffly he said, "Be right next door if you need me."

As the sheriff backed away, Harrow eased to the left, putting himself between the man on the porch and the retreating lawman, halting the pissing contest between the two armed parties before it came to Carmen—or any, or all of them—getting killed.

Shelton was still trying to keep an eye on Gibbons as he receded into near-darkness.

"Look at me, Mr. Shelton," Harrow said. "I'm the one you wanted to talk to—here I am. Look at me."

Slowly, the killer's attention shifted to Harrow.

"I'm here," Harrow said. "You don't need to send any more messages."

From behind Carmen, who looked only slightly more relaxed by having the sheriff in the next yard, Shelton said, "You . . . you know I've been sending messages?"

"Sending messages, and creating a target. Yes."

"Lebanon," Shelton said, his head popping out just momentarily, revealing an extraordinarily awful smile in an ordinary face. His blue eyes didn't seem to blink much. "The center point. Where it began. Where it ends."

"Was there no easier way, Mr. Shelton? Did my family have to die to make up for the loss of yours? Did so many families *have* to die?"

Shelton was quiet for a long moment—night sounds, insects, birds, rustling trees, provided an eerie orchestration.

Finally, the man holding Carmen managed, "Sacrifices had to be made. Innocent blood is always part of a sacrifice. I'm sorry about your family, Mr. Harrow. I'm sorry about all of them. But they did not die in vain. You *are* here. And my message will be heard."

"What *is* your message, Mr. Shelton?" His voice seemed calm, but within him, Harrow was waging a battle with his emotions, fighting the instinct to rush this sick bastard and blow his demented brains all over that porch, and if Carmen weren't in harm's way right now, that's exactly what he'd do.

From behind the wide-eyed Carmen, Shelton blurted words like pus exploding from a squeezed boil: *"They killed my wife and son!"*

"Easy," Harrow said, and patted the air, trying to calm both Shelton and his hostage. And himself.

"*That* is my message," Shelton said, his composure back. "Those selfish, evil bastards murdered my family, and left me in a world of pain."

"*Who* murdered your family, Mr. Shelton?"

"Brown, Gibbons, their deputies—the whole wretched lot of them . . . They're in it *together*."

Carmen's expression begged Harrow to be careful.

"Mr. Shelton—you need to put the gun down, and talk to me. I promise you will have time in front of my cameras to deliver your complete message to the public."

"You'll edit it to—"

"No! You are too important now. You have sent messages that have been heard all over this land, but not *understood*. This is your chance to correct that. To explain."

Shelton seemed to be thinking this option over. Harrow couldn't see much of the man, with Carmen a helpless puppet in front of him; but perhaps Harrow's words were getting through. . . .

"You know, Mr. Shelton, some say *you* killed *your* family."

"Don't *ever* say that!" The one eye visible flared. "I'll kill her! I'll kill her right now and—"

Carmen was holding her breath, frozen in fear.

"I am not saying that, Mr. Shelton! I am saying that the messages you've sent seem to say you'd be capable of such a thing. I know all too well that you *have* killed other men's families . . . why not your own?"

Carmen's eyes narrowed, questioning Harrow's tack.

"*Stop saying that!* Stop saying that. You're wrong; you're misinterpreting everything I've meant to say."

"That, Mr. Shelton, is why you need to put the gun down, and go in front of our cameras and explain yourself to the world. Explain that you would never have harmed your family."

Almost entirely hidden behind his hostage now, Shelton spoke in a clear but oddly small voice in the quiet night: "How did you *feel*, Harrow, when they accused *you* of killing your family?"

". . . I felt terrible. It made an unbearable sorrow more unbearable."

"Well . . . I'm sorry for that. But you *did* get the message, didn't you?"

"I . . . I did."

"And now you know that I didn't kill my family. Because I know you didn't kill yours."

This logic was nothing Harrow wished to spend time exploring. All he wanted right now was to talk this pathetic but so very dangerous creature into giving up and letting Carmen go.

A vein twitching in Harrow's forehead was the only hint that under his calm exterior he was fighting the urge to jump the rail of the porch and shove the nine millimeter in the man's mouth or maybe just strangle him; the desire to destroy the monster that killed Ellen and David coursed in him like lava, burning through his every capillary, vein, and artery.

"You can take my word," Shelton said, "as the man who killed your family, I did not kill my own."

Carmen's eyes were wide with fear, but managed to convey to Harrow that she didn't understand this insane reasoning any more than he did.

Only Harrow *did* understand. It reflected how twisted his own path had been that he knew damn well Shelton confessing the murders of Ellen and David, freely, was a gesture of sorts, a blood-stained olive branch.

They had a bond. And only the lunatic on that porch, and the man below who'd been driven half-mad by the lunatic's actions, could understand that bond.

"I believe you, Mr. Shelton. Why don't I come up there, and we'll discuss this further?"

"I like you where you are."

"No, you need to meet me halfway. You let me take Carmen's place, and we can work the rest of it out. It'll be a show of good faith."

A bit more of Shelton's head became visible over Carmen's shoulder as the killer got a better look at Harrow.

"All right," Shelton said. "You take a step at a time and wait for me to say take another."

"Fine."

"And I want your hands up!"

"Fine."

Harrow approached the stairs—six of them—and took the first one. Shelton moved back, closer to the front door, but the angle of the moon put him in more light. Carmen's eyes weren't so wide now; she seemed almost relaxed, or as relaxed as a person could be with a gun snout to her forehead.

"All right, another step."

Harrow took it.

"Another."

Harrow did so.

Then Shelton's eyes darted right, and Harrow realized the killer had seen something he didn't like.

"You stay *put*, Herm!" Shelton yelled. The arm around Carmen's waist tightened and she made a sound, like a child picked up too roughly. "You stay the hell *put!*"

Harrow glanced over and saw Gibbons at the edge of the shadows of the house next door—he was motionless, but for the weapon in his hand, dropping by degrees.

"Back off, Sheriff," Harrow said, loud, firm. "Mr. Shelton is complying with everything I'm asking. Let me *do* this."

Gibbons dissolved into the darkness.

After several long seconds, Shelton said, "Okay, Mr. Harrow. Take another step."

He stepped, and in the earpiece whose occasional cop chatter he'd been ignoring, Harrow finally heard something worth registering: "Suspect in better light. Still no shot."

The voice of the deputy, Colby Wilson.

The sniper was probably deep in the shadows of the houses across the street or possibly on a rooftop. Harrow risked a glimpse right, and caught sight of a boom mike peeking out at the back corner of a porch—either Hughes or Ingram had moved in pretty close. Harrow had gotten away with the glance because the killer's attention was still on Gibbons, or anyway the darkness where the sheriff lurked.

So Harrow risked a quick look in the other direction, and thought he saw a part in the curtains on the first floor of the nearest abandoned house. The sniper? Or the unblinking eye of a camera?

"Mr. Harrow! What are you looking at?"

Harrow's eyes snapped back to the killer. "I'm just nervous."

"Don't con me. You try conning me, and she's dead and you're dead. And I'm dead, but I don't care because I died a long time ago, so don't you *con* me."

Harrow gestured easily with the upraised hands.

"I was checking to see if my camera crew was in position and getting this."

The slice of his face visible behind Carmen's included an eye that widened. "*Are* they? That would be good."

"Yes, it would. It would get your message out in a much better way."

"Are they out there?"

"I don't know. You said, *don't con you.* I *think* so. But I just don't know."

Shelton allowed Harrow up the final few steps, and then Harrow was facing Carmen and her captor—perhaps four feet separating them. Ivory washed over Carmen, and she looked fragile and lovely and, of course, terrified.

In Harrow's ear, the deputy said, "If Harrow'd move a step to his left, I could cap this sumbitch."

But Harrow moved not an inch, his eyes on the slender wall of flesh that was Carmen, behind which her captor hid, only barely visible there.

What had happened to Jenny Blake? Where was her intel?

Harrow felt the situation slipping like sand through his fingers. Maybe he should dive left and let Gibbons's man take the shot. . . .

"Okay, Mr. Shelton. Here I am. Let her go, and I'll be your hostage."

"I let her go, and a sniper takes me out. Probably that shit Wilson. *He's* in on it too, you know!"

"We had a deal. . . ."

"I want a TV camera. You said I could talk to a camera."

In his left ear, Harrow finally heard Jenny: "Shelton's wife was named Cathy and his son Mark."

Harrow said, "How do you think Cathy and Mark would feel about what you're doing? About what you've been doing for the past ten years?"

The eye on view flinched, but the killer's comeback was quick: "How would *your* wife feel about you tracking me down, all over hell and TV and gone?"

"She'd hate it," Harrow said.

"Like mine would what I've done."

"And yet you kept on."

"I did. And you're here, aren't you? What our gentle wives would have done is beside the point. You and me, Mr. Harrow, we're men. Screwed-up men. We do what we can. We do what we have to do. Anyway, the dead don't get to have opinions. And your opinion is, you'd like to kill me."

Carmen's eyes pleaded with Harrow. He wasn't sure what she was begging him to do. He wasn't sure she even knew.

"Maybe," Harrow said. "Maybe not. We both know this much—nothing brings them back. Not revenge, not justice, nothing. I'd guess you know that better than anybody, Mr. Shelton."

"Sheriff Gibbons was lead investigator," Jenny whispered in his ear. "Shelton was his only suspect."

Wondering why the sheriff had omitted being the lead investigator, Harrow said, "Why does Gibbons think you killed Cathy and Mark?"

"He doesn't—he was in on it. *He's* part of the conspiracy."

"I need to hear about this conspiracy. America needs to hear. It's time to let Carmen go, Mr. Shelton, and get those cameras up here and—"

But Shelton was somewhere else: "They wanted the land, all the land," he was saying. "The ones that wouldn't sell, they drove out."

"But you *did* sell," Harrow said.

His face flashed from behind Carmen's and his brow was clenched and his mouth twisted. "Only after they killed my family! That money they gave me, their *blood* money, *that's* what's financed my deliveries. Oh, I bought that little crummy shack on the other side of town, but the rest, the insurance money for Cathy and Mark, every dollar and cent's been used to deliver my message to the world. To let everyone know the kind of greedy goddamn grubbing that's been going on in the center of America."

"And what *is* going on, Mr. Shelton?"

"I told you! They want all the land."

Jenny whispered, "Shelton sold out to Castano Developments."

"So Castano Developments wants all the land in this neighborhood?"

"Not just here! Everywhere."

"The whole town?"

"Everywhere, all of it!"

"They want *all* the land."

"*Now* you're getting it."

"And they kill people to get it."

"Yes, yes, yes—and they're using the deputies and cops, and maybe even the state police as their hatchet men."

"The state police?"

"Yes, them too. I went to them after Cathy and Mark were killed. They came back and said they couldn't find anything either. That meant *they* had to be in on it too. Maybe even the FBI—they listened nice and polite when I drove up to Kansas City, to tell them all about it. But they didn't do a goddamn thing. Didn't even pretend to do something, like the state police did. *No one* has . . . not till you, Mr. Harrow. Not till you."

Carmen's eyes begged him: *Stop him . . . end this. . . .*

"When did you talk to all these people?"

"In the weeks and months after the murders, but they didn't do a damn thing. *That's* why I started delivering the messages myself. I knew sooner or later *someone* would come to my rescue."

Harrow knew these were the ramblings of a lunatic mind. Shelton thought the evil developers were after his land, and everyone's land everywhere, and that all of law enforcement had conspired to kill his family.

At this point, the only remaining question was how to get Carmen away from this crazy, before the man decided to deliver one last message. . . .

"Mr. Shelton, how long have you been after these people? Ten years?"

"Ten years."

"Well, I've been investigating this for only a few months. I did look into my family's deaths, but it took me all these years, and some corn from this county, to bring me to this porch. So if you want us to stop them, you've got to share the information you've found. That's going to take time, and we can't do it here, not like this. We'll get you in front of a camera, and you will tell your story, and you will tell it in detail."

Shelton said nothing. The hand with the gun seemed to be shaking, just a little. Was that good, or bad?

"You can't stay on this porch with a gun to my friend's head forever," Harrow said. "Let her go. I'll stay with you as your hostage, until the cameras can come in."

Shelton swallowed. "We could go inside and talk. Where this started. Where they killed them. That would be . . . dramatic, right? Good for TV?"

The gun dropped from Carmen's temple, but Shelton's arm was still looped around her waist as the man shifted, about to ease out from behind the woman, if Harrow was any judge.

And in his right ear Harrow heard: "I've got a shot, do I have a go order?"

From the darkness, where he was shouting into his radio, Gibbons's voice registered for all to hear: "*Go!*"

"Bastards!" Shelton said, and ducked behind Carmen again as the sound split the night and the shot thunked splinteringly into the front door between Harrow and the captor with his hostage.

Shelton's sudden movement caused Carmen to stumble and the two went down in a heap, Carmen screaming, Shelton making animal sounds as they hit the old wooden slats of the porch. Then Shelton was on his knees, pulling Carmen's hair as he tried to bring her up as a shield again, his gun-in-hand rising to take its place at her temple.

Looking down at them, Harrow didn't hesitate—his hand whipped around his back and came back with the nine millimeter, which he aimed and fired in one smooth motion, the bullet punching through Shelton's forehead, the crack of his skull audible, the gunshot itself a thundercrack that seemed to shake the old house.

The gun clunked from the killer's hand to the porch as limp fingers released Carmen's hair, and the self-styled messenger slumped to weathered wooden slats, dead as his family, dead as Harrow's family, oozing brains that had been damaged long prior to the bullet.

Then Carmen was in Harrow's arms, sobbing, holding him tight, as they sat on the bottom porch step. For his part, he just stroked her hair and let her cry.

Chapter Thirty-six

Hathaway and Arroyo were next to Harrow and Carmen, filming even before Gibbons and his men got there.

"Byrnes broke in on *America's Wackiest Wedding Videos*," Hathaway said, obviously stoked. "That's the network's second-biggest show, you know."

Arroyo said, "Whole thing went out on the network live—seven-second delay, of course, in case somebody got shot."

"That's entertainment," Harrow said, and Carmen interrupted her crying to snort a laugh, then returned to her tears.

Even as the cameramen spoke, they never stopped shooting. The audio personnel were moving in now, as well.

Laurene and Choi appeared, and managed to each get in the way of a camera as Harrow helped Carmen to her feet. With Laurene, getting in front of a camera was accidental; with Choi, Harrow wasn't so sure.

Finally he asked Carmen, "How are you doing?"

Her tear-smeared face had a bitter cast. "You talked him down. They didn't have to take that shot."

"I know. Bastards risked both our lives."

"You gonna do something about that, boss?"

"You bet your . . . paycheck."

She managed a feeble smile. "You think I could go back to being a PA now? Stardom suddenly doesn't look so good."

"No going back, Carmen. We're both stuck."

"Are your ears ringing? Mine are."

"You were close to that gunshot. It'll ease up."

That was when Carlos Moreno came up and cornered them, microphone in hand. Apparently Gibbons's perimeter was as secure as a sand castle at high tide.

Moreno thrust the microphone at Carmen.

Harrow was about to slap the goddamn thing aside when she pulled away from him, stood upright.

Moreno said, "Carmen Garcia, we're on live on UBC. How do you feel?"

And the former hostage was instantly "on."

"Well, Carlos, I can tell you this—it's good to be alive. I owe everything to J.C. Harrow, who has to be the bravest man on the planet."

"What about the alleged killer who held you captive?"

"Carlos, I feel bad for Mr. Shelton. He was a very troubled soul. He lost his family, much as J.C. did. . . ."

Harrow had heard enough. He moved toward the sidewalk, where various official vehicles were pulling in.

Sheriff Gibbons came up to him. "You did good, J.C."

"You didn't," Harrow said.

The sheriff's expression might have been the aftermath of a slap. "What the hell . . ."

"Your goddamned deputy tried to gun him down just when I'd talked him into coming in peacefully."

Gibbons took a step back. "We didn't know—we couldn't hear. . . ."

"Hell you couldn't," Harrow said. "You were right next door and heard everything. And the second your guy Wilson had a shot, you told him go for it—risking *my* life, and Carmen's, needlessly . . . and robbing us of a suspect who might clear up countless murder cases."

"Goddamnit, Harrow, he had a gun on the Garcia woman! You would have done the—"

"Same thing? Don't think so. He was *surrendering*, you dick. Your man, and your *go* order, put the two of us in the line of fire. Then I had to do your dirty work for you."

"Well, J.C., I'm sorry you feel that way, but I feel we did the right thing. You'll cool off, and you'll think about it, and—"

Harrow had heard enough of *that* bullshit, too. He walked away from the increasingly noisy scene, needing some silence. Heading toward the crime lab semi, he felt someone fall in next to him.

Laurene Chase.

She gave him a sunny smile. "Rough day at the office?"

He shrugged. "Same-o, same-o."

"Carmen's alive," she said. "*That's* a good day at the office, no matter what else went down."

He nodded, not knowing if he really agreed. He was thrilled Carmen was alive, but he had been so close to bringing in the suspect the same way. . . .

Up ahead, Pall and Anderson were pacing like expectant fathers. Jenny Blake stood off to herself a little, arms folded. They all fell in line behind their boss and his number two, following like puppies.

Harrow's cell vibrated. Checking the caller ID, he saw: DENNIS BYRNES.

Holding out the phone to Laurene, he said, "*You* talk to him."

She took the phone, and he went up the metal stairs and into the crime lab to be alone.

He closed the door and sat down in a chair. The man who had killed his family was dead, killed by Harrow himself. But Ellen and David were gone forever, and any sense of closure was not revealing itself.

Why did he feel so goddamn empty?

And why did this long journey still feel unresolved?

Chapter Thirty-seven

Once Harrow was tucked away in the semi, Laurene Chase and Billy Choi stationed themselves at the stairs, blocking the way, as the other three team members—Pall, Anderson, and Blake—went off to check on Carmen.

The cell Harrow had handed off was throbbing away in Laurene's grasp. Finally she took the call.

Dennis Byrnes's voice exploded in her ear: "Harrow, that was bloody *awesome*! You are the *man*!"

"Mr. Byrnes, this is Laurene Chase. J.C. isn't taking any calls right now. He's winding down. You're obviously aware of what he's been through."

"I am, Ms. Chase, and let me share my enthusiasm and delight with you. You tell J.C. that the UBC switchboard is lit up like Christmas, and the website's crashed, so many viewers trying to get through. This is the moon landing and the final episode of

M*A*S*H and the Super Bowl with Lee Harvey Oswald and Jack Ruby tossed in for good measure."

"And that's a good thing?"

"It's a fantastic thing. This goes beyond our network—every other broadcast network and all the twenty-four-hour news channels are breaking into their regularly scheduled programming, and why? To advertise UBC and *Crime Seen!* You tell J.C. that I don't know how he managed this, but—"

"He didn't 'manage' anything, sir. He did what he promised you he would—he tracked down the murderer of his family and let you broadcast it."

"Ms. Chase, you tell Harrow I want him back in LA tomorrow. We have to get to work and figure out what we're going to do for November sweeps to take advantage of this wave of publicity."

"You do realize, sir, a man is dead, and one of our reporters almost got killed."

"But she *didn't* get killed," Byrnes said. "The star of my show saved her. Christ, Chase, don't you know a happy ending when you see one?"

Laurene clicked off the call, and turned off the phone. Suddenly the lowlifes she'd dealt with back in Waco didn't seem so bad.

Glancing in Choi's direction, she said, "Seems the show's a hit."

The young man shrugged. "You know what they say—give the people what they want. All we need to do to stay popular? Shoot somebody every week. We could take turns."

Laurene didn't smile at that. "That's a little dark, Billy."

"You think? We did something good here, boss lady—we shut down one of the worst serial killers in history. Yet I still feel like I could use a shower."

"I know," she said, and shivered. "I know."

Chris Anderson got to Carmen, with Michael Pall right behind and Jenny Blake trailing. But they all had to wait while Moreno finished his interview with the rescued star.

Hathaway and Arroyo were shooting from different angles, bright lights atop each camera catching their subject in a cross fire, both Hughes and Ingram grabbing sound, with Carmen's teammates media savvy enough by now not to interrupt.

Distant sirens howled and grew closer, and the darkness was alive with headlights heading their way—and not just emergency vehicles, Pall knew. The media, no matter how far they'd have to travel, would get there so fast you'd think they beamed down from a starship. And there would be gawkers too, from hither and yon. The three hundred souls of Lebanon, Kansas, would be waking to find their hamlet grown by ten times or more, and they'd be in the geographical center of not just the United States, but an international media storm.

"Thank you for your time, Carmen," Moreno was saying, giving his co-worker his most earnest look. "I know you must be as exhausted as you are relieved that this ordeal has ended."

Carmen managed a wan smile for the reporter (and the camera), which didn't fade till Hathaway said, "And . . . we're clear."

Moreno gave her a lopsided grin and shook her hand. "Great job, Carmen. Very brave to come straight out of that mess and be so professional."

"Thank you, Carlos," Carmen said, but Pall could tell the weight of it all was starting to settle on the woman. On camera, she'd seemed quietly strong, and her delivery had been halting only when it aided the story she was telling.

But with the camera off, Carmen—in the sweatshirt provided by her late captor—looked battered, as if her legs might give way under her at any second.

This was lost on Moreno, who soon was off in search of the sheriff or Harrow, or some other interview, with Hathaway, Arroyo, and the audio team in the star reporter's wake. But Pall, Anderson, and Blake ringed their co-worker protectively.

"What do you need?" Pall asked her, touching her shoulder lightly, gently.

"I need," Carmen said, trying to smile, but Pall could feel her trembling, "out of these awful clothes. Can I *please* get out of these awful clothes?"

"Let's get you to the bus," Pall said, and put a hand on her far shoulder and the other hand on her near elbow. To the others, he said: "I'll take her— you two make sure no one bothers us."

Uniformed officers seemed to be everywhere, directing traffic and trying to get an ambulance in for Shelton, even though everyone in the United States with a TV knew there was no real rush.

Pall and his charge reached the bus and got up inside, Jenny leading the way, and Anderson staying outside to guard the door.

Jenny had been prepared for this—which impressed Pall—and had a fresh change of clothes ready from Carmen's own suitcase, underthings, jeans, a Juicy Couture shirt and sandals. Carmen went into the restroom, was in there a while, presumably washing up, and emerged, if not a new woman, a fresher-looking one.

Jenny led the former hostage to a chaise lounge and sat with her, while Pall brought Carmen a bottle of water, which she gulped greedily, twice, then just stopped and seemed to be letting her stomach settle. Pall sat down on the lounge opposite, sitting forward, watchfully.

The three sat in silence for several minutes, Carmen starting to sip the water again. Jenny was rubbing the woman's arm lightly, as if letting Carmen know she was not alone. Again Pall was impressed with Jenny, whose quiet, loner demeanor seemed to be slipping away.

Finally, her eyes unblinking and almost dead-looking, Carmen said, "You know, he didn't *have* to die."

Pall blinked. "Of course he did. J.C. had no choice—the guy was about to shoot you. Harrow saved your life! We all saw what happened."

"No, I know. J.C. saved me—I owe him my life, I really, really do. But before that? Just ten seconds before that, Shelton was going to give himself up. He'd already let loose of me. He was about to go with J.C. and be questioned. And then they took a shot at him, and everything changed."

"In hostage situations," Pall said, "cops make tough calls like that all the time."

"It feels wrong," Carmen insisted. "J.C. was talking to him. Settling him down. Bringing him over."

"Carmen, the man was a—"

"They'd been talking about the company that was buying up the land." Carmen's eyes were bright now. "Harrow got him talking about the developer, the company—*what* was it?"

"Castano Developments," Jenny said.

"That's it," Carmen said. "Shelton really wanted to talk about that company. He wanted to open up. All of the killings, they were messages. Shelton was—in his sick, sick way—trying to tell us something. Only, then somebody took that shot."

"Sniper missed," Pall said.

Carmen shook her head, firmly. "No reason for him to shoot. Shelton was surrendering."

"The sniper couldn't possibly have known that."

"But the sheriff was nearby," Carmen insisted, getting worked up. "*He* gave the order."

Jenny slipped an arm around her and said, "Honey, you need to rest. You've been through so much."

Carmen swallowed and sighed and, finally, nodded.

"Why don't you stretch out right here?" Jenny suggested. "Just rest and maybe even sleep a little."

"I'd rather sit," Carmen said.

"Well, that's fine, too. . . ."

"I've been lying down a lot lately." She gave them a weak smile and then began to cry. Jenny had tissues ready, and Pall sat on the other side of her and was there when Carmen folded herself to him, sobbing.

Pall told Jenny, "Go ahead and go. I'll stay with her."

Jenny nodded. "I have some stuff I need to do anyway."

She squeezed Carmen's shoulder and went forward to the little office area behind the front seating.

Really, Jenny had only scratched the surface of Castano Developments, getting Harrow some key facts to use in the showdown with Shelton. But she was not one to leave stones unturned, and was anxious to get back to it.

Castano Developments, it seemed, was really little more than a shell company owned by something called Braun Realty, in turn owned by something called Marron Holdings, itself a partnered company with a firm called Brun Limited, a subsidiary of Kahverengi International, whose CEO was listed as someone named Danyal Braz.

And that was when she figured it out.

Soon she was off the bus and running. On informal guard outside the semi, Choi and Laurene saw her coming, and both wisely cleared her a path.

Within the semi, she found Harrow, sitting at a work station, his head in his hands. He heard her rush in and glanced up.

"Not now, Jenny. I need time to—"

"No time for foolishness, boss." She fired up the computer adjacent to him and sat.

He was frowning at her. "*What* did you say to me?"

She almost smiled, the implied "young lady" so strong.

"Boss—Shelton? He was right."

"What Shelton was," Harrow said, "was crazy."

"No argument. But he was also right."

Interested now, Harrow asked, "What was he right about?"

"He said the deputies were the muscle for the company that wanted to buy the land, didn't he?"

"He did, but he also included the state police and the FBI in on the conspiracy."

"Take a gander," she said, pointing at the screen.

Harrow scooched his chair closer and peered at the monitor. "Danyal Braz?"

"Funny spelling, huh?" Jenny said.

She pulled up the list of the companies she'd traced to and from Castano Developments.

"Here they are," she said, "the whole chain of shell companies, subsidiaries, and partnered companies . . . all run by the same man."

She hit the print button and, when the list popped out, handed it to Harrow.

He read aloud: "Castano Developments, Braun Realty, Marron Holdings, Brun Limited, and Kahverengi International."

"Notice anything?" she asked.

"Yeah," Harrow said. "Tongue twisters."

"That's because," Jenny said, "the names are all in different languages."

Harrow's eyes tightened. He glanced at the list, then back at her. "Go on."

"Castano, Braun, Marron—pronounced Mar-ón—Brun, and Kahverengi," she said. "Castano? Italian. Braun? German, Marrón? Spanish. Brun? Portuguese. Kahverengi? Turkish. And Braz? Polish . . . but they all translate into English as the same word. . . ."

"Brown," Harrow said.

She smiled like a slightly demented pixie and nodded the same way. "The CEO of Kahverengi International is Danyal Braz—translated from Arabic and Polish, you get Daniel Brown. As in former Lebanon *Sheriff* Daniel Brown."

"And that's probably not a coincidence," Harrow said dryly.

"My guess is," Jenny said, "when I track down the board of directors and stockholders of Kahverengi International? There'll be *more* familiar names."

"Get on it," Harrow said, rising. "I've got someone to see."

"You got it, boss."

"Oh! One more thing—track down the ubiquitous Daniel Brown. If he *is* on his way back to town, as the current sheriff says, I want him met at the city limits."

"By the police?" Jenny asked.

"No. Have Chris Anderson do it—tell him to lay on the Southern charm. Brown should be told we want to interview him for the show—as an outstanding citizen of Lebanon. Tell Chris to get him in front of a camera crew and just stall his ass with local color questions."

"Cool," she said.

Chapter Thirty-eight

Harrow came down out of the trailer like his hair was on fire, and Laurene and Choi fell in with him.

"Where we going?" Laurene asked.

"To see the sheriff."

"What for?" Choi asked.

"To ask him about a land deal."

The trio moved down the middle of a street crowded now with bystanders, reporters, state cops, and God only knew who else. The *Killer TV* teammates were heading toward the house where Harrow had lately confronted a serial killer of record proportions.

Gibbons was holding court in the front yard of the Shelton house, his deputies around him in a semicircle, the stocky sniper Colby Wilson immediately to Gibbons's right.

Carlos Moreno and the two camera crews were off to one side, taking a brief break, until they saw

Harrow coming. Then they all jumped to their feet at once, and the red lights came on, little demon eyes burning in the night.

As he approached the conclave of uniforms, Harrow received a thin-lipped smile from Gibbons, who said, "There's the man of the hour."

With Laurene and Choi behind him, Harrow positioned himself a few feet from Gibbons, facing the semicircle of local law enforcement. The camera eyes and microphones moved in, keeping their distance, but—like snipers—with their targets well in view.

"We haven't really had a chance to talk, Sheriff," Harrow said pleasantly. "There'll be some follow-up, of course. My firearm killed a man. You'll want to take my statement."

"Of course," Gibbons said, good-naturedly. "But that can wait till tomorrow, J.C."

"Sure. There'll be a lot of do tomorrow. For example, we'll need to dig into this whole Kahverengi International matter."

Gibbons flinched at the foreign word, then squinted as if he hadn't understood. "Afraid I don't know what you're talking about, J.C. This is Kansas. We don't deal with international anything, except maybe Harvester."

His deputies chuckled.

"You're being modest, Herm. You have a distinguished local citizen, ex-sheriff Daniel Brown, who does considerable international business, and land development all over the map . . . including right here in Lebanon."

"I suppose that's so. But it doesn't have anything to do with this tragedy tonight."

"Well, Gabriel Shelton thought it did. Just the mad ravings of a serial killer, though, right? If we were to take his lunacy seriously, then we'd have to believe Sheriff Brown and his deputies, ten years or so ago . . . *you* were one, weren't you, Herm, a deputy of Brown's? You'd have to believe a crazy story like deputies strong-arming local people into selling out when they didn't want to, all because the sheriff thought a new highway was coming through, and that land would become valuable . . . Ridiculous. Crazy on the face of it."

Gibbons and Wilson, and several other of the deputies, were getting fidgety, glancing at the cameras and boom mikes that were picking this up.

"J.C.," Gibbons said tightly, "this needs to wait for another day. It's not the kind of thing to air in public, now, is it? I mean, a person could get in trouble with libel or slander or that kind of thing, with fool talk like this."

"Oh, but Gabe Shelton's way past getting sued. Your crack shot, Deputy Wilson, almost killed him, and the attempt put me in a position where I *had* to. So you'll understand why his words kind of . . . haunt me. I don't take them seriously, of course, but we learned by studying his 'messages' that there was a method to his madness, as the saying goes."

"You need to put a lid on this, Harrow. You are on *very* shaky ground. . . ."

"Way I see it, Sheriff? Shelton was a monster, all right, but it took some greedy, violent bastards to turn him into one. Shelton's family, mine, twenty-some families, all torn to pieces just so some solid citizens could own some land, and maybe make some money, for themselves and their own families."

Gibbons turned away from Harrow and pushed the air with his hands. "Gonna have to ask you folks from the media to move back now—this is a crime scene."

"It's a *crime* scene, all right," Harrow said. "If Shelton's to be believed, his wife and children were murdered by three men in black ski masks driving a vehicle that belonged to the local sheriff's department. He thought deputies had come into his house to threaten his family—maybe things got out of hand, and murder wasn't the intention. But murder was born that night—murder on a grand scale, because Gabe Shelton . . . who must have had his problems all along . . . had something inside him break, and something else inside him trigger. A serial killer was made that night, formed out of other men's greed and brutality. A damaged soul went out and did terrible things, including murdering my wife and family . . . committing the crime done to him, again and again, screaming for attention and justice through his twisted deeds."

Gibbons swivelled and pointed a finger at Harrow, obviously wishing it could be a gun. "Now this talk is going to stop—*right now*. It's inappropriate, and you are embarrassing yourself, Harrow. You need to pull it together and—"

"You don't understand, Sheriff. I'm a TV personality. I just want to interview the lead investigator into the deaths of Cathy and Mark Shelton—and that's *you*, right? And my first question is—why didn't you mention that pertinent fact to us, Herm? Why did I have to find out for myself?"

Gibbons came up very close to Harrow. "You need to go, Harrow. Now. Or I will take you into custody for disturbing the peace."

"Like you did Gabe Shelton?" Harrow whispered; this was for Gibbons, not the microphones or cameras. "That unmarked car he saw was real. The men in the masks were real. I wonder if *you* were one of them?"

The sheriff's eyes popped; his mouth twitched, and he backed away. Then he said to his deputies, "Let's cordon off this crime scene and get these media types out of here! We have work to do!"

The deputies flew into their jobs, and the sheriff came back over to Harrow.

"J.C., you are wrong about this. You are embarrassing yourself. This ended tonight. You killed the man responsible for taking your family away from you. You need to be grateful."

Harrow, calmly, coldly, said, "I wonder if I'm *looking* at the man responsible for taking my family away? Certainly one of them."

Gibbons swallowed, and turned his back to Harrow and went about loudly supervising his deputies as they worked the yellow crime scene tape and batted the media back.

Suddenly Harrow sensed someone at his side: Jenny Blake. She handed him a slip of paper. He read it.

Then Harrow made an announcement in a voice loud enough to freeze the deputies in their motion, and to bring the various cameras and microphones his way again.

"*Excuse me!* I have important information related to the aftermath of this case!"

Pin-drop silence.

"Former Lebanon sheriff Daniel Brown has left the country. His passport was okayed by Homeland Security tonight. He's flying to South America."

Across the yard, the sheriff turned toward Harrow with the look of a wet hound. "That son of a *bitch* . . ."

"Looks like he left you holding the bag, Herm," Harrow said genially. "Who knows? Maybe you can get immunity."

Harrow was having a smoke outside the semi when Deputy Colby Wilson, with the hangdog expression of all time, came tentatively over. The heel of a hand was on his holstered revolver.

"Can I talk to you a second, Mr. Harrow?"

"What do you want, Colby? I've said my piece."

"I, uh . . . haven't said mine. What you said about immunity . . . you think that's a possibility?"

"I do, for the first conspirator who comes forward and comes clean."

He laughed, but it was humorless, more a cough. "Is that what I come to after all these years? Being a conspirator? Who do I go to, Mr. Harrow? Who do I talk to?"

"I'll get someone from the state police," he said, and did.

Because of his knowledge about the case, Harrow was asked by the state police not only to sit in on the interview, but to conduct it. It was irregular, but there was a moment that needed to be seized: right now, Colby Wilson wanted to talk, and he didn't ask for a lawyer to be present.

The interview was held in the *Crime Seen!* lab, since the state police did not under the circumstances wish to borrow facilities from the local authorities.

Colby Wilson said, "I was one of the guys in the car that night—Gibbons knew about it, but he wasn't there."

Harrow asked, "Who else *was* there?"

Wilson gave him three more names, all current Smith County deputies.

"Why kill Cathy Shelton and her boy? Doesn't make sense, Colby."

"We didn't mean to." He wasn't able to look at Harrow. "It was an accident. We went there to scare them. Put the fear of God in 'em, or anyway the fear of Sheriff Brown. We shook her and slapped her around, broke some knickknacks, even some furniture . . . but she had this gun she got to, that we didn't know about. When she aimed that thing at us, we didn't have any choice. It was sort of like . . . self-defense."

Sort of like, Harrow thought.

"And the kid had seen us . . ." The beefy deputy shrugged. "Things got out of hand."

Harrow said nothing.

"At night, I close my eyes, and I see that kid," Wilson said. "I didn't shoot him myself! I didn't do that! But I'll never get past that."

"Some things," Harrow said, "you never do get past."

Chapter Thirty-nine

The north-south highway turned out to be no rumor—the I-80–I-70 connector was due to start construction next year, and would be completed in less than three years, making the land Brown and his cronies owned worth tens of millions. Brown and his partners had also bought land in and between every small town along the route of the new highway. A major indoor mall and the United States museum in Lebanon were part of the master plan.

The show on the eighteenth had gone well, particularly a crowd-pleasing segment of Harrow and Laurene Chase on hand when a certain South American government, led by a president who "never missed" *Crime Seen!*, turned over a morose Daniel Brown to Interpol.

Jenny Blake had been surprised by how normal Brown looked—seventyish with a white beard and long hair, like somebody's grandfather, not a monster at all. In profile, a little pudgy, he'd have made a good Santa Claus.

Now, on Monday afternoon, driving back to LA on the *Crime Seen!* bus, gliding across I-70 westbound, Jenny was with Pall, Anderson, Choi, and Carmen, watching satellite TV as Harrow did yet another in an endless parade of interviews.

If he'd gained national attention saving the President (and losing his family) and had become a reluctant star by getting his own crime-busting show, J.C. Harrow was in a galaxy of his own now. Many bad guys had been shot on national TV, but rarely a real one, by a real hero.

A backlash from gun control advocates was already well under way, and fringe types proclaimed (mostly online) that Shelton was either a hero or a victim. *Not a hero certainly,* Jenny thought, *but a victim.* Also a monster—as her friend Carmen could attest.

Valerie Jenkins, the missing bartender with the stray license plate, turned up in Omaha, Nebraska, with a new life that included another bartender gig and a trucker boyfriend she'd followed there.

But other loose ends would be much harder to tie up—twenty-some family killings that would challenge and bedevil law enforcement agencies all over the killer's target-defaced map for months and even years to come.

On the screen, Carlos Moreno held the UBC microphone toward Harrow's rugged movie-star features. Jenny wondered if Carmen wouldn't rather be doing the interview herself; on the other hand, the reporter had declined a plane and requested that she ride back with the team.

Maybe we make her feel safe, Jenny thought.

Anyway, after her ordeal, Carmen could use a little downtime.

Moreno was asking Harrow, "How does it feel, getting an early pickup for a third season?"

"Gratifying," Harrow said. "The team's worked hard so far this season, but we never expected to wrap up our first case in three weeks. Still, we'll have something special ready for November sweeps."

Jenny shook her head. What could they possibly do to top their first three shows?

"You'd be considered a hero just for stopping Gabriel Shelton," Moreno said. "Yet you've kept digging, working to put away the men who wronged the killer of your own family. Why would you do such a thing?"

Harrow paused. Then: "Shelton's family were the first innocent victims. They deserved justice too. Also . . . he said something odd to me, that's stayed with me—he said I'd 'come to his rescue.' Maybe in a way I did."

Chris Anderson came up the aisle and plopped into the seat next to Jenny. They hadn't dated or anything, but Carmen and Laurene might be right— Chris *did* seem to like her. He took her hand.

She shook free from him and said, "Not yet."

"What?" Chris said in his lazy way. "I was just bein' friendly."

Out the windshield, Jenny saw what she'd been

looking for since they left Lebanon—a sign that said WELCOME TO COLORADO.

Sitting back, smiling, Jenny took Chris's hand in hers.

"*Now* it's okay?" he asked, clearly bewildered.

"Sure." Her smile widened. "We're not in Kansas anymore."

Crime Seen! Tips

Thanks to crime scene analyst Chris Kauffman, CLPE, retired lieutenant of the Bettendorf (Iowa) Police Department, who has been so much help to the authors in the past. Thanks also to computer forensics investigator Paul Van Steenhuyse, retired lieutenant, Scott County (Iowa) Sheriff's Office.

Insights were also provided by profiler Steven R. Conlon, retired Assistant Director, Division of Criminal Investigation for the State of Iowa Department of Public Safety; and Matthew T. Schwarz, CLPE, Identification Bureau manager, Davenport (Iowa) Police Department. For behind-the-scenes TV production matters, we were helped by our longtime film and video collaborator, Phillip W. Dingeldein.

Among books consulted were: *Practical Homicide Investigation* (1996), Vernon J. Geberth; *The Encyclopedia of Serial Killers* (2000), Michael Newton; *Mindhunter* (1995), John Douglas and Mark Olshaker; *In the Minds of Murderers* (2007), Paul Roland; and *Profile of a Criminal Mind* (2003), Brian Innes.

Special thanks are due the following: our editor, Michaela Hamilton, who was enthusiastic from the start and supportive throughout; agent Dominick Abel, for his friendship and professionalism; and our wives, Barb and Pam, in-house editors and support systems.

Max Allan Collins, a frequent Mystery Writers of America "Edgar" nominee in both fiction and non-fiction categories, has been hailed as "the Renaissance man of mystery fiction." He has earned an unprecedented fifteen Private Eye Writers of America "Shamus" nominations, winning twice for his Nathan Heller novels, *True Detective* (1983) and *Stolen Away* (1991), and receiving the PWA's Lifetime Achievement Award, "the Eye," in 2006. His other credits include film criticism, short fiction, songwriting, trading-card sets, and movie/TV tie-in novels, including the *New York Times* best-sellers *Saving Private Ryan* and *American Gangster*, winner of the International Association of Tie-In Writers "Scribe" award.

His graphic novel *Road to Perdition* was the basis of the Academy Award–winning feature film starring Tom Hanks and Paul Newman, directed by Sam Mendes. A nominee for both the Eisner and Harvey awards (the "Oscars" of the comics world), Max has many comics credits, including "Dick Tracy"; "Batman"; "Johnny Dynamite"; and his own "Ms. Tree."

An acclaimed and award-winning independent filmmaker in the Midwest, he has written and directed the Lifetime movie *Mommy* (1996) and three other features, including *Eliot Ness: An Untouchable Life* (2005). His produced screenplays include the 1995 HBO World Premiere *The Expert* and *The Last Lullaby* (2008) from his novel *The Last Quarry*. He lives in Muscatine, Iowa, with his wife Barbara, a writer with whom he collaborates as "Barbara Allan" on the award-winning "Trash 'n' Treasures" cozy mystery series.

MATTHEW CLEMENS has authored or co-authored numerous short stories in such anthologies as *Private Eyes, Murder Most Confederate,* the *Hot Blood* series, the *Flesh & Blood* series, and *Buffy the Vampire Slayer.* With Pat Gipple, he co-authored *Dead Water: The Klindt Affair,* a regionally best-selling true crime book, and has written for such magazines as *Fangoria, Femme Fatales,* and *TV Guide.* He has worked as a book doctor on over fifty novels, and assisted the late Karl Largent on several best-selling techno-thrillers.

Clemens is also co-plotter and researcher for Max Allan Collins on books based on the television series *CSI: Crime Scene Investigation, CSI: Miami, Dark Angel, Bones,* and *Criminal Minds.* Collins and Clemens have also written graphic novels, computer games, and jigsaw puzzles based on the successful *CSI* franchise. Many of their collaborative short stories were gathered in *My Lolita Complex and Other Tales of Sex and Violence* (2006). Clemens lives in Davenport, Iowa, with his wife Pam, a teacher.

Don't miss the next page-turning thriller by

MAX ALLAN COLLINS

and

MATTHEW CLEMENS . . .

Coming from Pinnacle in 2011!

GREAT BOOKS, GREAT SAVINGS!

When You Visit Our Website:
www.kensingtonbooks.com

You Can Save Money Off The Retail Price
Of Any Book You Purchase!

- **All Your Favorite Kensington Authors**
- **New Releases & Timeless Classics**
- **Overnight Shipping Available**
- **eBooks Available For Many Titles**
- **All Major Credit Cards Accepted**

Visit Us Today To Start Saving!
www.kensingtonbooks.com

More Books From Your Favorite Thriller Authors

More Nail-Biting Suspense From
Kevin O'Brien

__Only Son	1-57566-211-6	$5.99US/$7.99CAN
__The Next to Die	0-7860-1237-4	$6.99US/$8.99CAN
__Make Them Cry	0-7860-1451-2	$6.99US/$9.99CAN
__Watch Them Die	0-7860-1452-0	$6.99US/$9.99CAN
__Left for Dead	0-7860-1661-2	$6.99US/$9.99CAN
__The Last Victim	0-7860-1662-0	$6.99US/$9.99CAN

Available Wherever Books Are Sold!

Visit our website at **www.kensingtonbooks.com**